FINDING

LONDON

Regina ~
Lots of Love!
Xo
8- Ellie Wade

ELLIE WADE

OTHER TITLES BY ELLIE WADE

Forever Baby
Fragment
Chasing Memories

THE CHOICES SERIES

A Beautiful Kind of Love
A Forever Kind of Love

PLEASE VISIT ELLIE'S AMAZON AUTHOR PAGE FOR MORE
INFORMATION ON HER OTHER BOOKS.

WOULD YOU LIKE TO KNOW WHEN ELLIE HAS
GIVEAWAYS, SALES, OR NEW RELEASES?

SIGN UP FOR HER NEWSLETTER. ♥

For Tammi, who is one of the most amazing women I know.
Your love and support mean more to me
than you could ever imagine.
I love you something fierce.
Thank you for loving me. ❤

PROLOGUE

Loïc

Age Five

Seattle, Washington

Loïc: (low-ick) of French origin; meaning famed warrior.

*"You named me Loïc because it means warrior,
and warriors are strong."*
—Loïc Berkeley

"I spy with my little eye something blue but not just one shade, many beautiful tones…like the blues of an ocean changing with each wave, each ripple, each ray of sunshine."

"Um, that book cover over there," I guess.

Daddy smiles and shakes his head. "It's round."

I scan my bedroom. *Blue and round?* "A marble in my toy box?" I beam with excitement because that has to be it.

"Nope. One more clue."

I jump up onto my knees, so I can listen very carefully, and my mattress bounces beneath me.

"You ready?" Daddy asks.

I nod my head.

"Sometimes, the blue goes away when you sleep"—he closes his eyes before quickly opening them again—"or blink."

I giggle because I definitely know the answer. "My eyes, Daddy."

"Blimey! You got it!" He pulls me into a hug.

As he tickles my sides, I laugh, and we fall onto my bed. I lay my head on his arm, and he hugs me into his chest.

"I love you, Loïc," he says.

I know that means he's getting ready to leave.

I'm not ready to go to bed just yet. "Daddy, can you tell me a story of London?"

He chuckles. "You sure are a cunning little devil, aren't ya? You know you've heard all my stories a hundred times."

"I want to hear them two hundred times then."

"Well, tonight, let's focus on one hundred and one," he says with happiness in his voice. "What do you want to hear about?"

"Nan and Granddad, your favorites, everything!"

I love Daddy's stories.

He came from a place called London that is super far away. It's across the ocean, and we'd need to fly in an airplane to get there. Daddy came to this country for uni—or as my mom calls it, college. That's where they met. Daddy said that the first time he saw Mommy, he knew that he would love her forever.

London is a magical place with a queen and princes and princesses. They have beautiful old buildings that tell stories. I can't wait to see the buildings and hear all their stories. Daddy's favorite food is fish and chips. He says that chips are fries but better. Also, it rains a lot in

London, but the rain makes it foggy and mysterious, like in a movie. He says that a lot of people take a train to work instead of a car. I've never been on a train before.

Nan and Granddad come to visit us every year at Christmas. They always stay with us for lots of days.

Nan loves to play card games with me. She's really good, but I always end up winning. I think she cheats, so I can win, but she says that I win by myself.

Granddad is so funny. Sometimes, he has conversations with the wall or starts to yell at something for no reason. I think he does it because he loves to make me laugh, but Daddy says that he's sick. Granddad has something wrong with his brain that makes him forget stuff. Daddy tells me that, someday, he won't remember who I am, but I don't know if I believe that.

I do know that Nan and Granddad aren't going to come for Christmas this year because she can't take him on the airplane anymore. I heard Mommy and Daddy talking about how Granddad threw his travel bag at another person on the plane on their way back to London last time because he thought the person was trying to steal Nan. If I thought someone was going to steal Nan, I would throw something at them, too. It's not Granddad's fault. He just really loves Nan.

I'm hoping they change their minds and decide to come this year, but at least I get to talk to Nan and Granddad every Sunday on the phone. I love them so much. I can't wait to go to London to visit them.

Mommy doesn't have a mom or dad anymore. She said they went to heaven when I was a baby. So, Daddy's parents are the only other family I have.

I'm never lonely because my parents are the best, but it would be nice to live by my grandparents, too. I wish we could live in England with Nan and Granddad. Daddy says maybe we'll move there when I'm a little older, if he can find a good job.

I can hardly wait to visit London, but Daddy says it is a lot of money to fly in an airplane. He is saving all his money, so we can go someday. He should have enough money soon because he works all the time.

We have to move a lot because of his work. He sells stuff for his job. Mommy says he is really good at it, too. She says he does so well because he is so handsome and charming. She really loves Daddy.

But I think he loves her most of all. Sometimes, I see him watch her when she's not looking. He always has a big smile on his face and looks at her like she's the most awesome Lego set he's ever seen.

His face is like mine was when I opened my Star Wars Millennium Falcon Lego set for Christmas. I was so happy. Santa got it for me because he knew how much I wanted it. It is supposed to be for nine- to fourteen-year-olds, but I got it when I was five. Daddy said that Santa knew I had been extra good, so he made an exception. It took me and Daddy a really long time to build it, but that's because we glued every piece. Daddy didn't want it to break after we'd worked so hard on it.

Daddy says when you really love something, you need to take very good care of it. He always gives Mommy foot rubs and makes her tea. That's another reason I know he loves her.

I think we don't have enough money to go to London yet because Mommy and Daddy spend a lot of money trying to have a baby. They want me to have a brother or sister, real bad. I hear Daddy telling Nan how much it costs. It sounds like a lot.

Daddy used to give Mommy shots in her butt every day. I could tell he hated doing it, but Mommy really wanted him to, so he would. Daddy says when you love someone, you will do anything to make them happy. Apparently, the shots make Mommy happy.

The happiest I've ever seen Mommy was when she had a baby in her tummy. But the baby had to leave for heaven before she could come out. That's the saddest I've ever seen Mommy. Daddy took extra good care of Mommy after that.

"Daddy, tell me the story about the bat at the cottage again!"

"You've heard that one so many times." He chuckles.

"I know. It's my favorite."

Daddy's main home growing up was right in London. He said it was a flat in the city. Mommy says that's like an apartment. Daddy said they lived there because Granddad worked nearby. But Daddy's grandparents had a cottage south of London on the English Channel, which Daddy says is like an ocean between England and France. Nan, Granddad, and Daddy spent all their holidays at the cottage.

Because the cottage was by the water, Daddy used to see lots of bats. He tells me all the time that bats are good creatures and that they eat all the bad bugs that sting us, like mosquitoes. But no matter how hard I try not to be, I'm very scared of bats. They're just so ugly and creepy.

I pull the covers up to my chin. This story always scares me even though I know what happens.

Daddy tells it the same way every time. "So, I'm looking from room to room because something feels odd. In each room, I open the windows, and the stale, musty air of the closed up space is replaced with the warm, salty air of the water. It blows through the cottage, making whistling sounds as it greets the old wooden beams holding up the roof.

"After each window is wide open, I look around. Everything looks the same. That's part of the magic of the cottage. Even though I am a year older since the last time I went, nothing within the cottage walls has changed. It is a charming place where time seems to stand still. There isn't the hustle of the city. It is just calm.

"Finally, I get to the last bedroom and open the window. I lean against the sill and look out at the waves hitting the rocks. A few minutes pass, and I stand there, deciding that I should go and help Mum with the bags. But when I turn around, I see that I'm not alone. Right beside me, hanging upside down is a…humongous…black…*bat*!" He says the last word loudly as he grabs my sides.

I scream like I always do.

"So, I quickly grab a sheet from the closet, and I open it up. Very slowly, I walk over to the bat until he is within reach. Then, using the sheet as a barrier, I wrap my hands around him. As swiftly as I can, I toss him out the open window, and I watch as he flies away."

I shudder from thinking about it. "I still can't believe you held a bat, Daddy."

He laughs. "Honestly, Loïc, it was only for a matter of seconds, and I didn't touch him because I had the sheet."

I shake my head. "I would never be able to do that. I'm not as brave as you."

He shakes his head and smiles. "But you are, son. You're braver than I could ever be."

"No way, Daddy."

"Why did Mommy and Daddy choose your name?"

"You named me Loïc because it means warrior, and warriors are strong," I repeat what they've told me many times.

"Not only are they strong, but they're also very brave, the bravest. No matter what happens in your life, Loïc, you'll be strong enough and brave enough to conquer it all. You were already more courageous than Daddy when you were one day old. Strength isn't measured by how many muscles you have or what you are or are not afraid of. Strength comes from within. It comes from your heart. It will give you courage to face things, even when you're afraid."

Sometimes, Mommy and Daddy tell me the story about how the mommy who carried me in her tummy couldn't keep me. Doctors said I survived on my own for two days after I was born, and then someone took me to the firefighters to find me a family. I was even in the newspaper. Mommy and Daddy said they cried so much when they got to take me home because I was the answer to their prayers.

Daddy leans down and gives me a kiss. "You, my little warrior, have the biggest heart I know, and that makes you the bravest."

ONE

London

"I already feel like a tramp with my girls on display like this."
—London Wright

"Ah!" I scream as the cool spray of water from the hose hits the small of my back, sending an unpleasant shiver up my spine.

My best friend's laughter saturates the hot, sticky air surrounding me. I rub my hands up and down my arms, the movement so out of place on this record-setting muggy spring day.

"You're such a bitch." With mock disgust, I turn to glare toward Paige's smiling face.

"Sorry. I couldn't help it. You were just standing there, and I have this and all." She nods toward the green garden hose in her grasp.

"Yeah. Maybe you missed the part about washing cars, not each other."

"Maybe." She shrugs, her auburn locks cascading over her shoulders.

"Just for that, you get the first car."

"No way. All is fair in love and war," she protests.

"Not really sure that quote applies here, babe." I huff out a chuckle. I grab the hair tie from my wrist. Raising my arms, I pull my now partially wet hair into a ponytail. "Can you believe this is our last philanthropic duty, like, ever?" I face Paige again.

We graduated from the University of Michigan three weeks ago, but months ago, we had signed up for this car wash as one of our required charity events with the sorority.

"No, it's so crazy. No more washing cars, raking yards, collecting disgusting cans of peas and soup, or selling raffle tickets to win lame-ass gift baskets. It's hard to imagine." She rolls her eyes. "And I can hardly wait." Her pouted lips turn up into a quirky smile.

I met Paige the first day I stepped foot on campus my freshman year. I remember walking into my dorm room to find a thin little thing with long dark hair, wearing gym shorts that barely covered her ass cheeks. She was fastening a bright pink boa to the shelf above her bed and turned toward the door when I walked in.

Her wide smile greeted me before she said, "Hey! You must be my new roomie. I hope you don't mind pink!"

I took a quick look around to find her half of the dorm room practically shining with a rose-hued glow. Everything from her bed to her desk was decked out with twenty shades of pink accessories.

I simply replied, "Not if you don't mind green."

It was the first color to come to mind that might clash with pink. In truth, I liked the color green even if I didn't actually own anything bearing its shade, and pink was my favorite color as well. So, I could tell immediately that this girl and I were going to get along just fine.

She simply replied, "Hey, whatever floats your boat."

I would come to see that Paige was full of one-liners, and she'd sometimes use popular sayings that didn't actually fit the scenario.

From that first meeting in the dorm room to now, Paige McAllister and I have been best friends. We were roommates all four years. We saw each other through wardrobe malfunctions, bad boyfriends, worse breakups, drunken nights, horrible hangovers, useless classes, and tedious tests. She majored in marketing, and I majored in journalism. The two degrees had a lot of the same coursework, so we took as many classes as we could together.

We rushed the Delta Delta Delta sorority together as well, which leads us to our current predicament. The Tri Deltas love to donate to various charities. This week, we are raising money for the local no-kill animal shelter, which is a great cause. Of course, I have nothing against giving money to those in need—especially puppies—but seriously, it's such a waste of time. If every girl in our chapter donated twenty bucks—basically pocket change—to our cause of the week, then we would have more money to give to each charity than we could make on any car wash.

Then again, as I look at Paige in her string bikini, this event might actually raise money.

"You look hot, BTW," I say to her.

Her lips press into a satisfied smile. "Thanks."

"I mean, you do look slightly like a hooker but hot nonetheless."

She laughs. "I'll take it. And as they say, *When in Rome.* You could join my hooker status if you would take off your shorts, you know."

"I think I'll keep them on, thank you very much," I say matter-of-factly. "I mean, I already feel like a tramp with my girls on display like this." I look down to my cleavage popping out from the top of my bikini.

"Your boobs are hot. With them, we'll for sure make some money for our furry friends. We should have made a sign with our slogan!" she says excitedly.

"What slogan is that?"

She puts her hand out in front of her. "Boobs for a cause. Raising money for puppy paws." She bounces her hand in the air after each word, as if she can see the slogan in lights.

"That's not bad," I respond with a chuckle.

"So, I'm doing the first car, right?"

"Um, yeah. You haven't forgotten your little stunt from a minute ago, have you?"

"No, that's fine. I was just checking. So, that means, you are doing the second one?"

"Um, yeah. Why?"

"No reason." She shrugs with obvious mirth in her voice.

Makeshift rows have been set up in a large parking lot behind a local bank. Some of our sorority sisters have already started their washing duties, but we lucked out and got the farthest row out. The persistent low grumble of a large engine alerts me to the fact that my time chitchatting with Paige is over. I turn to face the two vehicles in our line, and I immediately understand Paige's jovial mood.

"No way," I protest.

"Yes way." She giggles.

It isn't the shiny little Toyota that catches my attention but the monstrosity of a dirty truck that is lined up behind it.

I stare, my mouth agape, at the mud-caked Ram Truck. The truck's size itself is overwhelming. I'm going to need a ladder to reach the hood. But the dirt…*seriously?*

"Oh, charity," Paige sighs, her voice rising an octave. "It just makes you feel so good inside, doesn't it?" She skips toward the first car and waves. "Have fun," she calls back toward me.

I close the distance between myself and the truck, internally preparing myself to greet the asshole who is sure to be inside it with a smile because I am a Tri Delt, after all.

The truck idles before me. My eyes scan from the wheels to the doors. Every inch is simply covered in a hard filth that appears to have taken up permanent residence on this truck. If the truck were taken care of, it would probably be quite an expensive vehicle.

My gaze continues upward, but I can't force my smile to come. Chalk it up to the fact that this is my last event with the sorority or maybe that it is eighty-seven humid degrees out or that the world's largest dick just pulled up, but I can't seem to force my Tri Delta classiness and jovial smile. So, instead, when my eyes finish traveling up the door to the window, I am wearing a verified pissed off scowl.

That is, until I see him.

His window is rolled down, and his arm is resting against it. He's wearing some type of military camouflage uniform—Army, I think—along with a hat of the same material, but it isn't the commanding presence of the uniform that has me speechless.

It's the face beneath the brown-and-tan camouflage cap.

Damn.

I don't find myself in this predicament often. Not much can rattle me to my core, but this Adonis before me has managed to steal every coherent thought I had.

The smirk across his face should anger me—normally, it would—yet I can't allow myself to feel annoyed when I find myself in the presence of his rugged face with those lips and deep blue eyes that seem to glimmer next to his sun-kissed skin. His sandy-blond hair is short and barely visible beneath the cap, but an image of my hand running through the hair at the nape of his neck flickers in my mind before I can stop it. He is manly perfection, plain and simple.

I'm lost in visions of hot, sweaty sex, a beautiful wedding, and making babies. Yes, loads of babies. It's official. I'm going to marry this man.

Movement before me pulls me out of the dream playing in my head, and I see Hottie's smirk has grown in width.

"Um…what?" I stutter ever so non-gracefully.

"I said, you should close your mouth before you swallow a bug. It's just mud. It will come off with a little elbow grease. You're not afraid to get a little dirty, are ya?" His deep voice sends a torrent of chills across my skin.

It takes a split second for me to realize what he's talking about. *That's right…car wash. Got it.* "Oh, I love getting dirty." I beam before internally cringing. A huge desire to kick my own ass rushes over me.

Enough of this middle-school-starry-eyed-girl syndrome. I'm a smart, attractive twenty-two-year-old college graduate. If I've learned anything in the past four years, it is how to get a guy to do what I want. And, right now, I can think of a lot of things I want this particular specimen to do.

I put on my sexy smile. "Hi, I'm London. London Wright. Sorry, momentary brain lapse there. Must be the heat." I shrug. *Why did I give the car wash guy my last name?*

"Yeah. It's hot as a bitch."

"Perfect day to make some poor college girl clean your filthy truck, huh?" I provide a smirk of my own.

"Exactly my thoughts. Although you're anything but poor, *London Wright.*"

I love the way my name rolls off his tongue.

"Maybe not. But it's not very nice of you."

His body is turned toward the window, and I catch his name patch on the right side of his chest on his uniform.

"Berkeley," I address him.

"It's Loïc. If you didn't want to wash cars, maybe you shouldn't have put up the sign. I'm just trying to do my part for the"—he pauses momentarily as he looks back at one of the posters—"puppies."

"Yeah, well," I say in my favorite flirty voice, "if you really wanted to help the puppies and me, you could just donate some money and drive through an actual car wash before picking me up for a date later."

His laughter booms through the truck cab as his head falls to the headrest behind him. "You're something else, London. Does that sort of line work for you often?"

"Well, to be honest, I usually don't have to work too hard. But I've found, when I see something I want, the best approach is a straightforward one." I pause. "And to answer your question, yes, my lines always work for me."

He takes me in, his beautiful blues squinting slightly.

I can't make out his thoughts, but the silence is uncomfortable, so I continue, "So, I hear a slight accent in your voice. Where are you from?"

"A little bit of everywhere, I guess."

"From the South?" I question.

"Partly."

"You're not giving much away, are ya?"

"Nope," he answers.

My eyes are drawn to his lips and the way they form a perfect pout after he finishes that word.

"Loïc...that's a different name. Is there a story behind it?"

"Maybe. Is there a story behind yours?"

"Yes, there is. Would you like to go out later, and I can tell you all about it?" I'm starting to get irritated with his evasiveness.

"Nope," he says again, putting emphasis on the P sound.

Oh, crap. He must *be married.*

My eyes dart to his left hand that falls from the open window.

A rumbly chuckle vibrates through his chest as he assesses me while I squint toward his ring finger. "I'm not married, London, and I'm not in a relationship."

"Oh," is my only response.

"I am in a hurry though and in need of a truck washin', so if you wouldn't mind getting started, that would be awesome."

My mouth drops open, but I quickly close it while rolling my eyes toward Loïc, God of Assholes—drop-dead gorgeous ones but assholes nonetheless.

"Right," I snap, turning to grab the hose.

Ugh, what a jerk.

Unadulterated fury powers me through cleaning the truck. In actuality, most of the crap comes right off with a simple spray of the hose, but the truck itself is inconsequential at this point. What is driving my rage is Loïc sitting pretty inside the cab of his truck, his fingers tapping away at his phone. He seems completely oblivious of me. Although I'm pissed, I'm still using every opportunity I can to get his attention.

Isn't watching a half-naked chick leaning over a wet truck some sort of fantasy for guys?

Yet, every time I glance his way to see if he's checking out my ass, I find that he's not. He's staring at his damn phone.

Maybe he's gay. He has to be.

But I didn't get that vibe from him in the least.

He's just some Army jerk. Why do I care?

I finish spraying his truck down and stand outside his closed window. He doesn't look up until I tap against the glass. When the window is open, a rush of urgency comes over me. I'm suddenly inundated with this longing to say something to keep him here, to make him want me.

Part of me knows that, when he drives away, I will never see him again. For reasons that escape me, that thought terrifies me. I don't know anything about Loïc besides that he drives a big truck, he might have lived in the South at some point in his life, and he's in some sort of military service.

But it's not about what I know of him. It's what I see in him. Behind his insane good looks is *something*. I'm not sure what it is, but I want to find out. I need to find out. And the fact that he doesn't seem to be interested is causing me to panic.

His right eyebrow rises. "All done?"

"Yeah, it's five dollars," I answer with a sigh.

There is so much I want to say to him, but none of it seems appropriate or, to be honest, sane. I shouldn't feel this range of emotions toward a stranger, and I'm starting to wonder if the heat is getting to my head.

He hands me a twenty. "Keep the change"—his deep blues send an electrifying current through me—"for the puppies. And, London?"

My eyes expectantly shoot up to his.

"Thank you," he says before pushing his gearshift into drive and pulling out of the parking lot.

TWO

London

"Why didn't he want me? I'm amazing."
—London Wright

I turn my attention from the *How I Met Your Mother* rerun that I've been watching to face my best friend, who is sitting at the other end of the couch. She is being awfully chatty at the moment and has been talking my ear off, ruining the better half of this show with her obsessive babbling. Granted, I've watched this particular episode at least three times, but that's not the point.

She must notice my less than amused look. "Listen up, girlfriend. You need to stop this little pouting session that you have going on. It's getting annoying. As they always say, *When it rains, it pours.*" Paige plops a corner of her frosted Pop-Tart into her mouth.

"What exactly do you mean by that? What's raining?" I ask, my eyebrow quirking up in question.

Paige looks at me like I have two heads, her face scrunched up in confusion. "How am I supposed to know? That's just what they say." She shrugs.

I chuckle. "Well, Paigey Poo, the entire point of using an expression like that is to have it make sense to the situation and, by extension, help in some way. Your sayings never fit what is going on, so there's really no point in saying them at all."

"I say them because I like to. It makes me sound"— she pauses, thinking of the exact word she wants to say— "smart."

I can't hold in my laughter, and an obnoxious roar of giggles comes from my mouth. "No, it doesn't." I wipe the few stray tears leaking from the corners of my eyes. "It actually has the opposite effect. You do know this, right?"

She plops another piece of her Pop-Tart into her mouth, her expression one of annoyance.

"It's just, when you say something that doesn't make sense, it makes you sound a little silly. I love you, silly and all…but I'm just saying." I give her a sheepish smile.

"You can *just say* all you want, but I will continue to say what I want even if you think I sound stupid." She narrows her eyes at me.

"I never said you were stupid."

"Yeah, you basically did," she huffs out.

I let out an exhale. "You're right. Say whatever the hell you want. I'm in a bitchy mood, and I'm sorry that I'm taking it out on you."

Paige crosses her legs underneath herself and leans in toward me, a wide smile on her face. "You're forgiven. So, are you really still all grumpy over hot Army guy?"

I sigh. "I think so. The whole thing is ridiculous. I don't even know him. I have no idea why his dismissal made me so mad."

"Well, I'm pretty sure this is what we call the first-time blues." She nods her head with her lips pressed into a line.

"Huh?"

Her hands flail as she talks, "It's obvious, isn't it? This is the first time you've ever been turned down, and your ego is throwing a pity party."

I absently chew on my lip, thinking about her words.

She continues, "It was bound to happen, London. You can't take it personally. Not everyone in the world will be attracted to you."

I squint my eyes toward Paige. Irritation lines my voice as I say, "You make me sound like a stuck-up snob."

"Well, the apple doesn't fall far from the tree." She shrugs.

"We're bringing my mom into this now?"

She's right. My mom is a total snob.

Paige looks at me in confusion. "Why would I bring your mom into this?"

"You said that the apple doesn't fall far from the tree."

"So?"

I roll my eyes. "That means that I'm like my parents."

"No, it doesn't." Paige shakes her head. "I don't know why you're bringing your mom into this. Yes, she is a little snooty, but you know I would never compare you to her."

I groan. "We're talking about my parents right now because your little saying implied that I was like them." My voice rises an octave with annoyance. "Did you mean to say, *If the shoe fits*? Because I think that might make more sense here if you meant that I can be a snob."

"Yeah, whatever. All I'm saying is, you have established certain expectations, and this Army dude didn't act accordingly, so you're butthurt. You need to move on. You know what they say, *The best way to get over someone is to get someone else under you.*"

I laugh. "'They'"—I raise my hands and bend my fingers in air quotations around the word—"totally do not say that, and now, you're making me sound like a slut. Have you always hoped your best friend would be a snobby slut?"

She giggles. "I'm not calling you a slut—or a snob really, for that matter. You know I love you exactly the way you are. I guess all I'm saying is, we need to go out tonight. You know, to get you out of your funk."

"All of that"—I raise my hand in the air, my finger drawing a circle between Paige and me—"was just to say that we need to go out?"

"Yeah!" She grins. "This awesome club band is playing at Necto tonight. Some of the girls were talking about going. I'm sure you could find someone to make out with. That would totally make you feel better." She winks.

"I could use a night out. Good plan," I say through a smile. "But, for the record, why didn't he want me? I'm amazing."

My phone buzzes against the couch, and I peer down to see my mom's face on the screen.

"Speaking of trees," I say to Paige.

"I thought we moved on to shoes?" She looks to me in question.

I laugh. "I can't keep track with you. Anyway, I'm going to take this, and then we'll pre-party."

"Yay!" She claps her hands together. "I'll get my shower out of the way."

I love our pre-party ritual that we've perfected over the past four years. It consists of snacks, music, drinks, and a couple of hours to style our hair and makeup to utter flawlessness. Someday soon, when we decide to grow up and get real jobs—or employment, period—I'm sure these nights are going to be few and far between. But, for now, I'm going to relish in the joy they bring.

"Hey, Mom," I say into my phone.

My mom doesn't call often. She usually communicates through text, so I'm sure she has some news to share.

"Baby girl! How are you? How's life since graduation? Anything exciting going on? Have you applied for any jobs?"

"No, not really. And, no, not yet."

"Oh, that's fine. You have plenty of time," she says with sincerity.

Exactly. I've only been out of college for a month. My mom gets me.

"Have you heard from Georgia?" she asks.

My younger sister is spending the summer between her junior and senior year at Stanford gallivanting through Europe with a group of her friends.

"Not really. I mean, you follow her on Instagram, Mom. You see the same stuff I do."

"I know. I just didn't know if she'd called or texted you. She has an international plan. It wouldn't hurt her to use it."

I chuckle. "Mom, she's having fun. She's fine. She posts proof-of-life photos every day. She'll call if she has free time, but I'm sure she's just busy with soaking in new experiences."

"I know. It's just weird not to get daily texts from her. You know your sister; she always needs something."

I can hear the smile in her voice.

"So, not hearing from her is a good thing. It means that she's figuring things out on her own."

"I suppose," she sighs.

"How's Dad?"

"Oh, you know, working himself to the bone, per usual."

My dad has made a name for himself in the business world—or at least, I assume he has based on how much money he earns. He's in the business of mergers and acquisitions. According to him, that means he buys, sells, divides, and/or combines companies in order to help them be successful.

My mom, on the other hand, doesn't work—at least at anything that brings in money. She keeps busy though. Her social calendar is always full.

"Oh, that's why I called. We're moving."

My parents currently live in New York City. They've actually been there for a few years, which might be the longest they've ever stayed in the same location. Growing up, it felt like we moved once a year on average. My dad goes wherever his job leads him, and my mom follows.

"Where to?"

"Louisville, Kentucky. We bought a house in a nice suburb outside of the city."

"Oh, that's great, Mom. How long will you be there?"

"Who knows? You know how it is." She chuckles.

"Please say you're going to keep your apartment in New York."

They have an awesome place downtown. It's within walking distance of everything, and it's so convenient when visiting the city.

"Yeah, I think we are—for a while. It's nice to have a place here, and your father always seems to have meetings here, regardless of where we're living."

"Oh, good. I love it there."

"Me, too. I'll miss it, but I'm sure the change of pace will be nice as well."

"I'm sure," I agree.

"Well, of course, our numbers will stay the same. I'll text you the new address. We're departing for Kentucky tomorrow. We'll leave everything here in the apartment besides some personal items that have already been moved. Other than that, the designers have the new house all ready. It's beautiful. I hope you can make it down to visit soon."

"I'll try, Mom. Not really sure what my summer plans are, but maybe I can fit in a trip."

"Thanks, honey. Oh, I have to go and get ready for this new acroyoga class I'm taking."

"Acroyoga?"

"Oh, yes. It's great. It's like yoga and includes all sorts of bendy positions, except I have a base—a guy beneath me. He lifts me with his legs so that all the moves are done up in the air. It's so fun. You should try it."

"It sounds slightly dangerous and a little scandalous. Be careful, Mom."

"Oh, it's fine." She laughs. "Talk soon, honey. Love you."

"Love you, too, Mom."

I shoot Georgia a text to tell her that I love her and hope she's having a ball. I end by telling her to give Mom a quick call when she can. I have no idea what time it is over on that continent, but she'll get my text at some point.

I turn on my pre-party playlist as I step into the shower. A smile crosses my face as the hot water falls over me. I am so ready for a night of fun.

THREE

Loïc

Age Ten

New Hope, Mississippi

"In the stories, the bars would keep the bad guys in,
but I'm praying they'll protect me, keeping the most evil man out."
—Loïc Berkeley

I spy with my little eye peeling flooring, dust bunnies, and a crack running up the cupboard—three things that don't matter, yet they calm my racing heart. The circumstances I'm in aren't the best. Actually, I can't think of much worse. But I know I have to continue to fight until they come.

They will come.

That's what I've been telling myself for 1,029 days. I've been here in this evil place for almost three years. I've been trying very hard to be patient, to wait…but it's difficult, and every day is so scary.

They will be here soon.

Until then, I play my game. I'm not sure why it helps, but it does. It reminds me of Daddy, which gives me strength. But it's more than that. I guess it forces me to focus on something that won't hurt me. There is so little that I have control over in my life, and so much of that unknown is painful.

I can't do anything about the crack running up the fake wooden cupboard door, but staring at it takes my attention away from the other things in the room that will hurt me. The dust bunnies—although, I suppose, if I inhaled them, they could present a problem—are safe. But the man standing in the dirty work boots next to the piles of dust and hair is anything but.

The kitchen, under the metal card table, is where I've chosen to hide. I close my eyes and imagine myself shaking my head. *Not the best choice.* I don't dare actually move though. I'm too afraid.

In all of his rage, he hasn't seen me yet, and if I get really lucky, he won't.

Please don't let him see me, over and over in my head, I pray…to whom I don't know.

I cautiously open my lids and see his worn leather boots. Once brown, they're now so caked with mud and dirt that they look a sad gray. He's facing away from the table. I listen to the familiar sounds of cupboards creaking open and being slammed shut. I hear the *glug-glug* of liquid falling into a glass. He gulps it down his throat, sighs, and pours another. He's swearing, ranting, and raving about something I don't understand. He's real mad tonight.

I shrink my shoulders down and pull my legs even tighter against my body. The smaller my presence, the less likely he is to see me. I'd disappear if I could. *I wish I could.*

As always, I continue to take stock of my surroundings. The rusted folding metal chairs that circle the table block me in. They remind me of what jail bars from long ago might have looked like in all the stories that Dad used to read to me of cowboys, Indians, pirates, and explorers. I loved the voices Dad would make when he told the stories. I especially loved the bad-guy voices he would use. He did the best at those. Lots of times, the mean men would end up behind bars, kind of like these rusted chair legs. In the stories, the bars would keep the bad guys in, but I'm praying they'll protect me, keeping the most evil man out.

There are flakes of green left on the chair legs, too. I guess they used to be green…at some point. It's hard to picture anything new and shiny in this house. Everything within these walls appears to be so old, so miserable.

I start counting all the tiles that I can see on the floor. I believe each square used to have a flower pattern, but those designs have all worn off. The flooring is like a big plastic piece of paper that was rolled across the kitchen. It's peeling back, curving up where it meets the walls. I could be imagining it, but I think it curls up a little more every day. Perhaps, one day, it will be lying in the center of the room, all rolled up, like a big treasure map. But there's no treasure here. There's nothing good at all.

In the corner of the room is one of Stacey's hair ties. I've never seen her wear her hair down. It's always wrapped up in a tie. Though I rarely see her. She's sad. I'm not sure why, but I know she is. Maybe it's this house? It's probably Dwight. He isn't nice to her either, and she's his wife. She stays in her room all the time, like she's hiding away.

I wish I could hide in my room, but he always finds me there, especially when he's mad. I have a better chance of avoiding him if I stay out of his sight. He's too lazy to actually look for me, but I'm sure he knows I'm here somewhere. But if I'm not in my room and he doesn't stumble across me in his rage, he usually just heads to his bedroom. I hope he doesn't hurt Stacey. He yells at her a lot, but I think he only hits me.

Dwight is looking in the refrigerator now. He's yelling about the lack of food. He's always screaming about something. I can see the side of the refrigerator, and I take note of all the hair balls wedged between the floor and the white appliance.

I memorize every little detail of my surroundings, and in this place where it is hard to find anything to be thankful for, I'm grateful that it's such a mess. There is so much here to see, so much to pull my attention away from the what-ifs, which are the scariest thoughts of all. In the time that I've been with Dwight and Stacey, this depressing I Spy game that I play with myself has proven to calm my fears the most.

I usually think about Mom and Dad, too. But dwelling on them makes me so sad. My chest has hurt since the day they died, and it seems to hurt more when I remember them. Some days though, the only thing that keeps me going is the memory of them. Although the memories hurt, they remind me that there is good and love in this world. It gives me hope that, if I'm strong enough, then Nan and Granddad will come, and they'll take me to London where I'll be happy.

I just have to wait a little longer. I just have to be brave.

FOUR

Loïc

*"I hate the fact that I'm in this dark bar
with endless things to look at, yet all I see is her."*
—Loïc Berkeley

"Enough, dude. The truck will still be there on Monday. Let's go." Cooper's voice cuts into my thoughts.

I had a dream about Dwight last night. I haven't thought about him for a while. But, like all my nightmares, they don't stay hidden forever. When I least expect it, they throw their ugly heads into my life in a way I can't ignore, and more often than not, it happens when I'm sleeping.

I slide out from under the Humvee that I've been working on. "Yeah, okay. I'll finish later." A change of scenery is welcome at this point.

"Good 'cause I promised Maggie we would go out with her tonight. She's been looking forward to it all week."

He casually snuck that in, but I know he conveniently waited until the last minute to tell me of our plans.

"Seriously, Coops?" I eye my best friend, David Cooper—aka Cooper, Coops, or at the present time, Dumb-Ass. "I'm really not in the mood to go out tonight."

"When are you? If we based our decisions on when you were in the mood to go out, we'd be hermits." Cooper shakes his head and hits me on the back as I pass. "You'll have fun. You always do."

I quirk my eyebrow up, looking over to him with a scowl. "I do?"

He laughs. "Yeah, of course, man. You just don't realize it."

Cooper is the only person in the world whose shit I'd put up with. He's more like a brother than just a friend. He's family—my only family.

I joined the Army on my eighteenth birthday and met Cooper during basic training at Fort Leonard Wood in Missouri. Our cots were right next to each other. I'll never forget Cooper's incessant talking. He yammered on about this or that at any chance he got. I completely ignored him for the first week.

I remember wondering, *Who does this kid think he is? And, for God's sake, can't he take a hint? Who holds a one-sided conversation for an entire week?*

David Cooper, the skinny kid from the outskirts of Detroit, Michigan—that's who.

I was a loner, had been for a long time. I didn't want or need relationships, but Cooper changed that. I found myself looking forward to our chats even if my responses were only in my head. Then, one night, I answered him out loud. Cooper didn't even miss a beat. He just kept the conversation going, as if I had always participated. And, since that night, I have—for the most part.

After basic training, we followed the same path, going to Fort Knox for AIT—Advanced Individual Training—then Fort Sill, and finally Iraq. After six years of active duty in the Army, we got jobs in a Special Forces unit with the National Guard in Ypsilanti, the city directly east of Ann Arbor. We have drill once a month and a two-week-long annual training, but other than that, we're stationed here in Ypsilanti. Our unit is up for deployment at the end of the year, so we'll be going somewhere else soon—at least for a little while.

Cooper convinced me that settling here, with this unit, was the route to go. I now know that, on one of his leaves home, he hooked up with his high school crush, Maggie, and fell hard. So, now, the three of us are playing house in the modest home we rent in Ypsilanti. I tried to move out into my own place, but Cooper insisted that I stay. I will for a bit, but once he proposes marriage and babies come, I'm out.

When we get home, Maggie is blaring music and dancing in the kitchen, putting away the dishes. Her face lights up when she sees us. "My boys!" she yells over the racket.

Cooper pulls her into an embrace, locking his lips with hers. I turn my attention to the stack of mail on the table and try to block out the smacking noises.

"Loïc," Maggie squeals my name. "Thanks for going out with us tonight." She hugs me from behind.

I tap my hand against hers that are splayed across my stomach. "You're welcome, Mags."

She lets go.

"I'm gonna go shower," I say.

I suppose, as far as female roommates go, Maggie is the best I could hope for. Cooper's a lucky man. Maggie's awesome. And I lied when I said that Cooper was my only family because Maggie is, too.

After my shower, I throw on a pair of jeans and a T-shirt, and then I make my way toward the laughter in the living room. Cooper is sitting on the couch, freshly showered and ready to go. He and Maggie are cracking up over something.

"What's so funny?"

"Oh, Berkeley, man…we were just talking about you." Cooper calls me by my last name as well.

"Oh, yeah? What about?"

Maggie chimes in, "Remember that time we went out and that stage-five clinger would not leave you alone?"

"The redhead?"

"Yep," Cooper confirms. "The one who was as hot as she was crazy."

"Hey." Maggie hits him in the stomach with a disapproving look.

"Babe, you know she was hot but not as gorgeous as you. No one is." He smiles sweetly at her before kissing her on her temple.

"Aw, thanks, baby," Maggie addresses Cooper before turning her attention to me. "Remember how she wouldn't leave you alone, no matter what we did?"

I roll my eyes. "How could I forget?"

I think back to the night that I just wanted to spend with Cooper and Maggie, and this chick wouldn't leave. She was so brazen, too. At one point, underneath the table, she grabbed my dick outside of my jeans.

I shake my head and chuckle. "Oh, the beer."

"I know! That's what we were just talking about!" Maggie laughs.

Cooper *accidentally* spilled his beer on this chick's shirt because he was so sick of her hanging around our table. Yet, instead of leaving, she simply took off her tank top, leaving her upper half in only her lacy red bra. She claimed that the bra could double as a shirt.

"After all, girls wear tube tops all the time," was her reasoning.

"You're like a magnet for crazy chicks," Cooper states with a chuckle.

"It's because he's so damn hot," Maggie says.

Cooper whips his head to the side and gives her an accusatory stare.

"Not hotter than you, baby, but the girls know you're taken."

"Damn straight," Cooper answers.

Maggie has a point in that clingy girls tend to find me and have a difficult time in letting go of me. I'm not a prude when it comes to hook-ups. Depending on my mood, I'm game for a night with a hottie in my bed, just as any other twenty-five-year-old guy would be. But, when a girl has a certain look in her eyes, I stay away at all costs. When her eyes are screaming *more*, I run.

I don't do relationships. I never have, and I'm not sure I ever will. It's just not me. I know what it feels like to be heartbroken, and I don't want to make someone else feel that way. So, if I get the vibe that the girl is looking for more than just a night, I steer clear.

The three of us hang out, chatting and laughing at one story after the next, while Cooper and Maggie have a few beers. I'm always the DD, and that works for me since I don't drink. I have no judgments toward people who do, but I decided a long time ago that it wasn't something I would do.

Growing up, I lived with a heavy drinker for a period—three years, to be exact. It was not only the longest I was ever placed with someone, but it was also, by far, the most difficult time of my life. At the age of seven, I learned what alcohol could turn some people into. I know it wouldn't have the same effect on me—I would never allow that—but getting drunk and losing myself has never interested me. Not only can the smell of liquor take me back to that very dark time, but the thought of losing any of my control is also terrifying. I need power over my life, my actions, in order to function.

So, of course, I picked the one profession where I have none. When the military gives you an order, you do it. No discussions. No questions. No choice. But, I suppose, where my job is concerned, having no control is actually calming in a way.

"You guys ready?" I ask Maggie and Cooper.

All the way to Ann Arbor, Maggie rambles on about the band we're about to see. I've never heard of them, but apparently, they are DJs with a techno flair. According to Maggie, that means they play a lot of covers of popular songs, but they spice them up a bit. Should be interesting.

I park in the parking garage, and we walk across the street to the club. Every time the bouncer opens the door to let someone in, the loud music escapes, sending steady beats of bass down the street.

The second we step foot into the club, Maggie is bouncing up and down, giddy with excitement. The place is packed. As we weave our way through the crowded space, I notice how each person seems to be holding or wearing something that glows in bright neon. Glow-stick bracelets, necklaces, headbands, and belts are apparently all the rage.

A smile crosses my face as we pass some chick laughing hysterically while she repeatedly hits some guy on the head with a foam glow sword. The ten-dollar cover was worth it just for the show the audience is bringing. Being the sober one is where it's at.

Near the back, we find a space large enough for the three of us to stand comfortably. Cooper says something to Maggie, eliciting a nod from her, before he heads in the direction of the bar.

Maggie is raising her hands in the air and swaying to the music as she shouts out the lyrics. Cooper returns and hands me a Coke.

"Thanks, man!" I yell over the music.

He nods toward me with a smile and wraps his arms around Maggie from behind. The two of them start dancing together without missing a beat. If I were honest with myself, I'd have to admit that I envy the relationship they share. Knowing them both as well as I do, I believe, without a doubt, that neither one would ever hurt the other. They are in it for the long haul. A tiny longing resonates within me. A small hope that I could find that sort of connection with someone enters my mind before I immediately shut it down. I've learned that any amount of hope, no matter how small, is dangerous.

Something pulls my attention toward the front of the club. My eyes scan the area—searching for what, I don't know. Yet it's there—a feeling, a presence, a whisper—and I can't ignore it.

It doesn't take me long to figure out what I've been looking for. There *she* is, like a beacon sending a signal meant for me. My hand grips tightly to the cool glass containing the iced pop, my thumb slipping across the condensation. The beverage begins to fall from my hand before I reposition my hold. Turning, I place it on a ledge and wipe my damp palms against my jeans.

What are the odds?

I stare at the wall. My heart is thrumming wildly in my chest.

I suppose it's not that surprising. This city isn't that big, and the fact that she would like the same band as Maggie isn't that surprising either. *But still.*

I haven't been able to get my mind off of her all week, and I don't understand it. *And, now, she's here.* If I were interested in finding someone—I'm not—she would be the opposite of the type of person I'd be looking for.

I breathe deeply, pulling the energy-charged hot air of the club into my lungs, before turning back toward her. She's probably thirty feet away, far enough that I can watch her without her noticing. And she hasn't realized that I'm here yet, as far as I can tell. She and another girl dance with abandon, similar to the way in which Maggie is moving next to me.

Her long hair is curled, the loose spirals bouncing against her bare shoulders as she moves. The kaleidoscopes of colors shining from the stage lights emit ever-changing bursts that alter the hue of her hair every few seconds. But I know the true shade.

I can close my eyes and picture it clear as day. I've imagined how silky her light-brown locks would feel against my skin. The color—so rich with varying shades of chocolate but with a hint of blonde when in the sun—has been present in my mind all week, regardless of my attempt to block it out.

I can't see her eyes from here, but I can picture them just as clearly. Her eyes mirror her hair with their different shades of brown. Every time she looked at me at that car wash, they appeared marginally different, an intriguing melody of browns with flecks of greens and golds.

I push my hand through my short hair in frustration. *What is wrong with me?* I shouldn't care less about the damn flecks of her irises or the freaking hint of blonde in her hair. I spoke very few words to her a week ago. I shouldn't even remember her damn name, but I do.

London.

If she only knew what that name did to my heart when she said it in the bank parking lot. But she wouldn't know. How could she?

It has to be the name that has me all jacked up over this girl. It's definitely not the girl.

London is gorgeous, no doubt, but she's not the type I would normally sleep with. She's too beautiful, and she knows it. Not to mention, I can't stand stuck-up, rich, entitled little bitches who think they are owed everything they want simply because they exist.

Those types of girls remind me of a family I briefly stayed with when I was in between homes in my early teens. The Bakerfields appeared to be living the American dream. They had a grand house that was entirely too big for the three of them, fancy clothes, and lots of expensive cars. They were rich, by most people's standards. They had this daughter who was a couple of years older than me, Caroline. Man, she was a cruel, evil bitch. I hated her. I'm not sure why they took in foster kids, no matter how brief. I think Mr. Bakerfield was in politics. It had to be for show—the whole charade of taking in poor, parentless kids—like a résumé builder of some sort. It definitely wasn't because they cared.

I realize I know little about the type of person London truly is, but I'd bet money that I'm right. I guarantee she's from a rich family who gives her everything she's ever wanted. She probably hasn't had to actually work a day in her pampered life. No matter how beautiful she is or how my body betrays me in its attraction to her, she will never be a girl that I want to be with.

I hate the fact that I'm in this dark bar with endless things to look at, yet all I see is her. Despite my attempts to stop, my focus is drawn to her. She seems to glow—and not because of the neon hues of the glow sticks. No, she's so much brighter. She's a light I can't ignore. I need to, I want to, but I simply can't.

She's no longer dancing, and her eyes are locked with mine. For a moment, she looks shocked, scared almost, but then her open mouth closes, forming a flirty smile. I yank my gaze from hers. I look at anything else and, at the same time, nothing else as my mind races with images of London. My stare betrays me as it finds her once more. This time, she is leaning in, talking to her friend. Her friend nods, and London starts walking with purpose and a huge-ass smile—directly toward me.

Oh, shit.

I find myself moving in her direction—if anything, because I don't want to confront her in front of my friends. I'd never hear the end of it. I guarantee that London's behavior will rival any of the crazies of the past. Red-bra-beer girl stories will be replaced with London stories, and if there is anything I don't want, it is to be reminded of her for the unforeseeable future every time Cooper or Maggie wants a laugh.

We meet halfway and face each other. And though we are surrounded by a crowd of dancing bodies, standing across from London this way feels almost…intimate. I can't stop my perusal of her, starting at her feet in strappy black heels to her skintight jeans to her equally form-fitting pink halter top to her cleavage that is pushed out on display to her breathtaking face and the way in which she is taking me in with the same amount of yearning.

"Loïc," she says as her hands splay across my chest.

I swallow, my mouth dry. "London."

"You remembered my name," she says with a smirk.

I shrug, my arms hanging loosely at my sides. I concentrate on her face, hoping that mine conveys complete nonchalance. I'm putting in a lot of effort to appear unaffected. But the reality is, I'm not. My heartbeats are uncontrolled, a pounding drum within my chest. My body is betraying me in every way possible with its reaction to London's touch, and all the focus in the world isn't going to make a difference.

What is it about her?

I grab her wrists and remove her hands from my chest. "Listen—"

Before I can gather my thoughts, she tilts her face to the side and asks sweetly, "Dance with me?"

I let go of her wrists, and she wraps her hands around my neck, pulling us closer together.

My hands ball into fists against my thighs. "London," I protest.

She glides one of her hands across my cheek. "It's just a dance."

Her touch feels so good, and I have to stop myself from leaning into her hand.

I don't want this moment with her. I don't want to feel this way when I'm around her. I don't want any of it, but for some unknown reason, I'm powerless to stop it.

I could stop it, if I wanted to. *Walk away. Just walk away.* That's all it would take.

Instead, my hands wrap around her waist. My body leans into hers. She nuzzles her face against my neck as I rest my cheek against her hair. Closing my eyes, I breathe in. She smells so good.

What am I doing?

I ignore the war raging in my mind between reason and want, and I allow my senses to fully take in this enigma of a woman in my arms. I will allow my brain and all the thoughts that I'm shutting out to have their say in a bit when I force myself to walk away. But, right now, I just want to dance with London more than I've wanted anything in a very long time. It doesn't make sense, and I'll rationalize it all later. For once, I'm going to permit my beating heart to win or at least have this small victory because the truth is, it's long overdue for one.

We move to our own rhythm. I don't even hear the band anymore. All my senses are fixed on London—the way she feels in my arms, her intoxicating smell, how beautiful she looks, the sound of her content sigh against my chest. We dance together like we've done it a million times before, our bodies moving seamlessly against one another. I press my lips together as an overwhelming urge to taste her comes over me, to kiss her…just once.

Wait! No. What is wrong with me?

It's lust, plain and simple. I'm giving this attraction more value than it's worth. There's no connection, nothing special about London. She's hot, and my body wants to fuck her. End of story.

End. Of. Story.

Yet, for more reasons than I care to admit, I won't be taking her home tonight. I step back abruptly. *Enough.*

I grab her shoulders and sharply push her away. "Listen…"

She opens her mouth to interrupt me again.

"Stop," I say more forcefully than I probably should have.

Her eyes widen in shock.

"I'm sure you're a nice girl and all," I say, trying to soften the blow some, "but I'm not interested."

Her brow furrows. "Why? Is it something I did? Something about me? Are you gay?" she fires off questions in rapid succession.

The last one makes me laugh. "No, I'm not gay. I'm just not a relationship kind of guy. Okay?"

She pouts her lips, her big doe eyes pleading. "I'm fine with that. We can just have some fun."

"No"—I shake my head—"not happening." My logic and senses are returning at full force. Though I know that a night in bed with London would probably be insane—the best kind of insanity—I can't.

"Why?" Her voice comes out in a whine.

I hate that I find the shrill sound attractive.

"You're just not my type of girl, and I'm definitely not the guy for you. You might not realize it yet, but I'm not. Trust me."

"Let me make that decision." She lowers her voice while placing her hand on my chest once more.

I remove it. "London, I'm trying not to be a dick to you. Believe me, it's a challenge because, in all honesty, I am one. But there are only so many ways I can say no before things start getting ugly. Lots of guys are here. A pretty girl like yourself won't have trouble finding one. It's just not me."

She bites her lip. "So, you think I'm pretty?"

I run my hand through my hair in frustration. "That's what you took away from what I just said?"

"Come on, Loïc," she purrs.

I glare down to her with a cold, frustrated stare.

Pulling back her shoulders, her chest rises with a large breath.

I watch her entire demeanor change. The soft features of her face morph into hardened resolve with, if I'm not mistaken, anger—and a lot of it.

She stands tall. One hand grabs her hip while the other one points an accusing finger at me. This is a completely different girl than the one I just danced with, and I despise the fact that I find this version equally as hot.

"What is your deal?" London barks out, her stare cynical. "Like, seriously? I know you find me attractive. I can tell in the way we just danced. This isn't me, Loïc. I don't beg guys to want me. It's always the other way around!"

She's furious, and I struggle not to smile because I find her rage completely adorable.

Oh, sod off, Loïc. Just stop.

This has gone on for long enough. I steel my features. Brutal bluntness is going to be the only way to get through to this girl. I need her to hear me because, honestly, I don't want to fight her anymore. I only have so much resolve. But I know that I'm no good for her, just as she's no good for me.

She stands before me, fuming. Her glare expectant, she's waiting for answers.

"I'm sorry, London," I say, though the tone of my voice communicates the opposite of remorse, "that you've lived such a privileged life that you don't understand the meaning of the word *no*." I pause to take her in one final time.

I spy large round brown eyes with specks of gold peering up at me with equal amounts of hope and fear, a face so perfect in its construction that it's more a work of art than a mere body part, and full lips that tremble slightly, begging me to kiss them. The sight before me brings more emotions to the surface than I've felt in years. And that's exactly why I have to go.

"Good-bye, London," I say with a firm finality. I turn away from her before she can protest.

I take the quickest route through the crowd to the spot where Cooper and Maggie are dancing.

"I'm out. Text me when you're ready to be picked up," I say to them.

"Who was that chick?" Cooper nods toward the space behind me.

"Not now. Text me," I say again before I head to the exit and out into the warm night air.

I pull my fingers through my hair, letting out a groan. I shake my head, trying to erase the last hour from my memory. I start walking. I'll have to be back shortly to drive my roommates home anyway. But I can't stay here. I need distance and some clarity. I'm hoping a walk and the fresh night air will give me both.

Yet, regardless of the physical distance I put between myself and London, I can't get her out of my head. She consumes my thoughts, and I hate it—or at least, I tell myself that I do.

FIVE

London

*"When multiple spa days, a mani-pedi, and the latest silver
Prada handbag don't bring a smile to my face,
it's time for a little self-reflection."*
—London Wright

I've been at my parents' new home in Louisville for the
past week, licking my wounds and healing my broken
heart. Okay, fine…it's my ego that needs healing. I get it.
I can't possibly love Loïc. I don't know him, so I can't be
in love with him. But my self-confidence took a few
blows at Necto a week and a half ago.

I think the thing that bothers me the most is that a
small part of me agrees with Loïc. I am a rich, spoiled
brat. I'm not used to being turned down by a guy, and it
sucks. It pisses me off. Yet it shouldn't. I'm not God's
gift to mankind. Of course there are going to be guys out
there who just aren't into me. Why should that upset me?

It's common sense. There are plenty of others who would want me...who do want me. Why can't I focus on that?

Nonetheless, I find myself at my parents' lavish house, getting pampered to soothe my bruised ego. Yet it isn't working. When multiple spa days, a mani-pedi, and the latest silver Prada handbag don't bring a smile to my face, it's time for a little self-reflection.

My mom has sensed my gloomy mood, and as always, she has tried to cheer me up with stuff. I know she means well, and normally, her efforts work, but this time is different. It's as if Loïc's rejection woke something up in me. It's difficult for me to make heads or tails of it, but I've changed. I'm not the same girl I was almost three weeks ago at the sorority car wash. I find myself wanting more. I want to do more, feel more, simply be more than the self-centered rich girl I am.

I don't know how a rejection from the hottest man in the world led to this desire to change everything about myself...but, for some odd reason, it just did. I take that back. I don't want to change everything. I know that, deep down, I'm a good person. I care about others, I'm kind, and I've never let my financial status in life make me feel entitled. Fine...that last part might not be true.

Whatever.

The point is, I want more out of my life. I think this empty feeling in the pit of my chest has less to do with a boy not wanting me and more to do with the fact that his dismissal of me altered the way I feel about myself. I will not accept anyone making me feel this way. The truth of the matter is, if I felt whole, it wouldn't matter who rejected me. It shouldn't change the way I felt about myself.

So, I'm going to fix that. I'm going to become the confident, whole person I want to be. I'm not exactly sure how, but I've come to the conclusion that the first step is to get a job.

I graduated from one of the best colleges in the country. I'm capable of securing employment. Why did I spend that time getting a degree if I wasn't going to use it? It's time I stop taking Daddy's monthly allowance and actually work for the life I have. Of course, I mean, I'll stop taking it when I have been working for a while and am making good money. Why struggle if I don't have to? Baby steps here.

"You shouldn't scrunch your brow like that, sweetie. It will give you premature wrinkles." My mom's dark chocolate eyes assess me from the entryway.

I relax my face. "Sorry, I didn't realize I was."

She makes her way over to the chaise lounge where I'm currently sitting. I watch her as she shortens the distance between us. She's always so put together. Even today, when we have no plans to leave the house, she's dressed to impress, her makeup perfectly applied. Her long brown hair is pulled up into a twisted updo. She's going to be fifty next month, but she doesn't look a day over thirty. Of course, she's had some surgeries to help her in that endeavor. But, plastic surgery or not, she's a stunning woman. When we're out together, people often think we're sisters. I've been told I look exactly like her, and she's beautiful, so I can't complain about the comparison.

"Baby, what is it? You've been so down all week." She sits near the end of the chaise beside my legs. She places one of her freshly manicured hands on my leg and squeezes gently. "You can tell me, honey."

"I don't really have anything to tell, Mom. I just have an unsettled feeling. I think I need to get a job."

"Do you need more money? You know your father will give you more." She sounds concerned.

I shake my head. "No, I have plenty. I'm kind of bored. I think a job will give me some purpose, you know?"

"I understand that. I try to keep busy, too. I have to with all the alone time I have. Even if you don't get a paying job, you can volunteer or organize a charity event."

My mom's life has consisted of organizing parties, charity events, and social functions. She's right in that she always seems to be busy. Then again, she's always alone, especially since Georgia and I went off to college. Even now, my father is traveling for work. He's gone a lot.

"Yeah, maybe," I say in an effort not to dismiss her suggestions. "I think it would be fun to use my degree. You know I love writing and reporting." I got a degree in journalism, and it'd be nice to use it.

She laughs. "Yes, you do. Do you remember how you used to report on everything? You'd run around the house, using your sparkly pink hairbrush as your microphone." She holds an invisible brush/mic in her hand and imitates my younger self, her tone serious, *"This just in. It appears Mom is currently making beef fajitas for dinner when she was planning on chicken cacciatore. Is something going on behind closed doors in the chicken industry that made her change her mind? We will be live at six with more on this story. Back to you, Bob."* Mom removes the nonexistent microphone away from her mouth and puts her hand back in her lap.

The two of us start laughing hysterically.

"I was so annoying," I say through my happy tears.

Mom wipes the sides of her eyes. "No, you were adorable. Still are."

I take a deep breath and let out one more chuckle, thinking back to my childhood. "That report must have been when you still cooked."

When I was in eighth grade, my parents hired a full-time chef to make our meals for us.

"Thank heavens we got a chef. I've always hated cooking."

"You were good at it though."

"Yeah, maybe. But I became way too busy with your and your sister's activities and all my volunteering. It was definitely easier when we got help."

"I'm sure it was."

I think back to all the recipes my mom used to make. Her meals were definitely more in the category of comfort food versus the low-carb vegan meals the chefs usually made. My mom has admitted that she wasn't the best cook when it came to healthy foods, but she made the meals Grandma taught her. I suppose that's how it goes. We learn from our parents.

Am I really like my mom?

Paige says my mom is stuck-up and self-absorbed, and maybe she is a little, but she's truly a good person. I think I'm a good person, so we have that in common. I'm not as self-centered as my mom—at least, I don't think I am—but that's an area I want to work on anyway.

"Hey, Mom, do you think you could make your chicken Alfredo for dinner once before I leave?"

"Oh, I don't know, honey. I haven't made that in years."

"But you still know how, and it is so good. Now that I think about it, I'm really in the mood for it. I'm sure it will cheer me up a bit." I smile big.

"Of course it will." Mom chuckles. "I suppose I could. It's just not really healthy, London. You know that, right?"

"Of course I do! That's what makes it so delicious. Let's live a little, Mom!" My voice is full of excitement at the thought of her Alfredo. It's that good. If I remember correctly, the sauce mainly consists of butter, heavy whipping cream, and Parmesan cheese. Okay, so it's definitely not the healthiest, but who cares?

"Fine, I'll prepare it. I can see how happy it makes you. So, back to your new job endeavor. Do you think you're going to try to get an on-camera job? The news stations always hire the fresh-out-of-college cute girls to give the morning traffic and weather reports. You could start there."

"No, I think I'm going to start off on the writing end of it. Being on camera doesn't sound as exciting as it used to. Now, I'm more interested in the investigative and journalism aspect. Maybe I will look into some freelance writing opportunities." My minor is in writing, and I've always loved telling a good story on paper.

My mom nods. "That sounds like a great place to start." She stands and looks back down to me. "By the way, when should I plan this meal for?"

"I think I'm going to fly out on Sunday, so before then."

"Sunday?" My mom's voice rises an octave. "You will not have been here for two weeks."

I stand from the chaise and wrap my arms around her tiny waist. "I'll miss you, too, Mom." I release my hug.

"But—" she starts to protest.

"Mom, I really need to get back and get my whole grown-up life started, you know?"

"Why don't you just move down here? There is nothing keeping you in Michigan. You graduated, and you don't have anyone up there."

"I have Paige, Mom."

"True, but Paige will always be your friend, no matter where you live. I just think it's time for you to move home."

"Home?" I laugh loudly. "Mom, have you even lived here for a full month yet? I don't know if I've been to Kentucky prior to this visit. This isn't home for me."

"Yeah, you've been to this state before—when you were little."

"Well, I've lived in Ann Arbor for four years now, which is the longest I think I've ever lived in one place, so it feels more like home there anyway."

"I guess I was thinking that home was where your family was."

"I get that, Mom. But Paige is my family, too. And, to be honest, you and Dad probably won't be here that long. So, what good would it do for me to get a job here just to have you move in a year? Then, I'll be stuck here, alone. At least in Michigan, I have Paige."

She sighs. "I see your point."

"How about this? I will look for jobs everywhere and pick the one that gives me the best opportunity. Who knows? I could get an amazing offer from a Louisville-based company."

"That would be great, London. Thank you. All I ask is that you keep your options open and give this area a chance."

"I will."

My mom seems lonelier than usual. She's always been too busy to care where I might end up. It's not that she doesn't care; she does. She just seems a little desperate for company here. I'm sure it will get better once she makes new friends, which she will.

"Mom, why did you have to move here if Dad's just going to travel? He can travel from anywhere."

"I know," she says quietly. "You know how it is."

I suppose I do, but I don't really understand my dad's work. I never have.

I decide to change the subject. "I say we go pick up the ingredients for fettuccini Alfredo, get a couple of bottles of nice wine, order that new release with Scott Eastwood, and have a girls' movie night."

My mom's eyes go wide at the mention of the actor's name. "Oh, you know I love him. He's such a great actor."

"I'm sure your adoration for him has nothing to do with the fact that he's insanely gorgeous." I teasingly roll my eyes.

"Well, you know it does. He's quite the specimen."

"Of course he is! It's about time you admitted it. Jeez." I laugh.

"Oh, stop." She chuckles and wraps her arm around my waist as we start walking out of the room. "Let's go buy you a load of fat to put on your noodles."

"Yum! Sounds delish."

I'm at the airport, sitting patiently at the gate until it's time to board.

The last few days with my mom flew by. I had the best time with her. I honestly can't remember the last time I spent so much one-on-one quality time with her, and I know I need to do it more often.

There's a walking contradiction pacing in the aisle in front of me. For the past eternity, it seems, this dude has been yammering away on his cell phone about trading stocks. Just a typical douche-bag businessman who thinks yelling his client's personal business into his phone at an airport makes him look cool, right? Yeah, that would be all he is—except he's wearing a blue short-sleeved polo shirt, a pair of bright orange running pants, and worn leather sandals with socks. It doesn't appear that he even attempted to comb his short hair when he got up this morning. I can tell that he sleeps with the right side of his head on the pillow. Furthermore, he keeps sucking on a straw that's in a cup of ice that, I'm assuming, used to have a drink in it, creating an obnoxious sound that echoes throughout the gate's waiting area.

What I see of this man and what I hear him saying into his cell phone are complete contradictions. It just doesn't add up. I've had a lot of time to watch him, and I've decided that there are two probable scenarios. One, there are hidden cameras somewhere, and I'm a witness to a hidden prank show. But I've looked around, and I haven't seen anything indicating a television crew. So, that leads me to my other guess. He's insane, like a literal crazy person, and he's talking into a phone that doesn't have anyone on the other end. In fact, it's probably not even charged. Scenario number two makes me sad for him.

Maybe I'm completely wrong, and he's just an eccentric-dressing douche-bag businessman. Yeah, let's hope for that.

"So, is that your next victim?"

I gasp when I hear *his* voice. I would recognize it anywhere.

I tilt my head up to see Loïc standing beside me. He's wearing his fatigues and carrying an Army green duffel. My mouth remains open wide. I'm so shocked to see him here. I can hardly process it.

"What?" I finally ask, not able to think of anything better.

"The guy you've been staring at for the last twenty minutes…you have your sights set on him?"

I ignore his question, knowing that he's joking. Instead, I skip to the real question. "What are you doing here?"

"I'm flying back to Detroit, same as you apparently," he says almost distractedly. His stare is focused on my lips before it darts back to my eyes.

"Right. I see that, but what are you doing here, in Kentucky?" I continue to gawk up at him, and although I'm in shock at the sight of him, I can't help but notice how incredibly mouthwatering he looks in his fatigues. *What is it about a hot guy in a military uniform?*

"I was down in Fort Knox for training this week. Why are you here?"

"My parents live here."

"Ah, gotcha. Do you mind if I take a seat?" He gestures toward the empty chair beside me.

I shrug. "It's a free country."

He chuckles. "Yeah, I guess it is."

He places his bag on the ground at his feet and sits beside me.

"There are other unoccupied chairs around, you know." My words sound snarky, even to my own ears. I suppose my ego is still bruised from our last encounter.

"I know, but I thought it would be a dick move to sit next to a stranger when you're right here."

My body bristles. I'm wary of this new friendlier version of a man who, prior to today, has wanted nothing to do with me. Even this minimal chitchat is out of his norm.

"We're basically strangers, Loïc. What's the difference?"

He regards me for one heartbeat and then another before he looks away. "Basically...but we're not."

We both sit in silence and watch Orange Pants continue to chatter away.

After a few beats, Loïc says, "So, what do you think his deal is?"

"I don't know. I'm thinking he's on a hidden camera show, he's crazy, or he's just a very odd, very loud, extremely impolite person. I'm leaning toward the latter."

"Yeah, I think you're right. Though I envy him in a way."

"Why's that?" I lean back into my seat and allow my gaze to drift from the man to Loïc. *Big mistake.* I put it off to the uniform and my newfound obsession with a man in camouflage, but my stomach flutters at the sight.

Loïc sports a genuine smile. He seems so carefree in this moment, and because I find the brooding badass version insanely irresistible, the man before me almost does me in.

"The whole package—his clothes, his loud voice— screams, *I don't give a flying fuck what y'all think.* I'd imagine it would be pretty freeing not to give a shit about what others think of you." His bright blues hold me for a second before they return their gaze to the topic of conversation.

I let out a small chuckle. "Yeah, I suppose you're right. Though I couldn't do it. I mean, socks with sandals? That crosses the line."

"Does it?" Loïc laughs.

I can't stop the way my heart picks up its pace at that sweet sound. He's always been so serious. Hearing his laughter does something crazy to my insides.

"Definitely."

"Noted. No socks and sandals."

"Honestly, I would suggest you avoid the entire ensemble. I get that it might be freeing and all, but I wouldn't recommend that look on you."

"Good to know."

"So, are we, like, friends now or something? At the club a couple of weeks ago, I got the impression that you didn't want anything to do with me."

Loïc locks his beautiful blues on me. "I'm sorry if I was rude, London. I didn't want to make you feel bad in any way. It's complicated, but know that it's my issue and not anything to do with you. I wouldn't say that we're friends. I don't really need any more friends."

"Everyone can use more friends."

"I don't believe that. But I can't say it's not a little unnerving that we keep running into each other like this."

I grin. "It must be fate."

"I don't believe in that either."

"Maybe not, but you don't have to believe in it for it to be real."

It takes some effort, but I pull my stare away from his. He's so handsome that it's disarming. I can only take so much.

After a few minutes, I stand. "They're going to start boarding in a few. I'm going to go get some snacks and magazines from the gift shop. It was nice running into you again, Loïc. Maybe we're not friends, but it was nice to be friendly. See you later."

"Good-bye, London."

Yet again, his words sound so permanent, and it makes my heart ache. I hate the way I feel around Loïc and how desperately I want him.

I'm so lost in my own private pity party as I walk away that I almost plow right into the loudmouth bed head.

"Excuse me," I say quickly.

My eyes dart down to the floor and his socks. I notice that there is a small hole in one of them, and the tip of his big toe is starting to pop through. I can't help the smile that crosses my face as I continue toward the shop. Maybe I could learn a thing or two from Mr. I-Don't-Give-A-Flying-Fuck because, to be honest, I wish I didn't care what other people—particularly Loïc—thought about me.

SIX

Loïc

"London has this way of making me want to be different.
She makes me want to try, and that is scary as shit."
—Loïc Berkeley

That wasn't so bad, I think as I grab a water from the cooler at the back of the store.

After London walked away, I thought a beverage for the plane sounded like a good idea. The fact that I chose to walk to another shop at the other end of this section of the terminal had nothing whatsoever to do with London. I just wanted to stretch my legs.

Keep telling yourself that, Berkeley.

But I do have to admit that my recent conversation with London went well. The sight of her sitting here, in Kentucky, waiting to board the same plane as me, is still baffling. When I saw her, I knew that I would have to do the social thing. Any *normal* person who ran into someone they knew would say hi and exchange a few meaningless pleasantries before boarding. Granted, I'm as far from normal as they come. Yet I did it. It might have taken me twenty minutes to steel my nerves to approach her, but I did. I was friendly, doing my civil duty.

Surprisingly, it was nice to just talk. The entire experience was made better because I wasn't going out of my way to be a total dick, and she wasn't putting her sexy hands all over my chest, trying to seduce me. If anything, she seemed timid, not her usual tactic. But I'd say it was a win-win.

She's just so beautiful. I can pretend all I want that every cell in my body isn't insanely attracted to her, but that would be a complete lie. Yet I'm proud of myself because, despite this crazy urge I have to take her against a wall—multiple times—I just had a pretty normal conversation with her and survived with everything intact. I'm starting to think she isn't the girl I pegged her to be—not that it matters. I might not have her completely figured out, but I know myself. Regardless of what type of person she might be, she isn't the one for me—or, more accurately, I'm not the one for her.

Chances are, after we land in Detroit, I won't see her again anyway. So, this nervous energy that's pounding through my veins will all be for naught. Then again, if I'm leaving it up to chance, then perhaps I will. Running into her three times in two weeks has started to make me wonder.

I make it back to the gate as the final boarding announcement sounds throughout the terminal. I do a quick scan of the area and don't see London. It's for the best. Get to my seat and get home—that's my agenda, plain and simple.

I hand my boarding pass to the attendant at the gate. She looks down at it before looking up to me with a wide grin. "Oh, Mr. Berkeley, one of the passengers wanted to thank you for your service and upgraded you to first class."

"Excuse me?"

"Here." She hands me a new boarding pass. "You've been upgraded to first class. Thank you so much for all you do for our country. You'll find your new seat assignment right there." She points to the letter and number indicating my seat number on the thin piece of paper in my hand.

"Right. Okay. Thank you." I take my new boarding pass and my duffel bag and head down the tunnel leading to the plane.

Don't they have free liquor in first class? A drink might calm my racing thoughts of London. Great idea—save for the fact that I don't drink. Bummer. Well, the extra legroom will be a bonus.

I step onto the plane, and my attention immediately goes to her. She sits tall in her first-class seat, beaming up at me. I don't have to check my ticket to know what my seat number will be. I toss my bag into the compartment above London before falling to the seat beside her.

"Thankful for my service?" I quirk up an eyebrow at her.

Her big doe eyes gaze up to mine. The corners of her lips rise slightly, hiding a smile. "I have no idea what you're talking about."

"Sure you don't." I stretch my legs and get myself situated, clicking the seat belt into place. The seats are definitely way more comfortable up here.

I scan the area. London and I occupy the first two seats on the left while an elderly gentleman, who is already asleep, is sitting in the farthest seat back on the right. The other nine extra-large leather seats remain empty.

"You seem different," I say to her, taking note of the huge grin on her face.

She's happy and flirty again, back to the London I'd met before at the car wash and club. The version of her I was just speaking to minutes ago was quiet and almost hesitant.

"What do you mean?" she asks thoughtfully.

"Just that your demeanor is different than it just was out there."

"I did some thinking on my walk to grab snacks."

"Did you?"

"Yep, I did." She grins at me but doesn't elaborate.

"And?" I chuckle.

"Oh…well, first, I couldn't decide if I should buy the gummy bears, gummy worms, sour gummies, or gummy Life Savers. But then I remembered that the Dove chocolate wrapper that I had yesterday told me to buy both."

"I'm sorry. I'm not following." I can't help the smile that comes to my face.

"Well, yesterday, my mom and I ignored our diets and bought a bag of Dove chocolates, which is my favorite. You know how, inside each wrapper, there's a saying or some words of advice? Well, my wrapper said, *Buy both*. I realize that the word *both* signifies two things, but in the shop, I was torn between which bag of gummies to get, so I bought all four. I guess, first, you should know that I have a crazy gummy addiction. I love them all, and I normally don't let myself eat them too often. Apparently, sugar isn't good for you. Whatever." She waves her hand in front of her, as if she's dismissing that logic.

At this point, she reaches into her purse, pulls out four bags of candy, and places them in between us. "Lucky for you, I share." She smiles before continuing,

"Well, my other wrappers yesterday said, *Do something that scares you, Forget the rules*, and, *Take a selfie with your grandma.* I obviously can't take a selfie with my grandma at this point because she's not anywhere near here. So, I'll have to put that wisdom on hold. But I've decided the other two pertain to you."

"Yeah?"

"Definitely. You and the whole brooding-jerk vibe you have going on scares me, and if I were to follow the rules of normal human behavior, I would take in the signs you've given and back away, leaving you alone to wallow in your moodiness on your own."

"But you're not going to?" I say as the plane begins its ascension into the clouds.

"No, Dove says not to. So, nope." She shakes her head, her long caramel brown hair falling in front of her shoulders. "I'm going to use the time we have together to talk. I've lived twenty-two years on this planet, and I have traveled all over the world, yet I've never met you until recently. Then, we proceed to run into each other three times in two different states within the same amount of weeks. I'm not sure what, but something—fate, destiny, the cosmos, or an all-knowing sparkly unicorn—wants us to know each other. In what capacity, I'm not sure. But let's start as friends." As soon as the last word is out of her mouth, she pulls in a long breath.

"I don't believe in sparkly unicorns."

"Apparently, you don't believe in a lot of things, Loïc, but that doesn't mean they aren't real nonetheless."

"I'm quite sure that omniscient unicorns with glitter coats are indeed not real. I'm willing to bet money on it."

She playfully swats my arm. "You're missing the entire point."

"To which point are you referring? That you take advice from chocolate, have a serious sugar problem, or believe in mythical creatures?"

London laughs, and that sound does something to me.

"That we're meant to know each other in some way. I'm suggesting friends, but I'm definitely open to other arrangements."

Her stare takes me in, ripping me raw with intensity. This kind of longing hurts. I've never experienced an attraction like this, and I'm convinced I don't like it.

"I told you that I don't need more friends."

At this point, I'm thankful the first-class section is practically empty on this flight. London and I aren't being loud, but we're not whispering either. I'm glad that no one else is taking part in our strange get-to-know-you session.

London continues, "I know you said that, but I also know that you didn't need to come up and say hello back at the airport. You could have ignored me, but you didn't. So, that right there tells me that you are capable of being a kind person, and that trait alone is enough for me in a friendship."

"I'll remember that next time," I say dryly in an attempt to seem uninterested when, in reality, I am anything but.

London opens each bag of candy and then grabs a gummy worm. She holds on to the end and puts it in her mouth before pulling it out, sucking it.

What the hell? I look away, rubbing my sweaty palms on my pants.

She finishes her weird gummy-worm-eating ritual and reaches for a handful of the sour ones. "Have some. They're so good."

"I'm fine, really."

She lightly pokes my side. "Stop being a douche, and just eat some damn candy. I'm prepared to eat it all by myself if I have to, but my thighs won't be too pleased."

Leaning my head back against the seat, I groan internally as a vision of holding London's thighs while she rides me shoots through my head before I can stop it. The flight from Louisville to Detroit is a relatively short one, but no amount of time will be quick enough at this point.

I think back to a few moments ago. "Why are you on a diet?"

London is goddamn perfection. She doesn't need to lose weight. If she's one of those chicks who starves herself to remain thin, it will turn me off—or it should.

"What do you mean?" She sounds confused.

"You said that you and your mom ignored your diets to eat chocolate."

Realization dawns behind her eyes. "Oh, I didn't mean it like that. I'm not dieting. I meant, my general diet doesn't usually consist of bags of candy. I'm a pretty healthy eater. I eat a lot—don't get me wrong—but I try to eat good stuff."

I'm happy with her response even though it's just another thing not to hate about her. *Damn it.*

"We should do a version of Twenty Questions," she says with excitement lining her voice.

"What do you mean?" I ask even though I know I'm not going to like her answer.

"Like, we'll take turns asking each other questions, and we have to answer honestly."

I was right. I'm not liking it.

"London," I say on an exasperated sigh.

"Fine, you can go first. Ask me anything." She practically bounces in her seat.

"Have you always been this annoying?" I bite out.

She shrugs. "Yeah, probably. Okay, my turn. Where were you born?"

"Berkeley, California."

"Isn't your last name Berkeley? So, your parents lived in the same city as their name. That's funny."

"Not exactly," I offer.

"Do explain," she says.

"Fine, but this is one of your questions. I'm only giving you twenty. I was born in Berkeley, but my parents lived in Lancaster, California."

"So, your mom gave birth to you when she was out of town or something?"

Before I can doubt myself, I just start talking, which is so unlike me. But there is something about London that makes me want her to know things about me, things that only Cooper and Maggie know. "I was adopted by my parents. I'm assuming my birth mom was from Berkeley. I was found on the steps of the Berkeley Fire Department."

"That's so crazy. It's like it's meant to be," she says with reverence in her voice. "My sister and I both have geographically themed names, too." When I don't question her, she continues, "We were both named after the places where we were conceived."

I huff out a laugh. "Really?"

She shrugs as her lips tilt up into a grin. "Yeah, my dad has always traveled a lot for work. My mom thought it would be sentimental to name us after our place of conception. My sister should technically be named Atlanta—so we're told—but they chose Georgia instead."

"My dad was from London," I let out before I can stop myself.

"Really? Have you ever been there?"

"No, I haven't."

"I bet your dad has the best accent. I love English accents."

"Yeah, he did." I can still hear his voice after all these years. At the time, I didn't realize he spoke with an accent. He just spoke like my dad.

"Where do your parents live?" she asks.

"Heaven, I suppose—if such a place exists. They're dead."

I can sense London stiffen in the seat next to me.

Her voice comes out broken as she says, "I'm so sorry, Loïc."

"It's fine. It was years ago. I was seven when they died."

"Can I ask how…what happened?"

"Car accident."

"Oh. I'm so sorry."

We're silent for a few beats, and I'm hoping that the questions are done. I try not to think about my parents and the life I lived after the accident. It takes me to a dark place, one that is hard to get out of.

I should know that, with London, nothing is comfortable.

Sure enough, she asks another question, "So, who did you live with after they passed?"

"Various people from all over." I feel her stare, and I turn my head to meet it.

She's so beautiful. Her expression is one of sadness, empathy, and confusion.

"I was a foster kid, London. I went from home to home until I was fifteen when I left and just lived on my own...for the most part. I joined the Army when I was eighteen.

"You see, infants are easy to find homes for. When I was left at that fire station, I was snatched up by my parents in a day. Everyone wants a baby. Nobody wants a seven-year-old boy with major emotional baggage."

London's eyes glisten with unshed tears, which I find comforting and irritating at the same time. Without saying another word, I stand and make my way to the tiny coffin, also known as the restroom.

I lean against the small counter with my head bowed and eyes closed. I take in the rumbling of the engine and the gentle sway of the moving airplane. My heart is beating rapidly, and my chest screams in pain. I'm so full of contradicting emotions.

London has me so screwed in the head. I've survived this life by closing off my feelings, locking them all up behind my tough-as-steel exterior. It's not an ideal way to live, but it works. Healing requires one to face their demons and let go of their pain. I might seem strong in many ways, but when it comes to that, I'm still the frightened seven-year-old boy who was left with no one. London has this way of making me want to be different. She makes me want to try, and that is scary as shit.

The announcement that we are starting our descent sounds through the speakers. *Thank God for that.* I exit the small enclosure and take my seat next to London.

"Loïc?"

I turn my head to meet her gaze. "No more questions, London."

She shakes her head. "I wasn't going to ask you any. I was just going to say that I appreciate you sharing with me. I'm a good listener, if you ever need someone to talk to. I know you aren't thrilled to keep running into me.

But I promise that I can be a good friend, if you find yourself needing one."

I pull in a deep breath. London's hopeful gaze penetrates into the most hidden parts of me. With just a look, she reaches places no one else has been before. It leaves me in awe but also with utter feelings of terror.

I know that, if I explore these newfound sensations, I am going to be setting myself up for devastation. I don't have proof to back up this theory, but staring into the eyes of London, I simply know. She isn't someone that I can come back from. When I lose her, I will never recover. Of this, I'm certain.

At the same time, with her eyes locked on mine, I'm finding it difficult to care about my inevitable future heartache. This connection gives me strength to push past the boundaries I've created and courage to ask the most important question of all.

I clear my throat. "I do have one more question for you."

"Sure. Anything." She beams, her full lips causing my heart to stutter in my chest.

"London"—I pull air into my lungs that feel as if they are suffocating—"will you go on a date with me?" I get out the words that I've never uttered before. *There's a first time for everything.*

"Of course!" she answers immediately.

I stare at her wide grin. It, like everything else about her, does something crazy to me. She makes me insane, and it's an insanity I've never felt before.

I have a feeling that I will be experiencing a lot of firsts with London. To prove my point, I lean in, and without warning, I take her mouth in mine. She lets out a surprised gasp, and then almost immediately, her lips move against my own. My entire body seems to vibrate in satisfaction.

This is the first time I've kissed a girl because I genuinely wanted to feel her lips and taste her sweetness. Kisses have always been a step I needed to complete before sleeping with a chick. The kiss has never been the priority, the core focus. But this right here, with London, is the motherfucking main event.

This is the first instance that I couldn't stop myself because my attraction to her lips was so overpowering that I'd lose my mind if I had to go another second without feeling them.

Yes, this is going to be the first of many firsts with London, and I'm going to enjoy them all...while they last.

$\vee$

SEVEN

London

"Well, you know what they say.
Better to have fucked and lost than never to have fucked at all."
—London Wright

"I still can't believe you ran into him at the airport. What are the chances of that?" Paige sits on my bed amid her pile of gossip magazines. Her attention is torn between the gossip of Hollywood's rich and famous and my own world of exciting developments.

"I know. It was meant to be. I really think so." I unclip another section of my hair from where it was twisted atop my head, so I can curl it. "I'm nervous though. He's so hot and cold. Well…he's pretty much all cold, except for when planes are landing at Metro Airport. Apparently, under those circumstances, he just wants to make out."

Paige and I burst into laughter.

"He's strange, for sure. He's lucky he's so damn fine." Paige returns her attention to the magazine in her hand. "Just remember, it's no use, crying over spilled milk."

I groan. "Nothing spilled, you dork. I know you're the proverb queen and all, but how about you stick with your own words when giving advice? They tend to make a little more sense."

She huffs, "Well, talk about the pot calling the kettle black."

I throw my hairbrush at her. "I hate you."

She uses the magazine to block the brush from hitting her. "You love me," she says with a chuckle.

"You're right; I do. But you do know that you kinda make me crazy, right?"

She shrugs. "It's a gift. What can I say?"

Ignoring her rhetorical question, I ask, "How do I look?" I spin around, displaying my date outfit for approval. I'm wearing my favorite skinny jeans and a baby-pink T-shirt. I finish the outfit off with glittery ballet flats. I'm hoping the outfit screams casual but cute in that I-don't-have-to-try-to-be-sexy-but-I-am-anyway vibe.

Paige peruses my entire look. "You look hot, but you're, like, naturally gorgeous without even trying."

"Yes! Thank you! That's exactly what I was going for. You're right; I do love you."

"Where are you going? Did he say?"

I grab my cell to check the time. He'll be here any minute.

"No"—I shake my head—"he didn't." I apply a few extra doses of my body spray and another quick run of my lip gloss.

"Well, you know what they say about surprises?" she asks.

I grab my clutch and a light jacket. It's a hot June day, and I doubt I'll need it, but it's better to be prepared. "No, Paige, I have no idea what they say about surprises. Please enlighten me with your wisdom."

"I don't know either. I thought maybe you'd know." Her response comes out in a giggle, and she winks at me.

"You're such a dork, really." I squint my eyes in mock disappointment when the doorbell chimes. I jump at the sound. Running my hands down my jeans, I say, "Here goes nothing. Bye, chica."

"Bye. Be careful. Don't do anything I wouldn't do," she calls to me as I exit my bedroom.

"I won't, Mom!" I call back as I walk down the hall to the front door.

"Love you! Be careful!" she yells from my bedroom.

"Love you! Don't wait up."

I hear Paige say, "Oh, I'm waiting up," as I open the front door.

I'm still laughing at my obnoxious best friend when the door swings wide, and I'm met with Loïc's beautiful blues. The intensity in them is so pure, so focused, that I feel my stomach begin to churn, and I can't remember for the life of me what I was laughing at a mere two seconds prior. The entire world around me has faded to black, and it's just Loïc standing before me in his spotlight of godliness.

I'm a goner.

"London." Loïc's voice is deep and, if I'm hearing it correctly, nervous.

"Loïc."

Our stuffy greetings feel out of place, but at the same time, it's so...*us*. None of our exchanges have been typical or followed the usual script of how two normal young twenty-somethings get to know each other. Yet it doesn't bother me. I think that's why I was so drawn to him in the first place.

None of the guys I've dated in the past compare to him. He is in his own category of intrigue. He belongs to his own club where he is the only member, and I desperately want to be the one who's allowed access.

Loïc runs his hands down his jeans and clears his throat.

He's really nervous. It's just so…adorable. Bad-boy Army guy, who has probably killed someone with his bare hands—okay, I don't know that; I'm just making assumptions—is scared out of his mind to go on a date with me. It's written all over his face. The contradiction between his usual hard-ass demeanor and this obviously timid man standing before me is so endearing. I can't put into words why I find him so fascinating, but, man, I do. He's trying to put on a show of nonchalance, but in this moment, I can read him like a book, and he's scared.

I take a step toward him, closing the front door behind me. Our upper bodies are a breath away. One more step, and I'm sure I could feel his heart hammering in his chest.

I grab on to his arms hanging at his sides. "Tell me the truth. How close were you to canceling our date?"

His face breaks into an amused smile. "Pretty damn close."

"I thought so." I grin up to him.

I've never met anyone like Loïc before, but he's still a guy, and I'm not ashamed to use the skills I've been given.

"I want to tell you something." Releasing his arms, I place my palms on his cheeks, cradling his face. I stand on my tiptoes and pull his face down to meet mine. Our mouths are close enough that I can feel Loïc's warm breaths on my lips. "I'm glad you didn't," I whisper before I push my mouth onto his.

Loïc's body stiffens for a fraction of a second before it melds into mine. His hands wrap around my waist, sprawling across my back and pulling my body closer to his. A groan comes from deep within his throat as his initially tentative lips begin to move with increased fervor. His lips, so perfect in their execution, ignite my entire body with a hum of satisfaction.

I have to hold back tears as our kiss continues. I feel like crying, which doesn't make sense, but each feeling within me is on high alert. His lips, our connection, bring every last one to the surface. I'm inundated with dueling emotions—happiness because this is happening, but sadness because I don't know if it will happen again. Desire pounds loudly through my veins, but along with it is fear. For all the highs I'm experiencing comes equally impactful lows because, though I barely know Loïc, I know he's broken. It's too soon, and I can't explain how I know, but I simply feel it down to my bones that, if this doesn't work out, if I don't get to keep Loïc, I will be left broken, too.

Eventually, Loïc pulls his lips away. He leans his forehead down and rests it against mine. Our chests expand against one another with each deep breath we take as we work to calm our bodies and settle our minds.

Loïc's gravelly deep voice breaks the melody of our entangled breaths. "I'm fucked. We're both fucked. You know that, right?"

Startled, I take a small step back. When our gazes connect, his eyes darken. A myriad of emotions flashes through them, but I know he won't share them with me. It doesn't matter because I see them anyway, and what I see is enough.

I take a deep breath and grin. "Well, you know what they say. Better to have fucked and lost than never to have fucked at all."

His frown morphs into a devastatingly gorgeous smile that leaves my knees weak. "Who says that?"

I shrug. "Not sure, but they sound very wise."

He chuckles. "It's not too late to back out. You can go back inside and forget all about me."

I shake my head. "Not gonna happen."

"You sure?"

"Positive."

"All right, but don't say I didn't warn you." He takes my hand in his, and we walk toward his truck that is parked on the street.

I'm giddy that he's holding my hand and of his own accord. I feel like the nerdy girl in school who is finally getting the quarterback's attention. It's a strange place for me to be. I've never been that girl. I've always been the hot cheerleader whom the quarterback would beg to date. But, with Loïc, I feel lucky that he's chosen me. He's a prize, and I won him—or at least, I'm on my way to victory, and there's nothing else more important to me right now.

"You know," he says, "I've never met anyone like you, London Wright."

"Is that a good thing?"

"I'm not sure yet," he says as he opens the passenger door.

I hop up into the truck, and before he closes the door, I respond with, "It will be."

A small smile crosses his face as my door closes.

As I watch him walk around the front of the truck, I can't help but ponder how serious this is—the start of this relationship or whatever it is that I have with Loïc.

This is only our fourth meeting, and each time has been so deep and intense. Maybe that's part of the intrigue.

But one thing's for sure. I've never met anyone like Loïc Berkeley before either.

We're in the truck for about an hour before we reach our date destination—a drive-in movie theater.

The drive consisted of a comfortable conversation. Okay, so it mainly consisted of me talking about myself. Loïc isn't a huge sharer, but lucky for us, I am. I told him about my parents, Georgia, and of course, Paige—my sister from another mister. I informed him of all the places where I lived before college. I talked about my ambition to be a journalist.

Now, we're parked with the truck bed facing the giant movie screen. Loïc transformed the back of his truck into a comfortable lounging area. We're seated on several fluffy blankets, and he brought a handful of pillows to lean against. He packed a cooler of food and drinks. It's adorable. All he's missing are the rose petals and candles, and it'd be perfection.

I'm sitting, cross-legged, watching Loïc get out the food. We have over an hour until it gets dark, and the movie starts.

He looks up from the cooler. "What are you smiling about?" he asks playfully.

"You," I answer simply.

"What about me?" The corner of his mouth tilts up.

"All this." I motion to our surroundings. "It's so sweet. I've actually never been to a drive-in movie before."

"Yeah, there aren't too many left. I found this one on Google." He puts our sandwiches on plates. "I remember going to one with my parents. I think we were living in South Carolina at the time. We packed a picnic, similar to this one." His smile falters. "It's a good memory."

"It sounds like it."

He hands me a plate of food. "So, is sweet a good thing?" he questions with an effort to sound nonchalant.

My heart hurts for him because, behind his tough-as-stone persona, I think he's a pretty insecure person. I can't wrap my mind around that because...well, he's gorgeous.

"Um, yes, sweet is an amazing thing."

I can see the relief on his face.

"You wanna know a secret?" he asks.

"Yes!" I answer a little too enthusiastically. I obviously want him to be a sharer, too—apparently, more than I knew. I crave to know everything there is to know about him.

He chuckles. "This is the first date I've ever been on."

"What? No!" I practically shriek, which makes him smile.

He nods. "Yeah."

"I don't believe it," I argue.

"It's true."

I shake my head. "How is that even possible? I mean, look at you!" *Okay, maybe I shouldn't have said that last part out loud.*

"You, London, are my first date."

Joy expands in my chest at being the first anything for Loïc, but I still don't understand it. "Wow. I never would have guessed..." My thoughts trail off to the how and why of this scenario. "I can't believe you've never been with a woman. It's just—"

Loïc laughs in his deep timbre. "I didn't say I've never been with a woman. I said I've never gone on a date."

I wrinkle my brow. "So, you're not a virgin?"

He throws his head back, his wide chest vibrating with laughter. "Hell no. Why would you think that?"

"Because you've never been on a date!" I feel the need to defend myself.

"One does not have to date someone to screw 'em, London."

My heart rate accelerates as those words fall from his lips—whether from jealous or lust, I can't tell.

"Yes, I realize that happens, but you *never* took any of the girls you slept with out on a date?"

"Never."

"And they were okay with that?"

He shrugs. "I don't know. I never asked any of them."

"Out of curiosity, how did you avoid that conversation? Because I know girls, and most girls wouldn't be cool with that."

"Well, after we fuck, I usually don't run into them again, and if I did, it wouldn't be a big deal anyway because they knew the deal."

Realization dawns. "Oh, so you're like a one-night-stand slut."

"What classifies a slut, London?"

I throw a slice of cucumber from my plate at him. "Oh my God, you're a man-whore!"

"And you're Mother Teresa?" He chuckles.

"Well…no…" I stutter. "But I usually get to know the guy between my legs—at least a little bit."

Loïc's eyes darken before he closes them and leans his head back. Eventually, he opens them, and his stare finds me. "Please don't ever say that again."

I giggle. "What? The part about having a guy between my legs?"

"Yes, that part," he growls.

"Why? You don't like to hear about other guys doing things to—"

He cuts me off before I can finish, "Damn it, London! Eat your food."

I'm sporting a giant smile as I take a bite of my sandwich. I swallow and then ask, "So, are we done with the slut conversation?"

"Yeah. Definitely."

"One more question," I plead.

His blues hold me, and my heart twists a little.

"What's that?" he asks.

"Why haven't you ever dated anyone before? There has to be a reason."

"I haven't found anyone who's worth it." His gaze pins me with something serious.

I want to ask, *Worth what?* I want to ask if he thinks I'm worth it, but I don't.

Loïc has shared a lot in this conversation. I have been gifted with one more piece to the puzzle that is Loïc Berkeley, and if I play my cards right, I'm hoping to gain another piece very soon.

EIGHT

Loïc

"Fate is a fucking lie, and destiny is its bitch-ass cousin."
—Loïc Berkeley

The conversation moves away from our sex lives, and for that, I am thankful. I barely know London, yet I have the incredible urge to pummel the face of every man she's ever been with. A rabid beast has awoken in me, and I just want to hurt anyone who has ever touched her. I've never been possessive over a woman.

Why now? Why her?

I'm not sure of the exact answer. One thing's for sure. London is different. From the first time I saw her face and heard her voice, I've felt something real for her. Maybe it's an extreme version of lust. If I'm honest, it freaks me the hell out.

I'm in uncharted waters, and I want out. I don't do well without control, and where this girl is concerned, I have very little. But I can't stay away. I tried to cancel today's date—she was right about that—but I didn't have the courage to do it. I had to see her one more time.

I bag up the food we didn't eat and put it back in the cooler. "Do you want more wine?"

"Sure," London replies, handing me the cheap plastic wine glass.

It's incredibly cheesy—the picnic, the plastic dishes, the bed of my truck made into some sort of chic country lounge—but she seems to appreciate it.

I pour her another glass of wine and grab a bottle of water for myself. We position ourselves against the pillows in the center of the truck bed.

"I'm surprised you're not drinking. You could use your tipsy state to cop a feel and then blame it on the liquor." She grins.

"And that move works?" I counter, raising an eyebrow.

"Depends on who's using it, I guess." She takes a sip of her wine.

I watch in awe as her cherry lips press against the glass, taking in the liquid. *Gah, what the hell is wrong with me?* I shake my head to get the vision of London's throat swallowing out of my mind.

"I don't need an excuse to touch you, London. If I touch you, it will be because you want me to."

Her eyes go wide at that statement. The corner of my mouth tilts up into a smile. London is such a strong woman, and she goes after what she wants. It's one of the aspects of her personality that I find so appealing. Yet I love when I say something that stops her in her tracks even if it's only for a moment. It's oddly invigorating.

The movie starts, and we set our drinks on the wheel well, so we can lean back against the pillows. The night air carries a bite, and I cover us with a light blanket. The theater plays back-to-back movies. Both of tonight's selections are action flicks, which I thought sounded good for a first date.

I'm on a motherfucking first date. London has another one of my firsts.

We both wiggle around to get comfortable, repositioning the blankets and pillows beneath us. Finally, I lay my inner arm out, and London falls back onto it, arranging her body tightly against mine.

Time passes, and I realize that I haven't followed a second of the movie. *Who gives a damn about the movie?*

Instead, I find myself listening to London's breaths while relishing the way her body feels against mine and the warmth it brings. It's a relatively still night, but the air that does move around us bears her scent. Her hair smells like vanilla paired with fruity sweetness. She's also wearing some sort of perfume that's as intoxicating as it is alluring.

Everything about this woman fascinates me. No amount of denial or refusal could prevent it. Most confusing to me is, the attributes I find appalling on other women, I find captivating on London.

I'm losing my mind. That's all there is to it.

I take in her facial features. It's dark, but with the light from the movie screen, I can see her profile. I scan from her chin to her full lips and move past her small nose to the long lashes that I know frame the most mesmerizing eyes I've ever seen.

She must feel the weight of my stare because she turns on her side so that we are facing each other. "Don't like the movie?" Her voice is a low purr.

"Something like that."

A storm of lust rises inside me. I position myself on my side so that my hands have access to her. I thread my fingers through her scalp. I pull her face toward me, and I meet her halfway before crashing my mouth onto hers.

The sexy whimper that comes from her fuels my desire, and I deepen the kiss. Our lips nip and pull. Our tongues twirl and taste. Our mouths devour, taking what they want. The kiss is desperate and sensual, loving and rough. It mirrors the short relationship that I've had with London—so back and forth at every step, full of equal parts want and fear. Most of all, the kiss is saturated with undeniable need, a need that only London has ever given me.

Beneath the blanket, our hands roam above our clothes. I feel the feminine curves of her body, and I draw it all in, committing every last detail to memory. I want to know everything about London. I want to remember every inch of her body—each dip, each curve, each beautiful piece. To me, she is perfect, and perhaps that's why I can't stop myself when I know I should, why I can't stop myself when I know I'll eventually hurt her.

In my life that has been full of disappointment, I've earned the right to be selfish, haven't I?

Yet, even as these thoughts fill my mind, I know that makes me as bad as all the rest of the people that I've encountered that put their cruel needs above the happiness of others. It makes me a monster. I'm no different. I'm taking what I want when I know I'll hurt her. What does that say about me?

I've strived so hard to be someone that my parents could have been proud of, someone different than the evil people I grew up with, I'm risking losing it all, losing myself, over a girl.

But she's not just any girl, is she?

And then there's the voice, the tiny whisper, that is barely audible. It tells me it could be different, I could be different, for her.

That small voice reminds me of the coincidental meetings, how the universe kept throwing her in my path. Words are heaved into my head—*fate* and *destiny*. I loathe those words because, if they were real, if they existed, then that means I was meant for the life I was given. I was meant to experience such sorrow and pain. And that doesn't sit well with me. No child should go through a fraction of what I did. Fate is a fucking lie, and destiny is its bitch-ass cousin. They hold no place in my world because, if they did, if I were destined for such loss, I probably would have given up a long time ago.

But that whisper gives me something else—hope. It's so miniscule within my soul that I can barely feel it, but it's there. It gifts me just enough hope to keep kissing her, just enough to continue to savor her, just enough to ignore the warning bells in my head, telling me that I should stop.

Just enough.

But, suddenly, kissing her isn't enough. I need more. I have to touch her. With the way she is rubbing herself against my body, I know that she wants me, too. She needs it as much as I do. We are two of the same. Our wants are desperate, and our needs overpower our reason while our lust screams the loudest.

My callous hand slides under her shirt, finding its way to her bra. I run my finger under the curve of the wire. She moans into my mouth, pushing her pelvis into my leg, begging me to continue. I put my hand underneath the wire and push the fabric up until I can feel the weight of her softness in my hand. I run my thumb along the taut nipple before pulling and teasing it between my fingers. She squirms against me.

Our lips continue their assault on one another as my hand moves to the other side and repeats my movements. After I've paid equal attention to both of her breasts, my hand roams down her smooth belly to the waist of her jeans. I run my fingers along the waistband, feeling the excited tremor of her skin.

I break our kiss and find her stare. Her eyes are hooded, her lips swollen, her hair tousled and sexy. She nods, granting me permission.

With one hand, I unbutton her jeans and push them down enough to grant me access. I slide my hand underneath her panties, and she closes her eyes on a soft moan, her head falling back onto a pillow. I push two fingers into her entrance, taking pleasure in the warmth that wraps around me. I drop my head to her neck and breathe her delicate skin in as my hand begins to move. She grasps my arm and back, digging her fingers into my skin. Quiet whimpers come from her lips.

I drag my lips up and down her neck, kissing and sucking, unable to keep from tasting her. My fingers continue to savor her as the palm of my hand moves against her sensitive skin.

Writhing against me, she bites her lip, attempting to hold in her groans of pleasure.

"Oh God," she whispers into the night air. "Please, Loïc, please," she chants.

I love the way my name falls from her lips, the way she begs me to touch her when that's all I want to do. It causes a storm of need to fill me up. My body threatens to blow with the sweet ache of all-consuming want. I've never wanted someone the way I want London. The intensity in which I need her is unsettling. It screams of devastation and loss, warning me to be cautious. But I ignore it all, except for her desperate pleas.

"Loïc," she breathes. Her voice is so needy that she sounds like she's in pain.

"I got you." I kiss her neck as my hand picks up speed.

Her body quakes, and I kiss her lips, catching her cries in my mouth. My mouth continues to caress her lips until her body stops quivering. Then, I move my kisses to her neck once more as she takes in breaths of air.

That was the single most amazing thing I've ever experienced, and I know where London is concerned, it's only going to get better.

I pull my hand from her pants and button her jeans back up. I'm propped up on one elbow as I stare down at her satisfied smile.

"You're good at this first-date stuff," she says, her voice airy.

I run my thumb across her cheek, simultaneously trying to figure out how I got here and how to never leave. I respond with, "I'm glad," for lack of anything better.

"We could go back to my place, if you want?"

I know what she's implying because I want it, too.

"Not tonight, London."

"But another night?" she asks hopefully. "There will be a second date, right, Loïc?"

"That depends."

"On?" she questions.

"I need you to know that I will hurt you. I won't want to, but I will. I have more baggage than you can imagine. This"—I wave my finger between us—"will end badly. You should know, I always end up losing everything I love."

Her eyes soften. "You love me?"

I shake my head. "Not yet." I pause. "But I will." The words shock me as they leave my mouth, but I know they are true. How could I not fall for London? It's only a matter of time, and I'm sure it's not much time at that.

"I want that second date, Loïc."

Her words penetrate me profoundly. My heart slams against the wall of my chest.

"Are you sure?"

"Definitely," she answers.

I lean my forehead against hers. Our chests expand as we both work to find enough air to satisfy the ache of emotions raging through our bodies.

Deep within my soul, the whisper of hope gets marginally louder.

"OMG…Loïc, we need details!"

Maggie's excitement is way too much for me at the moment. But seeing as she makes Cooper and me giant breakfasts every Sunday after our long run, I can't be irritated.

Cooper shoves an entire sausage link into his mouth. Chomping on it, he says, "Yes! Details," in an attempt to mock Maggie's tone.

"So, you really didn't sleep with her?" Maggie questions.

"No."

Her eyes go wide. "And you plan on seeing her again?"

"Yes," I answer. Although I know it to be true, it doesn't sit well with me.

She places her hand on Cooper's arm. Her voice is low and sweet when she addresses him, "Babe, our boy is growing up."

Cooper, in turn, slowly taps my hand while shaking his head. "That he is. That he is."

I want to be annoyed, but I love these idiots.

I swallow a mouthful of pancakes right before a laugh erupts. "Stop."

"So, tell us, what's she like?" Maggie asks.

"And why didn't you fuck her?" Cooper adds.

With a scowl, Maggie immediately slaps his arm.

"What?" he addresses her. "It's a valid question. It's not his typical MO."

Maggie seems content with his answer, and they both turn their attention to me.

"Well, like I told you, I've run into her a few times."

"Yep, the car wash, the club, and the airport." Maggie ticks them off on her fingers.

"Yeah, and she's different," I continue.

"What do you mean by *different*?" Maggie questions.

Cooper sighs. "Just let him finish. Save your questions for when he's done."

"I just wanted to clarify some stuff. Stop being mean," she whines.

I cut off their bickering, "She's...I don't know. I guess it isn't so much that she's different, but I'm different when I'm around her...if that makes any sense."

Maggie nods, as if she knows exactly what my rambling means.

"She's hot," I throw in.

"Of course." Cooper nods.

Maggie hits his arm again.

"She comes from a rich family, and she might be a bit spoiled."

Both of their faces scrunch up with repulsion.

I chuckle. "I know. Believe me, I know. But, somehow, on her, I find it…cute." I shrug.

"Cute?" Cooper questions, lifting a brow.

"Yeah, something like that."

"Okay, so you didn't sleep with her because…she's spoiled?" Cooper clarifies.

Maggie chimes in, "No, he didn't sleep with her because he likes her."

"I'm so confused." Cooper forks a large piece of pancake into his mouth.

"You and me both, brother," I admit.

"Well, I think it's adorable," Maggie says. "It's about time you found a girl who makes you all confused. That's when you know it's real."

Cooper turns to look at her, his mouth agape, like she's an alien sitting at the table with us. "They've been on one date, babe. Let's not get all serious here."

"Loïc doesn't date, so that's how we know it's serious. Plus, you knew you loved me almost immediately. The first time we spoke our junior year, when we were lab partners, you knew."

"I knew I wanted to screw you. I was a horny seventeen-year-old, not Casanova. It took us years to get to where we are now," he disagrees.

"It took years because you were immature, but you knew immediately. We both did. Loïc isn't a boy, like you were. He's a man."

Cooper drops his fork onto his plate. "I don't like how you said that."

"Which part?" Maggie questions.

"The *man* part." His voice is low.

Maggie and I both laugh.

She says, "Oh my God, would you stop? I mean that, at twenty-five, he's more mature than you were at seventeen, so it's not going to take him as long to figure things out. He is technically a man, as most guys your age are."

Cooper eyes her with a glare of speculation before he nods, apparently satisfied with her answer, and picks up his glass of orange juice.

"Wow, I can't wait to have a relationship someday," I say dryly.

Maggie grins, placing her hand on Cooper's. "I know. It's the best."

I chuckle—not because she's making a joke, but because she isn't.

"So, when are you taking her out again?" Maggie asks.

I roll my head back and sigh. "Not sure."

"I'm putting ten bucks on never," Cooper states.

"You're horrible!" Maggie complains.

"No, I'm realistic. I don't think he's there yet. These things take time," Cooper says, explaining himself.

"He's had time. I get it; I do. But the only way to heal is to keep going forward. Staying idle won't help anything." Maggie turns her attention from Cooper to me. "Moving forward can be scary, but it's necessary," she says with kindness before standing and grabbing her plate.

This exchange seems normal, but a part of me thinks that maybe it isn't. Yet this is the way it is. The three of us are open books around each other. If other people were to give me advice, I'd take offense. But there's none taken here. These two are my family, and as unconventional as we are, I know that they have my best interests at heart.

Despite my automatic tendency to side with Cooper, I know Maggie's right. It's time.

NINE

Loïc

Age Twelve

Marion, South Carolina

"These words are my sanity. They make me feel less alone when I am so very lonely."
—*Loïc Berkeley*

I spy with my little eye…white, white, and more freaking white.

I sit at a wooden desk, surrounded by four stark white walls. This square cubicle—also called my bedroom—is just big enough to hold a twin bed and this desk. The small hand-me-down dresser—that has probably been used by more kids than I can count—sits inside the closet because the room is too small to contain it. And all of it—the desk, the bed, and the dresser—has been spray-painted…white.

I think, when one kid leaves, Glenda spray-paints everything to prepare the space for the next one. Maybe it's her strange version of cleaning. White is known to be a sanitary color—or noncolor, I suppose. But it's so odd to be in a room with zero color. If I were in a mental institution, I could understand it, but I'm not crazy—yet. Depending on how long I'm at this placement, I might be when I leave.

I can't complain though. This home is much better than Dwight and Stacey's in New Hope.

New Hope…what a joke.

I can see the irony of it all now. Boy's parents die in a tragic car accident, and he is sent to live with a happy young couple in a town rich in new beginnings. The one thing that city didn't have was hope—at least, until Dwight drank himself into a coma, making Stacey call an ambulance.

In the chaos before the ambulance came, there wasn't time to tidy up the house and put on the faces of a joyful family. The paramedics got to see the home for what it was—hell. The staged joyful home that the foster care workers had been presented with at the few visits they made during the three years I was there was nowhere to be found. I'm not sure exactly who figured it all out and told the proper people, but I'm so thankful. Sometimes, I get the feeling that it was Stacey. She actually seemed mildly pleased to see me go—not in the way that she was glad to be rid of me, but in the sense that she was happy for me.

It's surreal to think that the glugging sounds that terrified me as I cowered, hidden underneath their crappy kitchen table on my last night in the house with Dwight, were actually the means to an end for my placement there.

I moved to this home three days after Dwight had been taken to the hospital. And while this placement isn't bursting with love, no one physically hurts me here. I live with Glenda and her five other foster kids. I've been here for two years now, and I've seen kids come and go.

To be honest, I pretty much stick to myself. I've tried making friends with some of the other kids, but that has never worked out for me. The few kids I've gotten close to have either hurt me by lying about me or stealing from me. Or they leave. Some were adopted, and others were sent to different homes for various reasons. But it doesn't matter why they go. It hurts just the same. It's simply easier to stick to myself and not get emotionally invested in anyone here.

If any truth has stood the test of time, it's that those I love always leave me in one way or another.

I'm currently writing in my notebook. The words within these pages are my sanity. They make me feel less alone when I am so very lonely. I write down the stories that Dad used to tell me. He was the best storyteller. I'm constantly scribbling down memories or moments with my family that I remember so that I don't forget them. I can never forget them.

Today, I'm writing a story that he told me about his favorite moment playing soccer. He made it sound like he was about the age I am now. I can close my eyes and still see him dribbling an invisible soccer ball across our living room floor as he gave me a play-by-play of how he'd single-handedly made the goal that won his team the game against their biggest rivals. I smile to myself as I recall how he ran around the living room, giving me and Mom chest bumps and high fives, as if we were part of his soccer team. He knew how to make Mom laugh. I realize now though that she was often sad, so maybe he was always extra goofy to cheer her up.

I'm glad that they died together. I don't think either one could have lived without the other. I just wish I could have gone with them. It's not fair that I was left here alone. Dad said that I was a brave warrior, and though I'm trying to be, I think I'm failing. I don't feel brave. I feel scared all the time. But Dad said that being scared and pushing through it anyway was part of bravery. So, I hope that he is proud of me. I hope he can see that I'm trying so very hard to have courage.

It's been five years since Mom and Dad passed away. I keep waiting for Nan and Granddad to come get me, but they haven't. I haven't heard from them at all. I haven't received one letter or phone call from them in five years, and I don't understand why. I know they love me. I felt it every time I saw or spoke to them. They called me their miracle baby, a gift. So, why haven't they come? Why won't they save me and take me back with them to England? We could spend half of the year in the city and the other half at the cottage. We could be happy.

Maybe they've been looking, but they can't find me. That's the only explanation that makes any sense. They aren't familiar with the foster care system in this country and are having a hard time locating me. I just have to stay strong for a little bit longer.

I finish writing my memory and then rip the paper out of the notebook. With each hand, I grab it at the top between my index finger and thumb, and I pull, ripping the page down the middle. I repeat this process what seems like eighty more times until my writing sits in a clump of indistinguishable letters on paper shreds on the desk. Then, I lift the white plastic trash can and swoop my hand across the desk until every piece has fallen in.

This is my ritual every time I write.

A year ago, a horrible girl named Jessica stole the notebook where I had written all my recollections. She started running around the house, and in a mocking voice, she read my private moments with my family to all the other kids. It tore me apart when they made fun of my prized memories.

I can still hear the shrill of her voice when she chanted with a whine, "Daddy calls me his little warrior, and warriors are brave." She proceeded to rip the pages out of my book, leaving them scattered all over the house.

That was the saddest I've been since my parents' deaths. Even the worst moments with Dwight didn't compare to how much her actions broke me. I suppose I'm more equipped to take the physical pain. I have methods of blocking it out, and I know it won't last forever. But nothing I could have done would have stopped the anguish I felt while listening to her words.

Emotional pain, at least for me, lasts forever. I'll never escape it.

So, that's my ritual. Every day, I write a page or two in my notebook. I keep my parents alive in that way, and then I make it so no one else can have access to it. No one deserves my thoughts. No one deserves to know how amazing my mom and dad were. My parents were mine, and I will keep them always. I will never let anyone tarnish their memory again.

And despite what Jessica thinks, I am brave and good. But she doesn't know what that even means because she didn't have perfect parents, like I did, to tell her. She's never had anyone to love her. And because of that, I hope to someday forgive her for being so weak and breaking my heart with her cruelty.

But it won't be today. I'm not that strong.

TEN

London

> "I desperately want Loïc Berkeley,
> and I'm used to getting what I want."
> —London Wright

I relax back into the large tan chair as the massaging balls beneath the leather roll up and down my spine. The contraption working my tired muscles isn't as divine as a real massage would be, but it's a close second, especially when it's paired with a pedicure. I let out a content sigh as a woman massages one of my feet with a soft scrub.

Just what the doctor ordered—and by doctor, I mean, me.

Paige and I love spa days. They're very healing. When we feel a moment's stress, our go-to fix is an old-fashioned mani-pedi—and by old-fashioned, I mean, one that takes place in the newest salon in town with the most attentive staff and state-of-the-art massage chairs. Oh, and free wine, not that piss water the cheap spas offer. This is real yummy imported wine.

Ah!

I shoot up, and my entire body cringes when the pedicurist rubs the rough brush across the sensitive skin on the bottom of my foot. My fingers grasp the sides of the chair. My knuckles go white from the force of my grip.

Paige chuckles next to me. "Your favorite part."

I can't reply or even give her a look. All my focus needs to be on enduring this small amount of torture on my way to perfectly painted nails and soft-heels heaven without drop-kicking the kind woman's face in front of me. The struggle is real.

Yes, I know…First World problems.

She finally finishes assaulting my feet and starts to massage my calves with a lotion that smells like coconut, reminding me of the beach.

Ah, this is more like it.

I release the breath I was holding.

Reaching for my phone, I swipe across the screen even though I know I didn't miss a message. But the pathetic girl in me checks anyway.

Nothing.

I set my phone back down in a huff.

"No message from Romeo?" Paige's question is rhetorical. She knows as well as I do that my phone hasn't chimed since I checked it ten minutes ago.

I sigh before answering her anyway, "Not yet."

I suppose I should be worrying less about text messages and spa days and more about finding a job. When I left Kentucky two weeks ago, I was hell-bent on growing up, obtaining meaningful employment, and being a better person. But my valiant motivation was stripped from me the second Loïc's lips met mine on that airplane.

Now, my entire life's mission is to continue tangling my lips—among other body parts—with Loïc's.

He's all I think about. We've been in each other's presence a total of four times, yet I'm a total goner. I'm not so naive as to think that I'm in love with the guy. More accurately, I think it's some sort of insane desire paired with an equal measure of obsession. It's not entirely his looks either. Though I'd be lying if I didn't admit that his good fortune in the appearance department had fueled my initial crush. I'm not certain if it was his tan skin, muscular arms, sexy bone structure, kissable lips, or those mesmerizing blue eyes. More than likely, it was the combination of each gorgeous attribute wrapped up like a fine little package of hotness in a military uniform. I only had to look his way once to be enraptured.

While all of that is still very much true and extremely lust-worthy in itself, he's more than a pretty package. I think I knew that almost immediately. From the start, something about him called to me. It was as if I could feel his pain, read his heart, and appreciate his struggles. It was as if he was put before me for *me*, and I, for him. It was as if I was the person he required to heal his wounded spirit. I've had this knowing feeling, all along, deep within, telling me that he needed me.

Am I crazy to think that? Maybe I am.

It might very well be true that I'm not destined to be with Loïc. Perhaps I'm having a post-graduation life crisis, and I'm clinging on to the hot Army guy, who is set on playing hard to get, as my own mission to sanity. Maybe I'm making this all into more than it should be. It wouldn't be the first time I've created drama in my life where none should have existed.

It honestly doesn't make a difference if it's delusional infatuation or once-in-a-lifetime true love because I'm already invested. Regardless of the origins of these desires, they're here to stay. I desperately want Loïc Berkeley, and I'm used to getting what I want.

I'm back to sounding spoiled again. I'm working on becoming the person I want to be. Rome wasn't built in a day.

"What's the last thing you texted to him?" Amusement lines Paige's voice.

"You know exactly what I said." I turn and give her my best attempt at an evil glare.

She just laughs. Obviously, I'm not as intimidating as I think I am.

"Tell me again. I just love it."

"I told him that his chicken-shit ass had better contact me today because he promised me a second date, and I expect him to deliver."

She slaps her hand on her thigh in a fit of giggles, startling the women working on our feet. "And you're surprised he hasn't responded?"

"I know. It wasn't my best moment." I sigh.

In my defense, I was slightly tipsy when I sent that text last night—and by slightly tipsy, I mean, wasted. In addition, it has been a week since our first date, and since then, I've received one measly text from him before nothing but radio silence.

The morning after our drive-in movie date—and one of the best orgasms I've ever had, I might add—I texted Loïc to tell him that I had a great time. He responded with, *Me, too,* and that's the last I've heard from him. I've texted him once or twice a day since then. I tried keeping my messages upbeat and nonchalant at first. I wanted to give him the I'm-a-cool-and-laid-back-kind-of-girl vibe.

But, after the fourth day of being ignored, my texts changed in nature, and somehow, they turned into the

I'm-the-type-of-crazy-that-you-don't-want-to-bring-home-to-mama vibe. Not that he has a mama. Ugh, wrong analogy.

I should cut him more slack than this. He obviously has issues.

Isn't his wounded heart part of my intense attraction to him? Yet would it kill him to text me?

Paige and I leave the coconut-smelling heaven. Our feet and hands have been buffed and lotioned to soft perfection, and our nails are painted a lovely royal blue—our current color obsession. My mom thinks that blue nails, regardless of the specific shade, look trashy, but I disagree.

We hop into my Mercedes, and I start the car, making sure the AC is on full blast. It's a hot and humid summer day, so immediate AC is life-and-death. Before I can put the car in gear, my phone dings. I whip my head to the side, and my eyes go wide as I look at Paige. She gives me a hopeful smile. I'm sure she thinks my Loïc obsession is a little odd, but as my best friend, she supports me one hundred percent. If I decide to jump aboard the crazy train, she'll be the first to buy a one-way ticket.

Careful of my freshly painted nails, I reach into my bag to pull out my phone. I have a text, and it's from Loïc.

Loïc: Pick you up at five. Be ready.

God, he's bossy, and damn, how I find that so hot.

I peer up to find Paige's expectant look, and I smile big and squeal. She claps her hands in rapid succession and squeals along with me.

There's a knock on the front door exactly at five o'clock.

He might be bossy, but I have to give it to the guy; he's punctual.

I quickly say good-bye to Paige and make my way to the front door. My knees go weak when I see him. He's just so beautiful in that closed-off, rugged, moody kind of way. He's wearing a form-fitting T-shirt, board shorts, and flip-flops. For some odd reason, the fact that I can see his feet creates intense lust-filled thoughts to storm through my mind.

I take in a breath and shake out the rogue hormonal desires that saturate my brain. *Focus.*

"You were going to cancel again," I say.

Yes, I've spent all week praying to the gods of dating that he would call and come through on his promise of another date. I admit, I've been almost desperate, which is so not me. Relief to have him in my presence again washes over me, flooding me with happiness, but that doesn't mean I'm not annoyed. Despite my longing to tightly hug him and thank him over and over for coming, I'm not that girl, and Loïc needs to know that.

"But I didn't," he says casually.

"You wanted to. More so, you wanted to avoid my texts altogether," I huff out in frustration. "You told me you wanted to go out again. We had a great time, and then you made me wait all week for a response. If you don't want to see me again, fine, whatever." *I don't mean that at all. Please want to see me many more times for all eternity.* "But don't play games, Loïc. I don't like them." I'm proud that I'm holding my ground.

Undoubtedly, this probably isn't the best way to start a date.

Damn it…I'm going to scare him away. Why am I not capable of shutting my mouth?

He smiles, and it's a full-on devastating event. Before I can register what's happening, his strong hands grasp the sides of my face, and he pulls my mouth to his. The second our lips connect, I lose all my pent-up annoyance and will to prove my point.

What was my point? I couldn't care less.

Nothing feels as right as Loïc's lips on mine. Nothing. The kiss is soft, void of crazed desire. It's sweet, communicating apologies and longing. It's a timid reunion of two souls so desperate to be together yet so close to imploding and finding themselves at a place from which they won't be able to return.

Loïc and I are on the fine precipice between utopia and a nightmare. We're at the thin space between unfathomable love and devastating loss. One step in the wrong direction would seal our fate, and we're too new, too fragile, to come back from it. I'm terrified of making the incorrect move, but the only option for me is to be myself. I'm not capable of anything else.

Thankfully, he doesn't seem to mind my earlier outburst because his lips continue to move against mine with such reverence that my chest aches.

When he pulls away, he continues to hold my face in his hands. Our faces are so close that I can see the multiple shades of blue in his eyes.

"We good?" he asks, his deep voice thick with desire.

I nod.

"Good." He leans in and kisses my forehead. Pulling back, he says with a chuckle, "And what are you wearing?"

"What?" I'm in black shorts and a flirty sleeveless top. "You told me to dress casual."

"You're wearing heels."

"Casual heels, and they match this outfit," I scoff.

"Heels aren't casual, London."

"They are to me," I protest. "What does it matter?"

"We're going kayaking. They're not what I would think of as appropriate footwear for outdoor sports." He smirks, and it's so adorable that I want to kiss him again.

"Listen, Berkeley"—I throw out his last name as a warning to the serious nature of choosing an outfit for a date—"if you tell me casual, I'm going to dress that way. Next time, perhaps tell me to dress in attire appropriate for kayaking." I offer him a glare though it's empty of annoyance, and he knows it. "So, should I change?"

He shrugs with a grin across his face. "It's up to you, but I would."

"Fine. Come on." I grab his hand and pull him into the house.

Paige is sitting, cross-legged, on one of the couches in the living room. She sports a knowing smile, and I'm sure she just heard everything.

"Loïc, this is my roommate, Paige," I introduce them.

They've seen each other a couple of times—at the car wash and the club—but they've never formally met.

They exchange a few words.

"I'm going to go change my outfit. Apparently, it isn't suitable for all the physical activity that Loïc has planned for me this evening." My face turns red as soon as the words are out. I meant it as a joke, but I'm painfully aware of the innuendo that came with that statement.

Paige giggles. "Good idea. I have some extra condoms in my top drawer, if you need them."

My mouth flies open as I shoot a scowl toward my best friend. *Brat.*

I'm not a prude or anything, but she knows that this is the first time Loïc has actually dated someone, and I don't want to scare him away.

Thankfully, he's laughing.

She's lucky.

"The outfit you were wearing the first time I saw you would work," Loïc offers with a teasing grin.

I recall the barely there bikini top and short shorts I wore for the car wash. "You'd like that, wouldn't you?" I shake my head in amusement. "You two had better behave." I point my index finger between them.

"All is well that ends well," Paige calls out as I turn to leave.

She's ridiculous.

After I've changed into a pair of jean shorts and a baby tee, I slide on my flip-flops and head back to the living room. Loïc and Paige don't notice me right away, and I have a few seconds to take in the scene before me. Loïc is laughing at something Paige said while she nods with a big smirk on her face.

She'd better not be telling secrets about me. I'll get to the bottom of this later.

What I can't take my eyes off of is Loïc—more specifically, Loïc laughing. That vision is a gift to my sight.

My heart tightens as I watch him. His wide smile, his eyes squinted in laughter, and his broad chest vibrating from the force of it combine into a perfectly constructed masterpiece. He looks so happy. More than that, he seems content within his soul. In this moment, he isn't thinking about his demons, overanalyzing the second-to-second details of life, or using his rough exterior to compensate for his desire for constant control. He's simply living.

There are still so many mysteries that surround Loïc. I'm sure I haven't even scratched the surface of what horrors reside in his memories. Oddly enough, that draws me toward him even more.

I've never been the type of person to seek out those in need of emotional support. It's not that I don't care about other people, but I'm not comfortable with dealing with others' issues. Maybe I'm selfish, but that's just not who I am. I'm here for my close family and friends, sure, but the rest of the world needs to find someone else to be their pillar of strength because I'm not qualified for the job.

Yet, with Loïc, it's different. All I want is to be there for him. I want him to trust me with his heart, to let me help mend it.

Finally, my presence at the entryway of the room is noticed. Loïc turns his attention to me. His laughter stops, but he still carries a smile. I shake off my deep thoughts revolving around Loïc's redemption and healing. I can revisit those later. At this point in my relationship with him, getting to date three is my first priority.

"Is she telling you my deepest, darkest secrets?" I question before shooting an accusatory look Paige's way.

"I guess you'll never know." The way he says it sounds like a challenge.

"Oh, I'll find out." I send a glare full of mock disgust toward Paige. I point my finger at her. "I know where you live, Paigey Poo. Don't forget that."

She laughs, which breaks my charade of anger as well, and I smile back at her.

With laughter in my voice, I add, "Remember where your loyalties lie, my friend."

She responds with, "You two enjoy all your physical activities tonight."

"I hate you," I say, shaking my head.

Loïc grabs my hand and leads us toward the front door.

"Lies! You love me!" Paige shouts from the living room.

"You're right. I love you," I call back, my free hand grabbing my purse from the table before we exit the front door.

Loïc chuckles beside me. "Girls are so weird."

"You're just realizing this?"

"I suppose not. Maybe that's part of the reason I don't date."

"You're dating me." He doesn't respond, so I continue, "I think a second date qualifies as dating, don't you?"

He lets out a noncommittal noise, letting me know that he heard me but, at the same time, neither agreeing nor disagreeing with my question. He opens the passenger door and waits for me to jump up into his truck.

After I've hopped up, I look over to him. "Why are you dating me, Loïc?"

He shakes his head and gives me a weak smile. "I have no idea," he says more to himself than anything before he closes my door.

His cavalier statement and the sound of the door shutting make me jump in my seat. I have the feeling that he didn't mean it as rude or hurtful but more speaking to his confusion about his feelings toward me. But I'd be lying if I said that it didn't sting.

It's about a thirty-minute drive to the river where we will be renting a kayak. We spend that time talking about our tastes in music. Loïc is a fan of varying rock. He likes classic rock, the hair bands—including the rock ballads of the eighties and nineties—and the alternative bands from the past two decades. He listens to a station on satellite radio that plays nothing but this type of music. The last three songs have been by Pearl Jam, Stone Temple Pilots, and The Smashing Pumpkins—and the only reason I know this is because each band's name shows on his radio display.

I, on the other hand, am a religious Top Forty Pop music fan. Loïc says I'm a sellout, and I have shallow tastes. I argue that my preferences are the best because I'm listening to what the majority of people like at the moment.

"The songs wouldn't be among the Top Forty most popular songs on the radio if they weren't good, right? My music is relevant."

"I'm gonna have to disagree with you on that one." He chuckles.

What does he know anyway?

Right next to the kayak rental is a mom-and-pop diner, so we each have a quick burger before getting started.

While Loïc is paying, I try to be proactive, and I attempt to lift the kayak. The first thing I realize is that, despite how light and welcoming the kayak looks with its colorful plastic appearance, it is extremely heavy.

Or I'm just a complete wimp.

I grunt loudly in an unladylike fashion as I hoist one end of the kayak off the ground, but my hands slip. In an effort to catch the thing, I stumble on the wet ground.

I let out a startled yell as my ass hits the slick earth, and the stupid wannabe boat falls on my legs.

Ouch! That's going to turn lovely shades of blue and purple.

My eyes water from the event. It's not as if I'm in excruciating pain, but it does sting a little, and my ego along with my shins are definitely bruised.

"London, what are you doing?" Loïc chuckles as he lifts the kayak off of me.

"I was trying to help." I sniffle, completely embarrassed.

My confession causes him to laugh some more as he grabs my hand and lifts me into a standing position against his chest. He hugs me, pulling me into his warmness, while one of his hands rubs soothingly up and down my back. Against my cheek, I can feel the vibrations of the laughter he's trying to hide, but I don't care. I'll fall more often to be held by Loïc.

I'm a true mess around him and extremely wishy-washy. One minute, I'm asserting my will, letting him know that I will not be walked all over, reminding him that I'm a strong, desirable woman who demands respect. The next, I'm a sniffling damsel in distress who's contemplating what other precarious situations I can get myself into, so he'll hold me like this again.

I'm an embarrassment to women's rights everywhere.

He releases his hold. His hands grab on to my upper arms and push me back a bit. His amused gaze finds my embarrassed one. "You okay?"

I nod.

"Good." He leans down and kisses my forehead before his grasp releases my arms. "Then, let's go. I'll handle the kayak." He winks.

Cocky bastard.

He points to the life jackets by his feet. "Can you grab those?"

I pick up the vests and then say, "You know, it's your fault."

He lifts the kayak over his head, like it weighs nothing. His shirt rises with the motion, and I can see his tight stomach muscles and the V that disappears beneath his shorts. I force my eyes upward, only to be met with the sculpted muscles of his arms as they tighten to hold the kayak.

"Oh, really? How so?" He chuckles.

My focus snaps to his deep blues as he waits for my response. "Oh, well…you made me change into flip-flops, and they have no traction, which caused me to slip," I answer petulantly.

He shakes his head in amusement and starts walking toward the water. "Right, and your heels would have been better?"

"Whatever." I follow after him.

"You know what, London? I think you have an issue with being wrong or corrected."

"I do not," I protest. *I so do.*

"You do, and it's kind of a big flaw. It makes you seem spoiled."

My mouth opens wide as I gasp in disapproval. Loïc sets the kayak down on the bank by the river.

"If you think I'm so spoiled, why are you here with me?" I ask firmly, my pride overruling my desire to shut up and be the girl that Loïc wants me to be.

Yes, I'm infatuated with him. Yes, I want him like I've never wanted anyone else in my life. But I'm not a good actress. I can't pretend to be someone I'm not. Loïc would see right through it. I just wish I were someone who knew exactly who she was. My attitude is all over the place. I'm composed of a myriad of opposing emotions. In the past few weeks, I've realized that I'm somewhat of a train wreck. No matter how badly I want Loïc, it'd be better for him to tire of me sooner than later, right? It's best to let my true colors shine.

Loïc takes a step toward me until we are a breath apart. He places his hand on my shoulder, rubbing his thumb across my collarbone. He stares at me with so much intensity that my heart begins to beat wildly in my chest.

"Do you know why I waited a week to text you, London?"

I shake my head, my eyes wide.

"It's because I'm fucked up. I have issues and not small ones either. I have real ones that prevent me from having too many true relationships in my life. I hate that about myself, and I wish it were different, but it's not.

"But then I saw this girl who was so insanely beautiful that I could barely breathe in her presence. From the moment I met her, I relied on the walls that I had put up to keep people out, but it didn't matter. She got in. Despite all my efforts, she penetrated my walls. She was constantly on my mind, and just when I figured I would lose my mind from thinking about her, I randomly ran into her.

"I fought hard to ignore her, to hate her. I wanted to detest her. I did. Longing for someone you can't have is nothing short of torture. So, I picked apart everything about her, looking for a flaw big enough to keep her from monopolizing my thoughts. Regardless of the negatives that popped up, the positives were always the loudest.

"I can't describe my attraction to her because it is so much more than physical. Something about her calls to me, beckoning me toward her. It's almost innate, unstoppable. So, finally, after deliberating so much that I thought my brain would burst, I decided to give it a chance.

"Perhaps, as she told me before, we're truly meant to be. Just maybe, I'm meant to have happiness in this life. I know she's not perfect. She has flaws, as do I. But I texted her back because what if my lots of fucked up and her little of fucked up can be fucked up together?" His other hand grasps my waist, and his fingers dig into my skin in the most delightful way.

He pauses a moment and regards me with burning eyes. "Maybe, where you have holes, I can fill you with my strength, and where I am ripped wide open, you can mend me. There has to be a reason that you're the first woman in my life whom I can't ignore. It's a lot to hope. But there's a small chance that, someday, we won't be fucked up together; we'll just be together."

All I can manage to say is, "Wow."

"I know." Loïc's voice is low. His hand releases its hold on my waist.

"I mean, like, wow, I didn't know you had all those words in you."

Loïc throws his head back in laughter. "I told you I've had a lot of time to think."

"I guess so. Did you have that all planned out? That's deep for a second date." I know I shouldn't be kidding with him after he just laid his heart and soul out for me, but I need a moment to process his words, and I'm pretty sure he needs it, too.

"No, it just sorta came out."

"You're a deep kinda guy, I guess."

"I'm definitely intense. You can add that to my flaw category."

"I'm digging your flaws." I smile.

"And I'm digging yours."

"Even the fact that I'm a little spoiled?" I quirk up a brow in question.

"Even that." He chuckles.

"There is one major flaw that I can't overlook." I press my lips together.

Loïc's expression goes serious. "What's that?"

I take in a big breath. "Well, usually, when a guy gives a sweet and sexy speech like that, he follows it up with an equally as hot kiss. I'm feeling cheated without a kiss, and that's definitely being marked as a flaw."

Using that deliciously low voice that makes my toes curl, he says, "Lucky for you, that's one I can fix."

Before I can think of a witty response, his mouth is on mine. He wraps his hands around my waist and pulls me in, so our bodies are flush as our tongues move desperately against each other. I thread my fingers through the short hair at the nape of his neck, pushing our mouths as close together as possible.

I can't get enough of Loïc. I don't think I ever will.

As our kiss continues, my mind returns to his words from seconds ago, and my heart swells with happiness. He said a lot, and I will take it all in later. But the one thing that rings loud and clear is that he is just as infatuated with me as I am with him. Nothing could make me happier.

ELEVEN

Loïc

*"Please forget my lame attempt at a joke. I'm not remotely funny.
It's one of my flaws."*
—Loïc Berkeley

"You've never done this before, have you?" I can't stop
from chuckling as I watch London struggle with the
paddle, like she's slaying a dragon with a sword.

"Um, no. Is it that obvious?" she calls over her
shoulder at me.

"Yep." I get the feeling that she really isn't an
outdoorsy type of girl. *One more flaw to add to her growing list
and one that I'll gladly help her with.*

I love being outside. There's something comforting
about being out in the elements, regardless of what they
are. I've lived all over the United States and been to Iraq.
It doesn't matter if I'm sitting beneath the lush evergreens
in Washington as it rains or in the Iraqi desert, covering

my face as the sand whips around me. Being outside calms me.

I spent way too much time inside as a child, hiding from my fears, trying to make myself invisible to the horrors that surrounded me. A large part of my childhood passed by with me feeling suffocated between strong walls that didn't protect me. I've learned that there are a lot of truly evil people in this world who will hurt others for their enjoyment. And that's the thing I love about nature; it's not out to get anyone. Yes, it can be powerful and even deadly, but it's not personal. It is a force to be reckoned with, but at least it's a fair force. And it's always beautiful, whether it's the waves coming onto the sandy beaches of South Carolina or a thunder and lightning storm in Georgia. Regardless of how serene or fierce its attributes are, nature is exquisite. I simply find it really intriguing.

Maybe that's why I'm so obsessed with London. I have to smile at the similarities. She can be as soothing as a breeze floating through the trees on a warm fall day or as dangerous as an ice storm on a busy highway during rush hour. Her mood shifts from hot to cold on a dime, yet both are equally thrilling. Through both, she's beautiful.

I think she has some growing to do as a person. I'm not sure she knows exactly where her place is in this world—not that I do either. But I'm hoping, when she finds it, she keeps her fire because I'd be lying if I said that I didn't find it extremely hot.

She stops wrestling with the water and wedges her paddle into the space down by her feet. She twists back, so she can see me. "I get the feeling you love all this sporty outdoorsy crap, don't you?"

I laugh and nod my head. "Yeah, I do."

"Are all our dates going to be outside?" she says with a sigh.

"Probably."

She groans and throws her head back with exaggerated effort, eliciting another round of laughter from me.

"You'll get used to it," I say.

"I think I should be in charge of planning some of our dates then. That's it. I'm taking you out next time."

"That's fine. It won't be as fun as this though." I offer her a wink.

"This isn't fun. My arms hurt," she says with a frown.

"How can your arms hurt? You've barely done anything."

"Hey!" She sounds offended, but I know she's just being dramatic. "I've been paddling…a lot."

"That's what you call it?"

"I hate you." She pouts.

"Keep telling yourself that."

London leans back as I continue to guide us down the river, which is fine by me. She wasn't that helpful anyway. We don't talk for a few minutes, and I take in the soothing sounds of the water.

After a while, I say, "You know that's kind of a flaw."

"What is?" she questions.

"Telling people that you hate them because they don't say or do exactly what you want them to."

"Is this, like, our thing? Pointing out what we don't like about the other person. 'Cause, if it is, that's not really good for building a relationship."

"Maybe you're right."

"I am right. And you know what, Loïc? You pointing out all of my flaws is definitely a huge flaw of your own."

"We all have them, London. No one is perfect. Wouldn't you like to know what yours are, so you can work on them?"

She huffs out a short laugh. "Not really. You know, growing up, my parents did nothing but tell me how great I was. I'm really good at listening to the wonderful things about me. You should try that move."

"Well, growing up, I was abandoned by the only people in the world who loved me. I was left to protect myself from predators who got off on hurting children and telling me how worthless I was every single day. I guess we come from different worlds."

London gasps, and I realize that my stab at wit about my past didn't end up humorous at all.

I'm such an idiot.

I wanted to keep the rest of the date carefree after my extremely premature deep confessions back when we were on the bank of the river.

"I'm sorry, London. I didn't mean to say that. It was a horrible attempt at a joke. Just forget it."

She nods, her expression one of sadness. She turns around, and we continue down the river in silence. She lifts her arm a couple of times, her hand moving to wipe something at the corner of her eye. I can't see her face, but I think she's crying.

Great, I made her cry. This is why I don't date—or at least, it's one of the reasons. I suck at it.

I steer the kayak over to the bank. A truck from the kayak rental place is there, waiting to take us back to where we parked, eight or so miles back.

After the kayak hits the sandy bank, I step out and pull it out of the water. Reaching down, I grab London's hand and help her get out. I hold her to me and hug her tight before lightly kissing her forehead. "Please forget my lame attempt at a joke. I'm not remotely funny. It's one of my flaws."

To this, she giggles, and I realize that it's definitely a favorite sound.

"It's definitely a flaw. You should really work on it," she responds.

"I know. I'll try," I say with mock seriousness.

I lift her off the ground so that her neck is level with my face, and I nuzzle my lips against the soft skin beneath her ear. I breathe her in, letting her sweetness fill my soul.

I've got it bad for this chick.

That fact both terrifies and exhilarates me.

London was right earlier. I did contemplate never returning her texts or taking her out again. In this short time that I've been talking to her, something has been happening to me. I'm having feelings that I haven't had to deal with in a long time. I'm thinking about people and places that I'd rather not think about. Hell, last night, I dreamed about Jessica, a girl from my foster home days whom I hated above all else—well, almost.

London came into my life, and so did a shitstorm of emotional baggage. It's as if I can't let my guard down to allow London access to who I really am without letting in all the sadness I've been keeping out. Apparently, my emotions are all or nothing.

As I said in my confession to her earlier—when all the feelings in my head decided to flow out of my mouth like vomit, unwanted and uninvited—for some reason, I think she's worth it. I've been closed off for so long. I've decided to face my fears for once, and after years of being a coward, I'm finally ready to show an ounce of courage.

We get the kayak loaded up and take a seat in the vehicle. The ride back to my truck isn't long. My fingers thread between London's as we hold hands. No words are spoken on the way back. We're both absorbed in our own thoughts. I would pay good money to know what she's thinking.

The truck drops us off. The sky around us is getting darker. I come to this area often to go kayaking, so I know that the state park nearby has a hill where we can park. We hop in my truck and travel a few minutes down the road until I park at the perfect vantage point to view the upcoming sunset.

After getting out of the truck, I start to organize the blankets in the bed of it.

London chuckles beside me.

"What?" I ask.

"I just had this vision of our entire dating future taking place outside."

"Sounds good to me." I finish laying out the blankets. "Do you have complaints about the last time we were in the bed of this truck together?" I raise my eyebrow in question.

That statement halts her snickers. "Um, no. Definitely not."

Even without the bright light of the day, I can see her cheeks redden.

"That's what I thought," I answer with a smug expression.

"Well, you know, we do live in Michigan, home of the eight-month winter. So, we're going to have to spend some time indoors eventually."

"Number one, I think eight months is a slight exaggeration. And number two, they make clothes to help with the elements—you know, snow pants, gloves…things like that."

"No way. Winter is unbearable, even with all that snow gear. My mom was trying to get me to move South the other day—or at least look for jobs south of here. I told her no because Paige was here, but now that I'm reminded of the winters, I just might."

The words have an almost tangible force to them as they come from her mouth. I feel them hit me in my chest, and I have to pull in a breath. I stare at her for a moment and imagine her leaving, moving away. I know I don't have the right to care—I barely know her—but the thought of losing her hurts for more reasons than I can explain.

Her gaze finds mine, and I see something flash through her eyes—regret maybe.

"I didn't mean that I am moving. I don't know. I haven't even started looking for jobs yet, to be honest. I'm going to apply to ones around here, too." Her words come out fast, rushed.

"London, it's fine." It's not fine, but there's nothing I can do about it this very second...except maybe give her reasons to stay. "Come on." I reach out and grab her hands, pulling her onto the blankets.

We get situated so that I'm leaning my back against the cab of the truck, and London lies between my legs with her back to my chest.

The night air is warm but not muggy. Michigan summers can be so humid that one sweats just from sitting outside. I'm thankful that it's not that way tonight because all my accolades over the joys of being outdoors would all be for naught if we were both sweating our asses off. This moment would have lost all of its natural romance, that's for sure.

London and I are silent as we watch the sun dip beneath the horizon among a sky of pinks and oranges.

When the big ball of light is gone and the sky is barely aglow with the fleeting colors, London turns around. She straddles my lap. "I don't think I've ever watched a sunset before. Thanks for that." She smiles sweetly.

"How can you never have seen a sunset in your twenty-two years of life? That isn't even possible."

"I mean, of course I've seen them, but I've never sat and actually watched one, like an event. It's a much different experience to be still and really appreciate the beauty of it, you know?"

"Yeah, I suppose it is." I raise my hand and brush a chunk of her silky hair behind her ear.

As my hand retreats, I grasp the bottom of one of her locks and run it between my thumb and index finger. It's silky. In all my experiences with girls in the past, I've never stopped to simply take them in. I guess I've never wanted to until now. It amazes me how soft they are, or maybe it's just London. Everything about her—from her hair to her skin to her lips—possesses an enchanting smoothness that is completely fascinating to me.

When my gaze lifts from her hair to meet her eyes, there's an air of scrutiny in her expression, as if she is trying to figure me out as much as I am with her. For two people in their twenties, we're relative babies in this dating game. I know she's dated before, but there is something different for her this time around. I can see it every time she looks at me.

I lift my hands to the nape of her neck and glide my fingers through her hair. The sounds of nature are around us with chirps of crickets and frogs in the distance. They all play the background melody to the crescendo of our breaths and the beating of my heart. Having London like this makes me insane with need. The way her body straddles mine and the short distance between our lips are maddening—in the best way. It's almost completely dark now, but I can still see the desire shining in her eyes, mirroring my own.

She closes her eyes and bites her bottom lip as her head tips back into my hands. My fingers grasp her hair tighter. The movement causes her body to grind against me and my rapidly growing need for her. Unable to physically keep my lips away any longer, I lean in to kiss her exposed neck. My mouth nibbles, sucks, tastes, and kisses over her salty skin. It's only the appetizer to the long meal that I know is to come, but just this small nibble satisfies me like nothing else has before. It's not enough—I definitely need more—but it's so good.

London groans into the night air. She grinds against me with purpose, and my lips become needier, urgently moving to sample every inch of her. I kiss up her neck until I've found her lips. I pull her face toward me, and my tongue plunges into her mouth. Her lips move passionately against mine. She tastes of pure ecstasy, pure heaven.

She's my London, my happy place. She's where I belong.

That thought paralyzes me, and I jerk back from her, hitting my head against the back of the truck.

Fuck. Look at that; I literally knocked some sense into myself.

A firestorm of unwanted memories invades my mind—all saturated with loss and despair. The overwhelming hurt floods my mind.

This can't work. It will never work.

"What is it?" London asks, startled.

It takes me a second to compose my thoughts. My ears ring uncomfortably from my head's firm meeting with the metal behind me.

"I just realized that we should probably get back," I say in a tight voice.

"What?" London sounds utterly confused.

I don't blame her. Two seconds ago, I was gearing up to fuck her senseless, and she knew it.

"Look, I just remembered that I have to work tomorrow, so we should go." I gently grasp her shoulders and move her off of my lap.

"Tomorrow's Sunday."

"Right, I know. I told Cooper that we'd get up early to go running. We have our PT test this week."

"Something tells me that you're not going to have any trouble meeting the minimal requirements given by the government, regardless of whether or not you train." Her voice is laced with blazing annoyance. "What's really the issue, Loïc?"

I jump down from the back of the truck. "Nothing. I'm just ready to wrap this up, is all."

London stands and walks toward me. "No, that's not it." She sits down before hopping off the tailgate.

I tug the blankets off and walk away from London. Throwing the bedding in the space behind my seat, I say, "It's that simple. I'm ready to go back. I have stuff to do tomorrow."

I turn around, and she's standing there. The light from the truck's interior shines on her, showcasing her aggravated stance, complete with crossed arms and a vicious scowl.

I don't want to deal with this. Pissed off London is not my favorite—albeit her fierce anger makes her even hotter.

Damn it. Focus.

"What are you hiding from? Why are you shutting down? I don't understand!" She raises her arms in frustration. "One minute, you're all but confessing your love for me, and the next, you're pushing me away faster than I can blink!"

"Hold up. I never said I loved you. We hardly know each other. Love isn't even in the same universe as us right now." I motion my finger between us, pointing from my chest to hers.

"Really?" she questions. "So, your little speech about barely being able to breathe in my presence, your attraction toward me that's so much more than physical, and something about me that beckons you toward me—oh! And let's not forget the part about the innate and unstoppable attraction! I thought we were going to be fucked up together, Loïc, until we weren't fucked up any longer but just together." Her harsh tone morphs into one of sadness at the end.

What? Does she have a photographic memory or some shit? What the hell?

Apparently, I can't have a moment of undoubtedly stupid weakness where I confess my deep-seated attraction to her without her rubbing it in my face.

I don't have the fire in me to fight her. I'll never win in a battle of words because hers will always make more sense. She will continually be right. I know I'm fucked up. I understand more than anyone that I hold on to irrational fears and block people out. Deep down, I realize that isn't the way to live. But knowing something and having the courage to do differently, to choose the hard and scary route, are two separate things.

Bottom line, when it comes down to the core of the issue, I'm weak. I've tried not to be, but my dad was wrong about me.

"I can't fight with you, London." My words sound pathetic, and I wish I could take them back and replace them with ones that would show that I'm strong and in control. But I'm not those things, so what does it matter? "Please, just get in the truck."

Her lip trembles, and I think she's going to cry, but she holds it in. Her face carries a frown as she all but stomps to the passenger side and gets in. I have to stop myself from smiling. I get that this situation isn't remotely funny, but, God, I love when she's all feisty, and her pouty attitude comes out.

I hop up into the truck. Starting the engine, I begin our trip back.

After a few minutes, London asks, "What does this mean? Do you just need to call it an early night? Do you need a few days to think about stuff? Or are we over?"

Are we over? Those words resonate in my brain.

We were over before we even started. One intriguing, drop-dead gorgeous woman isn't going to heal a lifetime of hurt overnight. I tried to avoid her. I told her no multiple times, but she wouldn't hear it. This frustrating, beautiful woman wouldn't take no for an answer.

Doesn't she know that I was trying to be a good person? That I was trying to stop her from feeling like this? And this is how we feel after a handful of meetings and two dates. Two. Fucking. Dates.

But I can't make myself voice my thoughts out loud even though I know them to be true. So, instead, I say, "I don't know."

London sighs beside me but doesn't say anything else the rest of the ride. She's the type of girl to battle for what she wants, but she's also prideful. I think she's found herself at the spot where she's put up enough of a fight to make sure I know how she is feeling. But she's not going to beg for me to like her either. Her stubborn pride is one of the many things I love about her...or loved, past tense—I mean, liked, used to like. Ugh, I don't know.

I pull into London's drive and opt for not being a total dick, so I walk her to the front door. She turns to say good-bye, and the tension between us is more than a little uncomfortable.

"Listen, Loïc," she starts to say, her voice sweet and kind.

"Just save it, London," I snap before I can stop myself. My walls and ability to be an eternal asshole are back in full effect.

Her eyes widen, but she quickly composes herself. She stands on her tiptoes and gives me a small kiss on the cheek. My body stiffens at the contact. She turns to leave, and her hand grabs the knob of the door.

But then, almost on instinct, she looks back at me. "I was just going to say that I really want to be fucked up together. And whatever reason you have for thinking you don't deserve someone to love you is wrong. I see you, Loïc, more than you think I do. You're a good person, and you deserve way more in this life than you're allowing yourself to have. I don't know why you're punishing yourself, but you should stop. Maybe I'm not the person you need, but you need to find the one who is. Everyone needs love, even a big, bad warrior. Not everything in life should be a battle."

I'm stunned, standing frozen on London's front porch, staring at the door she just closed behind her.

What the hell? Those three words are on repeat inside my head. I grasp the back of my neck and turn to leave. *Seriously, what the hell?*

This entire day consisted of 351 reasons why I don't date. I can barely think clearly enough to put one foot in front of the other to get off this porch.

I just need to get home and go to bed. Then, in the morning, I'll work on forgetting that I ever knew a girl named London.

TWELVE

Loïc

Age Fifteen

San Antonio, Texas

"Hope is a powerful thing.
It always kept me fighting for every tomorrow."
—Loïc Berkeley

I spy black mold running along the caulk on the back of the sink, a sponge that is more gray than the teal color it's supposed to be, and a sink full of dishes that should have been washed last week.

I think back to Glenda's house. I haven't lived there in two years, but I'll never forget the maddening whiteness of it.

But which is worse—disgusting grossness or insanity-inducing starkness?

I think I'm going to pick black mold for $500, Alex.

Yep, I'd take the white over this any day.

I smile as I think of Mrs. Peters, the sweet old lady I stayed with for a few weeks before coming here. To say that she had an obsession with Alex Trebek would be an understatement. She recorded every episode of *Jeopardy!* onto stacks of VHS tapes and then would watch it all day long, every day. She would pause it to make meals and cookies. She made the best oatmeal–chocolate chip cookies in the entire world.

Oh, I miss Mrs. Peters.

I wished that I could have stayed with her for a long time. She was the nicest person I've stayed with. I didn't have the nerve to ask her, of course, but I think she knew that I was happy there. Before my caseworker came to bring me here, Mrs. Peters explained to me that she was just too old to have kids full-time. She said us kids deserved better and that she could only be a temporary placement situation.

If she only knew.

After leaving Glenda's, I stayed in five homes before coming here. I'm hoping this one will be temporary as well, but if we're basing my stay off my luck, I'll probably be here forever. I haven't been here long, but I already know I don't want to be either.

Bev and Carl seem nice enough—not really. *Nice* is a relative term, and in my experience, it signifies not cruel more than it stands for kindness.

Carl is overweight and just kinda gross. When he's not at work—I'm not sure where that is yet—he's sitting in the brown-and-yellow plaid armchair in the living room. When he's gone, you can still see the outline of where his body sits. The fabric and cushions are completely worn down in a perfect Carl-shaped form.

Bev reminds me of a witch, like the one who tried to eat Hansel and Gretel. She comes off as decent, but there's a part of her that's off, that scares me. It's like she's being accommodating enough so as not to frighten me away, and then she'll attack. She knows that I have nowhere else to go anyway. So, if it is indeed an act, she should know it's an unnecessary one.

I have a feeling that Bev and Carl are going to be a permanent placement.

They have another foster kid named Sarah who's been here for three years. She's shy and quiet. I tried to talk to her last night, which goes against my usual behavior. I'd stopped trying to be friends with the other foster kids a long time ago. But something about Sarah makes me think she could use a friend. I didn't get much out of her last night, other than the amount of time she'd lived here.

But I don't like the way she acts around Carl. She never looks at him. The second she enters the living room, she keeps her eyes focused in the opposite direction of where he sits. I have the impression that she's petrified to look at him, and that's weird. I mean, he's pretty ugly, but I think it's more than that.

"Boy, the dishes aren't going to wash themselves." Bev's presence in the kitchen startles me.

"I know. I'm working on it."

"To me, it looks like you're just standing there," she snaps.

And just like that, the witch is here.

I don't say anything else as I continue to scrub the mildew-infested gray sponge against the caked-on lasagna pan. I've learned, most times, it's best to be quiet.

"You know, it's hard to find placements for teenage boys. I would think you'd be a little more grateful when people take you in." She continues yammering, but it's almost as if she's talking for her own benefit.

135

I try to block her out as I continue to scrub.

"We're always offered teenagers, and nine times out of ten, they're boys. You see, girls are adopted much earlier—at least, the good ones. Unless he's a cute little baby, no one's standing in line to adopt a boy. Did you hear me? I said, boys are useless. No one wants them."

I know she's expecting a response, but I don't have the desire to play this game. I've played it too many times before. So, I simply nod.

Apparently, that's not the response she wants because, in a clipped tone, she adds, "What do you expect? Even your own parents didn't want you."

"Shut up," I say under my breath, barely containing my rage.

"Excuse me?" she spits out.

I turn and throw the disease-infested sponge on the ground. Through gritted teeth, I say, "Shut up." My hands clench at my sides, and I have to talk myself out of hitting her in her big, crooked nose.

I've had it with these excuses for human beings who sign up to take in kids. *Why do they do it? Money? It surely can't be that much. I mean, look at this dump. Power? They obviously get their thrills from kicking someone else when they're down. But it still doesn't add up.*

I can't take it anymore. Years of bottled up despair and anger threaten to explode. *And what if it does? What can these people possibly do to me that hasn't already been done? Kick me out? Being homeless doesn't seem too bad. Send me to jail? Sounds good to me. Is Carl going to hit me? Hardly. I can outrun him any day. Fat ass.*

I'm done.

"My parents died, you stupid twat, and I haven't been adopted because my grandparents are looking for me to take me back to London."

She laughs. It's a deranged sound, and it sends unpleasant chills down my spine.

"No one is coming for you. Are you that stupid? Your grandparents have long forgotten about you. They left you. Even your own flesh and blood didn't want a piece of shit like you. There's only one reason a boy your age is still in foster care, and that's because you're worthless. The state has to pay people money to put up with you. You're lucky that there are people like us, willing to take you in."

"I don't need you."

She takes a step toward me until her thin finger is in my face. I can smell the stale rot of her breath.

"Yes. You. Do."

I hate this woman before me. I hate her more than I've ever hated anyone. I despise her more than Jessica, and up until this moment, she had hurt me deeper than anyone else. But, now, the stupid witch Bev has taken the most evil crown. She earned it fair and square. In one breath, she managed to take the little bit of hope that I'd had left, and she obliterated it.

A frail combination of hope and love was all I'd had left. I'd held on to it like a shield, and for years, it had kept me going. It'd turned me into a survivor. I'd learned quickly how to navigate this horrible nightmare I'd been living in. Like a badge on my chest, I'd worn the knowledge that they would come, and it had given me strength to keep going day after day. I'd only had to make it one more day because, the next day, they would be here to save me.

Hope is a powerful thing. It always kept me fighting for every tomorrow.

I'd believed, and because of that, I had known that tomorrow would eventually come. And when it did, it would be worth it.

All of it.

My grandparents would be my saviors, and they would take me to London—a little boy's vision of heaven, happiness, love.

I always believed that they were out there, fighting to rescue me, but the witch is right. No one is coming. No one is going to save me. Love is a joke, and London's a lie.

The only person I have looking out for me in this world is me. I'm furious that it took this evil person before me to tell me with such bluntness before I got it, but I hear it loud and clear now.

She's totally right. They're not coming for me. They never were. The only two people left on this earth who were supposed to love me have left me completely alone.

I have no one.

I haven't had anyone for a long time.

My heart shatters beneath my aching chest. I can't believe I never saw my reality for what it was. I suppose I had to believe—at least when I was younger—so I would have the strength to get through each horrible day. Maybe my mind is finally ready to accept the truth because I'm old enough now.

I don't need to suffer in these homes until I'm rescued. I need to save myself.

Complete clarity envelops me. For the first time since I stepped foot in Dwight and Stacey's home when I was seven years old, I have control—or at least, I will.

I don't bother to say anything else to Bev as I step around her and march to my makeshift bedroom, which also houses the thirty-year-old washer and dryer. I shoot a quick glance behind me to see if anyone followed me. I'm relieved when I see that no one is there. It wouldn't have mattered, but it just makes things easier.

Before reaching my sleeping space, I duck into Sarah's room. "Hey," I whisper.

Startled, Sarah whips her head up from the book she's reading. Her long, curly strawberry-blonde hair swooshes over her shoulders, and her big blue eyes are open wide.

"I'm leaving. Come with me."

I don't know why I'm including Sarah in my plans. I need to focus on myself. But something deep in my gut tells me not to leave her here. This place is slowly killing her. I barely know her, but I know that much.

"I…I can't." She shakes her head.

"Look, I don't really have a plan, but we'll figure it out. I don't want to leave you here, alone…with Carl."

Her body visibly shudders when I say his name.

"Please come with me. I won't hurt you. Grab a bag. Pack the essentials—clothes, toiletries, your personal stuff, a jacket, and maybe a blanket, if you can fit it. Just get what you can carry. We're leaving in ten minutes."

She stands, and I exit her room before heading to mine.

This is insane. My behavior is completely reckless, yet this is the happiest I've been in a long time. Hope grows in my chest, and it's not of the delusional variety. I'm taking control of my life, and regardless of what happens when I leave this house, it will be of my doing. Who knows? Maybe I'll starve to death. But who freaking cares? It will be because of my actions and no one else's.

I feel a wave of caution come over me as I think about the fact that I'm involving Sarah in my rebellion. But then I realize that she'd probably rather starve to death than stay here with Carl any day.

I've packed up all my belongings into a backpack and my duffel bag. I've even managed to swipe a blanket and pillow. Something tells me that I'm going to be glad I did.

In the bathroom, I find several unopened toothbrushes, a brand-new tube of toothpaste, deodorant, and shampoo, so I take them, too. I have no idea what I'm doing, but I'm trying to think of things that I'll want the most while homeless. I realize that food will probably be at the top of that list, but I know that good old Bev isn't going to let me raid her pantry when I leave, so I'll have to figure out the food issue later.

When I pack everything that I think I need—at least the items I have access to—I meet Sarah in her room.

"You ready?" I say in a low voice.

She looks terrified, but she nods her head.

"I got some bathroom things, but did you grab stuff that you'll need, like a brush or something?" I have no idea what goes into being a girl, but looking at Sarah's hair, I know a brush must be involved.

She nods again.

She's so sweet. I hardly know her, but I feel like it's my duty to protect her. I think that involves being honest.

"Look, I don't know if I mentioned this before, but when we leave, we're probably going to be homeless." I think that seems important to mention.

The corners of her lips turn up slightly, and if I'm not mistaken, for Sarah, that's like a smile.

"I know," she answers quietly.

"And you still want to come?" I decide to give her an out.

She nods once more.

"And you packed everything you think you'll need for a life on the street?" Okay, I admit I'm being a bit dramatic.

For all I know, we'll be picked up by the police before we get a mile away. But the mere chance that we won't is so exciting.

"Yeah, I think so," she answers.

"You know, I know we've only known each other for two days and all, but I sense a lot of trust growing here," I kid.

I actually joke, and she giggles softly, which leads me to one of my ultimate goals in life. I will make Sarah I'll-Ask-Her-About-Her-Last-Name-Later laugh at least a few times per day. I'm liking this new version of me.

I stretch out my free hand, and Sarah grabs it. The two of us walk toward the front of the house. As we get closer to the living room, she squeezes my hand. I squeeze hers back, trying to reassure her that she'll be okay. I am not leaving this place without her.

"What do you two think you are doing?" Bev shrieks over the TV.

"We're leaving," I say firmly.

Bev cackles. "And where do you think you're going?"

"Doesn't matter. Not here."

"You aren't going anywhere!" she yells.

I ignore her and continue to walk toward the door.

"You stop right there, you little shit." Carl's voice booms from behind me.

I turn to watch him lifting his fat ass out of the chair.

"You can leave all you want, but you're not taking her with you." He storms toward Sarah.

I feel her quiver beside me.

I let go of her hand and step in front of her. "If you touch her, I will kill you."

My threat doesn't faze him, and he continues toward us. I've recently grown a lot, but Carl is still bigger than me. I might be able to take him though. He's pretty out of shape. I decide to play it safe, and the second he's close enough, I swing my leg back and kick him between the legs with every ounce of strength I have. He immediately falls to his knees with a howl of pain.

"Stop!" Bev screams, charging toward us.

I raise my fist like I'm going to punch her, and she stops.

Her eyes bulge, and she breathes heavily. "You are such a worthless piece of shit," she spits out.

"Fuck you. This piece of shit is already so much more than you'll ever be. And you'd better tell your husband to keep his dick in his pants. I will be watching you. If I find out that he's hurt another girl, even once, I will murder you both while you're asleep, and I will make sure you suffer," I say in the evilest voice I can muster.

It must do the trick because her eyes go wide with fear.

With this, I grab Sarah's hand, and we run out of the house. I've never said so many swear words out loud in my life, and it's so invigorating. I totally lied to Bev. I don't plan on ever coming within thirty miles of this place again, nor could I ever kill anyone, but I hope I was convincing. I hope I scared her enough to have a serious talk with her child-molester husband.

Sarah and I run, hand in hand, until our chests ache, and our lungs burn. Finally, after what seems like miles, we stop. We stare at each other, wide-eyed, and I'd be lying if I didn't admit that we are a little scared. But when our gazes meet, we bust out in sidesplitting laughter. The two of us laugh until we have tears streaming down our faces.

Eventually, just like we ran ourselves out, we've laughed ourselves out.

Sarah holds up her fist and says in a low voice full of mirth, "I will kill you."

She sounds more like Arnold Schwarzenegger as the Terminator than she does me, but it brings a genuine smile to my face.

"What? I didn't have you convinced?"

"No, but I think they kinda believed you. That's all that really matters." She shrugs.

"True." I smile at this girl in front of me.

Already, she's so different. It's very strange what a little bit of hope and control can do for a person.

I understand what it feels like because that same surge of optimism is blooming within my chest, too. I know that Bev's words and my subsequent realization about my life will come back to haunt me. I don't know how to get over that type of abandonment and loss. But, for now, I'm not going to mourn it. Instead, I'm going to let this newfound sensation of empowerment engulf me and carry me along for as long as it can.

For the first time in eight years, the smile on my face is genuine.

"Well, I think we should get a little farther away and then maybe find somewhere to sleep. That's what homeless people do, right?"

"I guess so." She giggles.

We walk at a leisurely pace now.

"Sarah, what's your last name?"

"Why?" she wonders sweetly.

"I was just thinking about it earlier, and I was curious."

"It doesn't matter what my last name was. It isn't one I plan on keeping, that's for sure. What's yours?"

"Berkeley."

"Did you have nice parents at some point?" she questions.

"The best," I admit sadly.

She thinks for a moment and nods her head. "My last name can be Berkeley then."

"Sounds good to me." I chuckle. "You can be like my sister."

"I like that." She nods. "I just hope they don't find me." Sadness returns to her voice.

I have a feeling that *they* is a lot more people than just Bev and Carl, but it's not important because I will keep Sarah safe. "They won't. No one will."

"Promise?"

"I promise."

I make a silent vow to always protect Sarah. No one stepped up to the plate to save me after my parents died, but I don't need anyone to protect me now. I have myself. But Sarah's fragile. She was close to breaking, and she's already improving. The sensation that comes along with knowing that I had a small part in healing a piece of her heart feels better than any sensation I can remember.

It feels a little like love.

THIRTEEN

London

> *"Loïc is and will forever be the only fish in my sea. If I can't have him, then I don't want another."*
> —London Wright

"The grass isn't always greener on the other side, chica." Paige provides her words of advice.

The two of us are lounging on my bed, each with a pint of Ben & Jerry's ice cream sitting on our shelves—also known as our boobs. Yes, we're dressed. My T-shirt-clad breasts provide the perfect place to place the fattiest flavor of ice cream I could find, which happens to be Chubby Hubby. My ultimate goal is to eat as much as I can, become extremely obese, and cry myself to sleep for the rest of my life until I die. At which point, I will have died sad, alone, and fat with hairy legs because I wouldn't have seen the point of showering either.

My mom always said I had a flair for the dramatic. She might have a point.

"You know, I think your advice actually has merit this time."

"Really?" Paige asks excitedly.

"I mean, given another boy or breakup, then, yes, that saying would work. But, unfortunately, it doesn't work for this scenario because Loïc is the one, Paige. I know it. The grass will always be greener where he is."

"I'm just trying to help you, so please don't get mad at me."

I eye her with an accusing stare.

"Stop. You know you get mad at me if you hate my advice, and it usually ends with, 'I hate you.' Then, you apologize and say that you don't."

"Okay, you might be right. I promise not to get mad. Continue." I wave my hand in the air.

"I guess I'm just wondering why you're so upset over this dude. Sure, he's fucking hot. I get it. He's nice enough, I guess. But the baggage? Apparently, he has a seven forty-seven full of it. Who wants to deal with that?"

"I do," I whine in protest. "I want it all."

"Why, babe? You barely know him. You haven't even gone all the way. I mean, I could see if you had been careless and gotten knocked up, then you would put some effort into making it work with your baby daddy. But, unless you're secretly with child and not telling me, I can't understand why you're so down about this one. He's just a guy. There are plenty more where he came from. There are other fish in the sea."

"First, I have to say, once again, that saying would be appropriate here, given it were another guy. So, kudos to you. I'm impressed. But Loïc is and will forever be the only fish in my sea. If I can't have him, then I don't want another. And, secondly, I hate you."

"London!" Paige smacks my arm with her hand.

"Stop, Paige!" I laugh. "You're going to make me spill my Chubby Hubby, and this might be the only hubby I get in life."

"You're so ridiculous."

"I know. I can't help it. But, seriously, I might love him, Paige. I would never tell him that because he would totally freak out. But he's unlike any guy I've been with. It's so hard to explain, and the entire thing sounds cheesy...like I'm pulling it from a Disney movie. But, when I'm with him, I just know. He needs me. We're perfect together. He simply has to get his head out of his ass and see it."

"All right, girlfriend, I'm stopping you right there. You do not love him," she says with a huff. "I don't know if you even like him. From what you've told me, he sounds like a mess who doesn't know which way is up. Isn't your head spinning? 'Cause mine sure is, like a teeter-totter."

"Teeter-totters don't spin."

"Okay, like a freight train on full speed," she says dramatically.

"Nope, still no spinning involved," I say with a straight face, trying not to laugh.

"A merry-go-round?"

"Yeah, that would work. Or maybe one of those spinny-top things," I offer.

"Okay, fine. So, my head is spinning like a merry-go-round from this shit. Isn't yours?"

I sigh. "I'm sorry; you lost me at freight train."

We both burst out in a fit of laughter, and it feels good. There's nothing better than laughing with your best friend until your sides ache.

Our laughter finally ceases, and I wipe my eyes.

Paige says, "My entire point, before you had to split hairs, is that you don't love him. You're obsessed with him because you can't have him. You think about him nonstop because he doesn't want you. His rejection is making you crazy. You, London, do not like being told no. That's what this whole thing is about."

I take a minute to think about her words. "Maybe you're right. Rejection sucks."

"Yeah, it does."

"So, how do I get someone who doesn't want me?"

Paige thumps the heel of her hand against her forehead. "Oh my God, I might as well be talking to a wall."

"Whatever." I don't feed into her dramatics. "Just tell me what to do."

"I don't have any more advice for you," Paige says in a resigned tone. "This whole thing is out of my advice realm."

"You can't be out of advice. I need it," I protest.

"I gave you mine, remember? I said, charter a plane without so much baggage. But, *no*, you want the baggage. I said, stop going after someone who doesn't want you back. But, *no*, you don't want to listen to that either. So, I've got nothing for ya. He's special...blah, blah, blah. Then, get him back, I guess."

I point my index finger toward her. "There are no *blah, blah, blahs* allowed in giving advice, but I think you're right." I pause and nod my head for effect. "I'm getting my man back!" I yell, lifting my spoon in the air in triumph. "London Wright does not back down from a challenge."

"Exactly! And we know London Wright's serious when she starts speaking in third person!" Paige cheers along beside me. "But before you go and hijack that seven forty-seven of hotness, can we please finish watching season five of *Downton Abbey*? We're so behind. I need to know what Edith is going to do with the baby, and then we need to move on to the final season. Paige McAllister has needs, too, and they're all going to come from that magic box right there." She points dramatically to my flat screen TV hanging on the wall at the foot of my bed. "And since my needs are more accessible than yours at the moment, I think I win."

"That's fine," I sigh. "You know these things take planning anyway. It hasn't even been a week yet. I'm going to give the boy at least a week to come to his senses, a chance to come back begging. But, if he doesn't, then game on."

"That's my girl!" she says with enthusiasm as she grabs the remote. "Now, which episode were we on?" she asks herself as she scrolls through the menu.

My tummy is about to explode from ice cream overload, so I set the pint down on my bedside table. Besides, I no longer want to become obese and die. Instead, I want Loïc back, and I'm going to fight to get him. He might not know what he wants, but I do.

An extremely happy and lively version of my sister fills up my laptop screen as she adamantly tells me of her latest adventure. I haven't physically spoken to Georgia in a month. All our communication has been over social media or text, so it is so great to see her and hear her voice.

It could be the color settings of my computer screen, but she looks so tan. I've never seen her with truly bronzed skin.

Georgia and I are opposites in almost every way. Where my skin darkens after just a few minutes in the sun, hers is pale, burning more than it tans. She has long blonde hair, opposite to my brown. She even has these brilliant blue eyes, which are in complete contrast to my brown ones. She looks nothing like me or my parents. Apparently, my dad's mother was pale-skinned with blonde hair and blue eyes. Georgia has always stood out at family events, oftentimes being the only blonde in the room. When she was little, she was like this little cherub with rosy cheeks and blonde ringlets. She always seems to be the center of attention—not because she is necessarily more beautiful than anyone else, but because she's different. She stands out wherever she goes with her angel-like appearance and exuberant personality.

I suppose we are similar in that way. We're both comfortable with being the center of attention. However, Georgia is more adventurous than I am. I love to experience new places in comfort. Paris? I loved our trip there, but while Mom and I were shopping and dining at the best restaurants in the city, Georgia was touring Les Catacombes—also known as the Empire of Death. Apparently, it is an underground tomb, complete with musty dark tunnels and neatly stacked bones, like skulls and such from dead humans.

No, thank you.

Georgia is talking a mile a minute as she fills me in on the last two months of her European adventures. Something she said catches me off guard.

"Wait, slow down. Did you just say you're in Brazil?"

"Yeah, I told you at the beginning that I'm in Manaus." She appears a little irritated.

"I didn't know what that meant. I figured it was a city somewhere in Europe."

She sighs. "No, it's in Brazil where Fabio's parents live." She looks so serious.

I can't hold in my laughter. "Fabio? You're seriously flying across the world with a guy named Fabio?"

"Jeez, London. Have you been listening to me at all?"

"I'm sorry. I tried, but you're talking so fast, and I've been kind of mesmerized by your tan. What's up with that?"

Georgia's face lights up. "I know! It's amazing, right? It's a spray tan, but it looks totally real, doesn't it?"

I nod my head. "Yeah, it does. It's so strange, seeing you with color. It's like I can't focus on anything else." I laugh.

She chuckles, flinging a lock of her long hair behind her shoulder. "Okay, because you were admiring my radiating skin, I'll give you a pass."

We both laugh, and though she's many miles away, she feels so close. In this moment, I realize how much I've missed not seeing her this summer. Our summers are usually spent traveling around with our mother. But Georgia wanted to gallivant around the globe with her friends, and I wanted to stay here to hang with Paige, ogle over Loïc, and apparently get a job. I'm still working on that last part—and by working, I mean, thinking about working on it. What can I say? This whole Loïc drama has been taking up a lot of my brainpower.

When our laughter settles, Georgia continues, "I'm going to go over the details again, but listen up this time."

I nod in agreement.

"So, I met Fabio in Spain when I was visiting Lolita."

151

We stayed in Spain one summer when we were younger, and my dad had business there. Lolita was the girl who lived across the street from our rental house. The three of us were inseparable and have remained in contact since then.

"Fabio was visiting his cousin, who is Lolita's next-door neighbor's boyfriend's friend from college."

"What?" I stare at the screen, confused.

Georgia waves her hand. "It doesn't matter. You know, everybody knows everybody over there. Lolita's neighbor had a party, and I met Fabio there."

"But doesn't his name weird you out?" I pull a face. "Wasn't Fabio the muscled guy on all of Mom's romance novels when we were little?"

"I don't care. I think it's cute. His real name is Fabian, but when he was young, his brothers used to tease him by calling him Fabio, and I guess it stuck. It's adorable." She sighs, content.

"You are coming back to the States next month to finish school, right?" I ask seriously.

She has one year left before she'll complete her degree at Stanford.

Georgia's lovesick eyes stare back at me. "Of course. I'm not stupid...but..." She trails off, looking sheepish.

"What?" I ask hesitantly.

"I'm probably just going to fly straight from here to Cali. I don't have to stop at home for anything. All my stuff is at my apartment. I know I promised to hang out with you and Mom for at least a week before school started, but I'm having so much fun. I just...I want this summer to last as long as possible."

"Wow. Someone's smitten."

She smiles. "I know. I totally am. I mean, who really knows if we'll stay together after the summer? I hope so, but you know how it is. I just want to experience as much as I can with him before I leave. Plus, we have so many things left to do this summer. Next week, we're flying to Peru to see Machu Picchu."

"Wow. You and Fabio sound like two adventurous peas in a pod. I get it. No worries. I will fly out this fall to spend the weekend with you. I'm sure Mom will, too. You enjoy your summer with your hottie. I've heard those Latino men are totally dreamy."

"That's an understatement. So, Mom tells me that you're all smitten for someone, too."

"Yeah, but he isn't as all in as Fabio seems to be. It's complicated."

"Well, tell me. I have ten minutes before I have to go. Fabio and I are going to explore this cave beneath a waterfall today. It's supposed to be amazing. So, give me the nine-minute version, so I have a minute for my advice."

I laugh. "Okay."

I rush through the details of the last month from the car wash to our two seemingly-awesome-turned-failed dates to my current plan to get him back.

"Oh, he sounds sexy. No wonder you are so hung up on him," she responds after I finished talking.

I can't help but chuckle. "You think he sounds sexy, not crazy?" I shake my head. "I don't mean crazy. It's just that he has issues."

She shrugs. "So what? He has issues. He's not your typical guy, so there must be something about him that makes you want to pursue him, and I'm guessing it's his level of sexiness. I think it's good that you're falling for him."

"Why's that?" I raise an eyebrow.

"You always date these perfect Ivy League type guys, London. Yes, they're always cute, and I suppose they're sexy in their own way, but they're all boring or douches. It's annoying. They never stand up to you. They're like your little show ponies. You parade them around while it suits you, and then you get bored and move on."

"I do not!"

Georgia doesn't flinch. "You do so. Loïc sounds drastically different than anyone you've ever dated, and for that reason alone, I like him. You need to live a little, London. I think Loïc can help you with that."

"Whatever," I say for lack of a better response.

"Don't get all pissy. You know you tend to err on the side of caution. You like to be in control, in charge, the boss—"

"I get it," I cut her off.

"All I'm saying is, I see why you're hung up on him. He challenges you. That's a good thing."

"So, where's this brilliant advice?"

"You said you were going to get him back, right?"

I nod. "Yeah."

"Perfect. Then, I say you already have a great plan."

"What should I do?"

She shrugs her shoulder. "I have no clue, but you'll figure it out."

"That's not remotely helpful," I protest with a pout.

Georgia laughs. "I gotta go. We'll chat later."

"Fine," I huff. "Go be with Fabio." I wave my hand while saying *Fabio* with the best Spanish accent I can offer.

"Keep me posted on your Loïc dilemma."

"I will. Love you. Be safe."

"Love you, too. And aren't I always?" She winks and blows me a kiss.

Before I can respond, she closes out of Skype, and I'm left with a blank screen.

What a little brat. I just love her.

FOURTEEN

Loïc

Age Seventeen

Phoenix, Arizona

"One person can only lose so much before he starts to realize that he's not strong enough to lose any more. "
—Loïc Berkeley

I spy one of the most beautiful creatures I've ever had the privilege to love.

Her thick, silky hair appears light blonde in the dim light, but I know, if we were in the sunlight, it would take on a reddish tint. With her recent haircut, it's shorter than I've ever seen it, but thankfully, it still covers her breasts as she leans forward on my lap, naked from the waist up.

I spy someone who breaks my heart every day, someone I don't know how to help.

"Sarah, what did you take?"

"Oh, just a little something to take the edge off. You don't need to worry about me," she says in a slurred voice, barely able to keep her eyes open. "Let me worry about you. Let me make you feel good, Loïc. Let me love you. I'll suck you, baby. I'll ride you, or you can go in from behind. Whatever you want. Fuck me, Loïc. I promise, it will feel good." Her words are desperate. They always are.

And, like always, I turn her down. "Stop it. You know you don't need to do that with me." I gently lift her off of me and set her down on the cheap hotel bed.

Lately, I've been lucky enough to secure some under-the-table odd jobs that pay a decent rate. We've been able to stay in this run-down motel for the past several months. It's nice, having a roof over our head along with a shower and a bed. The motel is located in a shady part of Phoenix, but Sarah and I are no strangers to bad areas. She can find drugs anywhere we go, if she wants them bad enough. More often than not, she does.

I don't know what to do to help her. She begs me not to turn her in. She swears that she wouldn't make it in another home, and I believe her. Sarah has been destroyed by all the monsters in her past—men who have abused her, scarred her, and left her with nothing but demons that invade her mind. She tries to fight them. I know she does. She doesn't like being like this, but she hurts, and I don't know how to make her better.

Over the past couple of years, Sarah has offered me sexual favors more times than I can count. But she only does it because she doesn't know how to show me that she cares for me in another way. She hasn't had healthy relationships in her life to use as examples. Being used by men is all she knows. She thinks she owes me some sort of payment. She can't grasp the fact that, because I love her, I could never take a piece of her. I would never accept payment in any form. She doesn't owe me anything.

And I do love her more than anything else in this world. She's all I have. I would do anything to save her.

Sarah and I panhandled and did various work around Texas until we eventually made it to Arizona. We never set out to come here. Honestly, we didn't really care where we ended up as long as we were together and not put back into foster care. Once we got here, we decided to stay. Under-the-table jobs are easy to get here, which is helpful. The fact that we don't freeze our asses off outside in the winter is also a strong check in the positives category. Sure, the hot-as-hell summers suck, but on the deathly hot days, we can find somewhere with air-conditioning to hang out. Even on the scorching days, the nights are manageable. But the biggest positive, especially for Sarah, is that it's not Texas. We'll never go back there.

I love Sarah like a sister. I always have. It's not that I don't find her attractive because I do. She is the most beautiful person I've known, inside and out. But neither of us is emotionally stable enough to be lovers. That's not what we need. What we both need is a friend, a confidant, someone to have our backs, someone who truly loves us…family. Sarah is my family, plain and simple. It's her and me against the world.

Unfortunately, Sarah doesn't do well when she's left alone, even when she promises me that she'll be fine. I try to be with her as much as I can. I try to find jobs that we can do together. But it doesn't always work out that way. She tells me that she's going to go panhandle or shop for food or anything else that sounds reasonable. But, more often than not, when I come back, she's crying and wasted. She doesn't tell me how she pays for the drugs, but deep down, I already know.

I know she's in pain and that sex and drugs are her methods of numbness, but it kills me a little more every time it happens.

I've spent countless days at the public library, researching ways to help her, both with her addiction and her mental well-being. But nothing I've tried works. I've been tempted to turn her in, so she can get help, but she told me that if I ever did that or left her, then she would kill herself, and I believe her. I can't lose her. The world can't lose her. She's good. She's pure. She's special. And when she figures out how to see all of that in herself and get better, she's going to make this world a better place. She has so much to give. I just have to figure out how to make her see that.

"Come on." I reach my hand out to her, and she takes it. "Let's get you in a nice warm bath."

Sarah loves baths. Up until we were able to afford this room, they had been few and far between. Even growing up in different homes, she hadn't been given the luxury of baths too often.

The tub in this room wasn't the most appealing when we first got here. But I went out and got some Comet and bleach, and I scrubbed the tub and the surrounding walls until they were shiny. Now, Sarah can take a bath whenever she wants.

I lead her to the bathroom, start the water, and pour in the lavender bath bubbles that I picked up for her at the Dollar Store. She loves the smell of lavender, even the chemical-imposter variety.

When the tub is full of water and bubbles, I turn to leave, but she grabs my arm.

"Please don't leave. Get in with me." When I don't answer, she gives me a pleading, "Please."

Sarah entered the bathroom in only her panties. So, after I strip down to my boxers, we both get in the water. I lean against the back of the tub, and she rests between my legs, her back to my front.

We sit in silence for a few minutes before I ask gently, "Do you want to talk about it?"

She shakes her head. She never wants to talk about it. I wish she would. I think it would help.

"Are you sure? You can tell me anything. I'm here for you. You know that, right?"

She nods, her long hair moving across my chest. "I know. Thank you."

I want to cry. I want to scream. I want to make her let me help her.

"We could splurge on a movie?" I suggest, willing to do anything to make her feel better, to take her mind off of all the horrors in her head.

We actually go see a movie a couple of times a month, but we usually go to a matinee because they're cheaper, and only one of us pays. The one who pays sneaks the other one in through a back Exit door in the theater that isn't monitored by cameras. Sometimes, we get lucky and spot a large group of friends walking in. We stick close to them, and when the attendant takes the pile of tickets, they assume everyone is accounted for.

For being homeless, we have a pretty good life. Well, I guess some things could be better.

I rest my head against the top of Sarah's, and she leans back into me. My arms wrap around her waist, and I pull her in tight, letting her know that I'm here, that I love her.

Finally, she answers, "No, not tonight. I'm not really in the mood."

"Okay." I kiss the top of her head.

"Loïc, promise me that you'll never leave me." Her voice comes out in a broken sob, and I know she's crying.

"You know I could never, would never."

"Promise."

"I promise, Sarah. I love you more than anything. I would never leave you. Nothing can tear us apart."

"Nothing can tear us apart," she repeats softly.

"Nothing."

"I love you, Loïc. I'm sorry about earlier. Can you forgive me?"

"You don't have to apologize, and you're always forgiven because I love you. Nothing you could ever do would change that."

She turns to the side now, her cheek resting against my chest. "You saved my life," she says softly. "No matter what happens, I need you to know that you saved my life, and I'm so thankful for you. You're the best thing to ever happen to me."

"You're the best thing to ever happen to me, Sarah. I don't know how, but I promise you that we'll get through this. It won't always hurt this much, okay?" I need her to believe my words even though I'm having a hard time believing them myself.

"Okay," she whispers.

Sarah falls asleep against my chest, and I hold her until the water goes cold. I wake her enough to dry her off, get her dressed in something comfortable, and get her into bed.

I fall asleep beside her, grateful that another storm has passed—at least for now. Tomorrow, I'm going to find a job that we can both do. I'm never leaving her alone again.

I wake with a start. The bed is moving violently beneath me. The room is dark, and I fumble to find the light switch above the bed. I click it on, and the space floods with pale light.

"Sarah!" I scream when I see her.

She's in the bed beside me, convulsing and spitting foam from her open mouth.

"Sarah!" I shake her. "Oh my God, Sarah! Please don't do this! Sarah! Sarah!" Tears fall down my face, and I pray to whoever will hear me.

I reach for the cheap motel phone screwed onto the wall. When I pick up the receiver and listen, I don't hear a dial tone.

I hate this fucking place!

I knew that the phone connection was hit or miss, but I've never cared as much as I do in this moment. I wiggle the cord attached to the receiver and push it up. Finally, I get a dial tone. I push 911 as fast as I can. Thankfully, the phone stays connected long enough for me to tell the operator everything that's happening. I beg her to tell the paramedics to hurry.

I don't know what to do to help Sarah. She's no longer shaking, but her mouth is ajar, and traces of spit are falling from it. Her eyes are closed, and she's motionless. Her arm is dead weight, hanging limply off the side of the bed as I hold her in my lap. I rock her back and forth and beg her to stay. I blink back tears and notice the empty pill bottle and glass on the end table.

Oh, Sarah.

I hold my hand against her chest, but I can't feel her heart beating. "Sarah! Please! Please! Please!"

I gently lay her on the bed. I hold her nose while I breathe into her open mouth. I have no clue how to do CPR properly, but I can't just sit here and let her die. I put my hands together and press against her chest, like I've seen done in movies. Nothing happens, but I keep going while begging her not to leave me.

There's a knock at the door, and I run to open it. The paramedics come in and get to work, putting her on a stretcher. I hand them the empty pill bottle and tell them what I think happened. In a matter of seconds, she's being loaded into an ambulance.

As they close the ambulance doors, I cry out, "I love you, Sarah! I'll see you soon!"

I will see her soon.

I run back into the room and get dressed. I don't know how long it will take me to get to the hospital if using the bus, so I opt to call a cab. I don't know why I didn't go in the ambulance. They didn't offer, and at the time, I didn't think I could, but people do it in the movies. Maybe they didn't extend an invite because they think I'm the one who did this to her. Or maybe they needed space to work on her. I know I couldn't have done anything to help, but I feel so lost without her.

When I get to the emergency room, I run in like a crazed person. The receptionist flinches when my palms find the counter with a smack.

"A girl was just brought in—Sarah Berkeley. Well, you wouldn't know her name if she's not conscious yet. She overdosed on some pills, I think. I need to know how she is doing." I think I might have frightened the lady behind the desk.

"Sir, you need to calm down. A minor was brought in, but I don't know what her status is at this time. But I will tell you that, unless you are her parent or guardian, then no one will be releasing that information to you."

"I am her guardian. I'm the only family she has!" I yell.

"Can I see your ID?" she asks calmly.

"I don't have an ID."

"I see. Well, why don't you have a seat? Then, I'll see what I can do."

Two days have passed. Not only did that bitch have no intention of helping me, but neither did any of the bitches to follow. I've never met a group of people so intent on following the rules as people who work in a hospital.

I can't prove to them that I have a right to know how Sarah is. I can't even prove who I am. I don't own a single form of identification. I've begged. I've pleaded. I've cried. I've screamed. I've been about two seconds from being arrested, but through it all, nothing. Not one word about Sarah has been given to me.

I haven't left the waiting room in two days. I've been living off of the drinking fountain and a couple of bags of chips from the vending machine—not that I've been real hungry anyway.

I'm not sure what I should do, but I know that leaving here isn't an option.

My elbows rest on my knees, and my fingers tug on my hair as I lean into my hands. I pray silently to Sarah, begging her to come back to me.

"Sir?"

I look up to see the older lady from the reception desk peering down at me. She looks like a wicked witch. Then again, they all do.

"She's gone. You should go."

Her words resonate within me.

I repeat them again and again in my head, trying to make sense of them, *She's gone. She's gone. She's gone.*

Using all the energy I have left, I stand and walk out of the hospital waiting room. I hope never to step foot in a hospital again. The lobby alone is the most depressing place I've ever been. I can't imagine what it would feel like to actually be in a room.

She's gone.

The words don't add up, yet I know them to be true. I think they've been true this entire time, probably before she even left our hotel room.

What am I going to do without her?

Without Sarah, I have no purpose. I have no reason to live. She was everything.

I was naive to think I could change her. I should have gotten her help sooner.

A million what-ifs, should-haves, and would-haves flood my mind, but in my heart, I know it doesn't matter now.

Nothing matters now.

Nothing will ever matter again.

As I walk away from the hospital and leave my only family behind, forever, I hear my father's words.

"Strength gives you courage to face things, even when you're afraid."

Well, I am afraid.

I'm afraid of loving.

I'm afraid of losing someone I love.

I'm afraid that, because of this fear, I will never truly love anyone ever again.

I'm afraid of a life without love because, despite the hard times, these past two years have been the best years of my life since my parents died.

So, I'm definitely afraid. *But am I strong enough to face my fears?* I don't know.

One person can only lose so much before he starts to realize that he's not strong enough to lose any more.

FIFTEEN

Loïc

"Apparently, I'm a selfish prick."
—Loïc Berkeley

The calm that comes over me at the firing range seems unconventional at best. The soothing comfort is completely at odds with the deadly weapon in my grasp, yet there is something to be said for the routine of it all. I know exactly what to expect during target practice. The sounds and movements of firing an M4 are so ingrained in my head.

I take in a deep breath before pulling the trigger. The tinging of the spent casings falling to the ground paired with the smell of the burned gunpowder engulf me in peace. Hitting my mark brings me purpose. Seeing the holes on the target in the distance rounds off a familiar and strangely relaxing start to my morning.

Here, I know where I belong. Here, I know what I am meant to do.

I'm a soldier.

I train. I take orders. And I complete missions to the best of my ability. Simple.

Although unforeseen circumstances arise out in the field, they seem uncomplicated in the scheme of things. There are orders and protocols. I follow them and do my best.

I like having a clear set of rules. I feel safe, knowing how the chain of command works, how missions work. I've trained with my unit, and the group of us works together like clockwork. There are no gray areas.

Sure, especially out on deployment, there are surprises, unexpected events. Even in those though, we have protocol.

With London, there's nothing but gray. There is no black and white when it comes to women. Relationships are a state of perpetually changing expectations. I'm a barely functioning man when I know what to expect. I have issues for days, and that's not including my London dilemma.

"Your shooting's on point, man," Cooper says beside me as the two of us stare at the targets.

"You, too."

Cooper's target of nothing but bull's-eye shots matches my own.

I bend one knee to the ground and pack up my weapon. Cooper does the same.

"Do you have the brief ready for this afternoon?" Cooper asks, referring to the group I'm leading after lunch.

"Yeah, there really wasn't a lot to prepare. Captain handed it to me in PowerPoint form."

"Really? It's one of those?"

I can hear the disappointment in Cooper's voice. I can't help but chuckle. As exciting as being in the Special Forces sounds, it's not all adrenaline rushes from high-action situations. Most of the days when we aren't on deployment consist of working out, shooting, lifting, and learning about something field-related. For me, it also includes presenting what I learned about to others.

"It's not that bad, I promise. Plus, I have lots of stories to liven this one up."

"Oh, good. The brief that Miller gave last week about the importance of proper reporting made me want to claw my eyes out."

I laugh. "Wasn't the hard part listening to it? Shouldn't you have wanted to complete some grotesque task on your ears?"

"Yeah, but the way he pressed his lips together, squinted his eyes, and nodded after every bullet point—like each little piece of information was so groundbreaking—made me want to hurl a stapler at his head. I couldn't stand looking at his smug face for an hour straight."

"You know he looks like that all the time. It doesn't matter if he's talking about the chick he hooked up with over the weekend or his mom's chicken potpie recipe; he has that douche-bag expression on his face. I don't think he can help it."

Cooper scoffs, "Maybe not, but that doesn't mean it isn't as annoying as fuck."

"True," I agree as the two of us pick up our duffel bags of supplies.

We start walking back to base.

"Maggie and I are going to see that new spy movie tonight. Do you wanna come?"

"Yeah, sure."

"You should invite London," he says, attempting to sound casual.

I can hear the optimism in his voice.

"Nah, that's okay. I don't think I'm going to see her anymore."

"Dude," Cooper sighs beside me.

"Dude, what? It didn't work out. End of story. Not a big deal."

"I don't believe that. You like her, Berkeley. I know you do. You owe it to yourself to give it a shot."

"I did. It didn't work."

"Then, give it another one."

"Hold up. Aren't you the one who said I needed time?"

Cooper waves his hand in the air in dismissal. "Maggie's right. You've had plenty of time. London's the first girl you've been remotely into, and you should take a chance. You don't want to miss out on something great because you're scared."

I decide to ignore Cooper's effort to goad me into proving that I'm not afraid by trying the dating thing with London again. I answer simply, "Relationships aren't my deal." I pause and slap Cooper on the arm. "Speaking of, when are you going to ask Maggie to marry you? You know she's waiting."

"I know that you're trying to change the subject, and this time, I'll allow it. But we will be revisiting London at some point."

"Yeah, whatever." I chuckle. "Maggie?"

Cooper lets out a breath. "I don't know, man. I'm going to. It's not like I'm not ready or anything. I just need to get my ass to a jewelry store and then come up with some romantic-as-shit way to ask her. I already feel committed to Maggie. She knows she's my forever. The ring and marriage just seem like an annoying nuisance, just some hoop I have to jump through to make something that's already a done deal official."

I shake my head and laugh. "Regardless of whether or not you find it annoying, I'm telling you that Maggie doesn't. Girls live for all that."

"Says the guy who can't make it past two dates."

"Fuck you."

"Fuck you," he retorts.

"Blow me, asshole."

"I'll pass. Thanks for the offer," he says with a smirk.

"Maggie deserves the whole deal...the nuisance."

Cooper nods. "Of course she does. I'm just a lazy prick. I'll do it soon, okay? Does that make you happy, Loïc 'I Went on Two Dates and Now I'm the Love Expert' Berkeley?"

"Just because I suck at execution in that department doesn't mean I don't know the rules."

"But you would figure it out if you just gave it more time."

"Cooper, enough."

"All right, I'll drop it for now." He changes the subject. "So, love expert"—the tone of Cooper's voice rises an octave in mock excitement—"do you think I should go with a round diamond or square, tear-drop, or maybe cushion cut?"

"Ha. So, you have been looking into rings?"

"Of course I have. There are just so many choices. It's tiring." Cooper drops his shoulders in a dramatic display of exhaustion.

"I think you can handle it." I chuckle.

"Yeah, yeah."

Toss.

   Catch.

   Toss.

   Catch.

My wrist bends back before the baseball spins into the air above my face. Right before it hits the ceiling, I watch as it starts to descend, falling back toward my bed. I catch it again before it hits my chest.

I've been lying in bed, throwing this ball for hours, it seems. This week has been brutal. I'm more fucked in the head than I care to admit. London has me all sorts of confused.

The walls I've put up, the bullshit I've been feeding myself about not letting anyone in for the past eight years since I lost Sarah—it's all starting to be too much. It was easy before London, but she's changed me. She's different. She makes me different. She makes me happy.

I don't know. Sometimes, I let myself wonder if it's all meant to be, even as much as I don't believe in that shit. But, just maybe, with London, it is.

Her freaking name is London. That has to be a sign, right?

Maybe it's time I pay my birth name some respect and show an ounce of strength and courage to fight for the life I want. Closing oneself off and hiding from the world is the cowardly move. It's the easy path.

What's the point of living if I'm constantly hiding from possible pain?

But I realize that my feelings of apprehension are more for London than they are for me. I can't guarantee her forever. With my issues, chances are, at some point, I will hurt her. I know that there is a risk of getting hurt in any relationship. It just seems that London will have a higher one with me. I feel selfish for wanting to ignore that gamble to be with her anyway.

There's a small knock on the door.

"Come in," I call out.

"Hey," Cooper says by way of a greeting. He leans against the doorframe, taking me in. "So, this London chick has really done a number on you, hasn't she?" He smiles, looking pleased. "I have to say, I wasn't sure I would see the day."

"You and me both."

"So, what's the issue, man?"

"I'm the issue, Coops. You know that."

"Who cares? So, you have a messed up past. You have a few issues. Who doesn't? No one is perfect. You're kidding yourself if you think anyone is. You have every right to be just as happy as the rest of us, Berkeley."

I throw my legs over the side of the bed and sit up. "Yeah, I guess."

"I don't guess. I know, brother. You've been dealt some major shit in this life. You, above all, deserve to be happy."

"I can't change who I am, and if I could, it definitely wouldn't be overnight. I don't want to end up hurting her," I admit.

"Nothing about a relationship is guaranteed. You know that. Heck, Maggie could leave me tomorrow, for all I know."

I chuckle. "Yeah, right."

He shoots me a wicked grin because, let's be honest, he and Maggie are perfect for each other.

"Okay, bad example. The point is, everyone who falls in love and goes into a relationship plans for it to last forever, but shit happens. Half of marriages end in divorce. You know none of those people were thinking about their future divorce on their wedding day."

"I'm talking about dating. I have no idea why you're bringing marriage into this. And how does anything you just said help at all?"

"Shit, man. I'm not Oprah. You get the point. No one knows the future. You like her. She likes you. Go for it. If it doesn't work, it doesn't work, and life goes on. Even if you were the stablest person alive and wanted to date her, you couldn't promise her forever. Getting to know someone is always a gamble. Sometimes, it works, and sometimes, it doesn't, but you won't know if you don't try. And it's about time to start trying, dude."

I sigh. "Maybe you're right. That was pretty Oprah-worthy though."

Cooper nods. "Yeah, that advice was definitely on point. I'm just that good. Who's the love expert now?" He smirks, lifting his shoulders.

"Whatever." I laugh. "Hey, guess who I've been dreaming about a lot lately?"

"Who?"

"Sarah."

Cooper and Maggie are the only people who know about Sarah.

"No shit?"

"I know. I try not to think about her, for the most part. Then, just this week, I've been, like, dreaming of her every night. It's fucked up."

The memory of Sarah invades my mind at some point every day. As much as I try not to think about her, it's impossible. I'm ashamed to admit that I intentionally push her to the side even though her memory doesn't deserve it, but it's still so painful to remember.

Cooper shrugs. "It makes sense. I mean, she was the last person you loved—well, besides me." He waggles his eyebrows.

I simply roll my eyes.

He continues, "So then, this London chick comes around, and you like her, which opens up all the touchy-feely emotional shit in your brain. So, of course, it's going to make memories of Sarah surface."

"I suppose that makes sense. You don't think it's my mind warning me that this whole thing with London isn't a good thing? That something horrible will happen?"

"Come on, Berkeley," Cooper huffs. "Do you regret the time you had with Sarah?"

"Of course not."

"So, I think it means the opposite. If anything, it's telling you that love is worth it even if you lose it. I know you think you're cursed or some shit, but that's ridiculous. People die every day. It's just shitty luck that many of the people you've loved died. But don't think for a second that London's just going to kick the bucket because you date her. That's not the way life works. Plus, would you rather have never known your parents or Sarah? If you'd had a choice at the beginning to know them even though they were going to leave you or to never have known them at all, what would you have chosen?"

"Of course I'd have wanted to know them."

"Exactly my point! *Dude*, come on!" Cooper runs his fingers through his hair in frustration.

I can't help but laugh. "Okay"—I chuckle—"I get your point."

He's right. I'm being a total idiot.

"Thank you!" He groans. "You good?"

"Yeah, I'm good."

"Thank God." He shakes his head with a grin. "Now, before I had to go all Oprah on your ass, I originally came in here to see if you wanted us to order you some Chinese. Maggie and I are going to stuff our faces and have a Mission: Impossible marathon."

"Nah, thanks though. I'm going to go get London back."

"Aw, that's my boy." He smirks.

"Shut up already."

"All right, all right." He raises his hands in mock surrender. "But, seriously, good luck, man."

"Thanks, Coops." I pin him with a stare. I don't say the words on the tip of my tongue because, let's face it, this brief conversation has been enough sentimental shit for one day.

But that's the thing with Cooper. I don't have to say the words for him to understand. He's always had this crazy ability to get me, oftentimes better than I get myself. He knows how much he means to me.

"Anytime, brother." He nods before stepping back and closing my bedroom door behind him.

I get what Cooper said. It all makes sense, and I know he's right. Deep down, I know that I didn't have anything to do with my parents' or Sarah's deaths. I understand, too, that all relationships are a gamble. But there's still that part, far within, that whispers that I'm being selfish. I have a real fear that, by dating London when I'm not a whole person, I will hurt her.

She's this bright light, the first one since Sarah, that's been able to penetrate my darkness. But, unlike Sarah—whom I loved like family—the feelings I have stirring within me for London are so much more. They are raw and hot, urgent and needy. They consume me with immense want. This week and every other day since she first washed my truck, I've tried everything not to think about her, but I've found it impossible.

London, for me, is unforgettable. Her light is so vivid that it refuses to be dimmed. I'm just terrified that somehow, though I won't mean to, not only will I dim her brightness, but I'll also extinguish it altogether.

So, yeah, maybe picking London is the selfish thing to do, but I'm going to take that chance anyway. Apparently, I'm a selfish prick.

SIXTEEN

London

"I'm fully aware that you have the potential to obliterate my heart into a million pieces, and I'm okay with that."
—London Wright

Exactly a week ago, I had an amazing date with Loïc, at which he all but confessed his love—if not love, then deep *like*—for me. We proceeded to watch a magnificent sunset and had an incredibly steamy kiss. Of course, that was followed by his internal freak-out and subsequent cutting off of the date and dropping me off at home early where I was left hurt, confused, and sad.

Ah, just a typical night out for me. No, not really.

If I've had an amazing time with a guy I like, it's always ended way better than that.

What is my fascination with Loïc? I truly, for the life of me, cannot begin to understand it. Pre-Loïc London would never have put up with this teeter-totter of craziness.

But therein lies the problem. Loïc isn't like any guy I've ever dated. He's different. Despite his plethora of issues, I'm drawn to him, almost instinctually. My attraction to him and desire to be with him aren't things I can control. I simply know we're meant to be. We have to be. It's the only logical conclusion to my obsession.

Here I stand, on the corner of Independence and Desire. The problem is that Desire is littered with lots of trash that I call desperation while Independence is covered in regret. *So, the million-dollar question is, is it better to risk falling to desperation to cure this immense ache of desire, or should I hold my head high on my lonely walk to independence?*

For me, at least with Loïc, there is no question.

So, now, I need to come up with a plan to get him back.

Yeah, that's a problem.

I sigh before plopping onto my bed, TV remote control in hand.

I've tried with Loïc. I've pulled out all of my charms. None of it worked on him because his mind was already closed off. I need to do something *more*. I just haven't figured out what.

Granted, bingeing on Netflix for a week straight didn't allow for much time to plan for my Loïc domination.

Paige is out with a guy, so I planned on using tonight to craft my ingenious plan, but I can't find the motivation. Perhaps, after a few episodes of a new guilty-pleasure show, an idea will come to me.

The doorbell rings, and I freeze. My mouth goes dry, and I swallow. I slowly sit up, throwing my legs over the side of my bed. My chest feels light, and I focus on my breathing.

It might not even be him. Calm down.

It has to be him, right?
Who else would it be?

I step into the hallway and hesitantly make my way toward the front door. The bell rings again, startling me, and I jump. At this point, I notice my wounded-heart ensemble—a thin tank top, short yoga shorts, no makeup, and my long hair thrown on top of my head in a messy bun. It could be worse. I actually showered today, so at least I don't stink.

Oh, well. I don't have time to glam it up at this point. It is what it is. Take me or leave me.

Wait, I didn't mean it. Please don't leave me.

My sweaty palm grasps the door handle, and I pull it open. My knees go weak, and I know that's cliché, but *gorgeous* doesn't begin to describe the man before me.

Oh, what he does to me…

He's here, and he's smiling. It's a cautious grin, but it's something. In his hands, he's holding a huge basket with an adorable pink ribbon wrapped around it. Inside the basket, among purple paper confetti, is bag upon bag of gummy candy. My eyes do a quick scan, and I see a variety of gummy goodness from worms to sour to original bears. I can't contain the wide smile that comes to my face.

"What's this?" I motion toward the basket.

"A peace offering. I was hoping to soften you up with a little sugar, so I could plead my case." The rich timbre of his voice never fails to still my heart.

"Your case?" I manage to keep my voice steady. I wouldn't be surprised if he could hear the rapid beating of my heart.

"Yeah, I was hoping I could take you out and kind of explain some stuff, maybe talk you into giving me…*us* another chance." He releases one of his hands from the basket and rubs the back of his neck. His beautiful blues dart from my lips to my eyes before peering toward the ground.

"I don't want to go out," I say.

Loïc's eyes pierce mine. A deep sadness resides behind them, and it makes my chest ache.

"But we can hang out here," I offer.

His expression is one of confusion. I know this groveling-at-my-door scenario that's going on is new and probably difficult for him.

I give him a comforting smile. "Come inside. We have the whole place to ourselves. You can plead your case here. You can even wait until I'm in a major sugar coma to do so, if you want," I say with a quirked eyebrow.

A slow smile forms on his lips, lighting up his eyes. I step back, and he enters. I close the door behind him, and he places the basket on the table in the foyer. He turns toward me, and before I know it, he pulls me into his chest, engulfing me in a hug.

My arms wrap around him, tightly hugging him. The tension rolls off my body, and I want to cry from the mere relief of having him this close to me.

He bends his head toward mine, nuzzling his face into my hair. "God, I've missed you," he groans, his voice so husky and needy.

His confession causes a torrent of goose bumps to explode over my body.

We stand this way, wrapped in each other's arms, for a long time. I think we're both afraid to let go. I haven't been this content in a week, and I'm terrified for it to end. I'm scared to death that something will trigger him to leave me again.

Eventually, he leans his head back, so our eyes meet. "You're so beautiful."

"Right," I say sarcastically.

"No, you are, London. You are the most beautiful woman I've ever seen."

His eyes hold a sincerity that makes my stomach flutter.

I lean my face against his chest. "So far, you're doing a good job in pleading your case."

His chest vibrates beneath my face with laughter. "Good."

"Come on, let's go to my room," I suggest as I take a step back from him, my body immediately regretting the absence of his warmth.

"Your room?"

"To talk," I clarify.

He laughs. "Okay. I thought you'd forgiven me awfully quick."

I grab his hand, entwining my fingers with his, and I lead him the short distance to my bedroom. "I've already forgiven you, but that doesn't mean we shouldn't talk."

I sit, cross-legged, on my bed. Loïc takes off his shoes and sits across from me.

"So?" I say as a lame attempt to get the conversation going.

"Right." Loïc sighs, obviously uncomfortable. "I guess it's probably best for me to tell you everything from the beginning. I don't know how else to explain my issues, but I think it's important that you understand them. I need you to know all of it, so you can decide if you want to take the risk and be with me."

I open my mouth to protest, but he raises his hand to halt me.

"Listen, London, truthfully, I don't know if it's in your best interests to be with me. I've tried to end it with you multiple times now because of that, but for some reason, I can't stay away from you. You should know all the details though, and you have to take it all in. You have to listen carefully when I tell you that I'm damaged. I'm broken, maybe irrevocably, and I don't want to drag you down with me. You need to hear me, so you can decide what's best for you."

He looks so serious. Incredible apprehension hides in his expression. I want to tell him that it doesn't matter what he says. Nothing will change my mind. But I think he needs this. Maybe if he confesses his demons and I choose him anyway, he'll stop running.

"Okay, tell me everything," I encourage.

He starts from when he was discovered at the entrance of a fire station. He talks of his parents and grandparents. He runs through every foster home he lived in and the horrors of each one. I have to stop myself from reaching out to hold him as he tells me about his grandparents and how he kept waiting for them to rescue him, but they never did. He tells me about the moment when he was fifteen and he'd had enough, so he ran away with Sarah. Then, he tells me about being homeless with Sarah for over two years and how he lost her. After Sarah's death, he turned himself into the foster-care system, so he could obtain the proper paperwork he needed to get an ID. Then, he got his GED, and the day he turned eighteen, he joined the Army.

His account is so sad, so incredibly depressing, that it's hard to fathom that it is real. But looking at his hollow eyes as he recounts the nightmare of his life, I know it is very real.

I understand why Loïc has commitment issues. He's lost everyone he's ever loved. I also see the fear residing within him. At twenty-five, he is this strong, masculine force to be reckoned with, but behind the tough exterior, he is a little boy who is afraid of having his heart broken.

Over the past hour, Loïc has told me his entire life's tale—or at least all the ugly highlights. I've listened attentively, and I've made a conscious effort not to interrupt him, to let him talk. Just from the little that I know of him, I realize how much courage it took for him to open up like that.

Some of the details I already knew, but most of them were new to me.

He finishes and expectantly looks at me.

I grab his hands in mine. "I'm so sorry that you had to go through all of that. It breaks my heart. I understand why you're hesitant to continue this thing that we have. I can't tell you what tomorrow will bring, Loïc. I can't promise you that we'll be forever. But I can tell you that I'm more attracted to you than I have been to anyone else in my life. I'm crazy about you, about all of you. I want this to work between us. I want it to be forever, but the only way we're going to know if it's real is if we try. The unknown is always scary, but if we end up making it for the long haul, I know it will be worth it."

"I'm going to hurt you, London. I feel it. A lifetime of issues can't be fixed overnight. I'm my own worst enemy, and I'm going to ruin you." His voice breaks. The despair that resonates from him is tangible.

"I don't care," I say simply. "You very well might. Yes, there's a chance that we won't make it, and my heart will be broken. But, Loïc, there's also a chance that we will. You're worth the risk."

"London…" he pleads.

I shake my head. "No. No more. Do you think that you're the only one on this planet who's damaged? You're not. We all have our issues."

"I have a flawed heart, London. I don't know how to love."

"I don't believe that for a second. And you know what? My heart is flawed, too. It doesn't know how to function properly when it doesn't have you. I need you, Loïc, for however long you can give me. I'm fully aware that you have the potential to obliterate my heart into a million pieces, and I'm okay with that. I'm letting you off the hook right now, releasing you from guilt. I'm going into this with my eyes wide open. I just need you to give us a chance. Please just try. No more running."

"No more running?"

"Nope." I shake my head.

Indecision lines his expression before his features relax and settle on acceptance. "Okay," he sighs.

I take in the significance of that word. "Okay?" I ask as my soul fills with joy. "So, if I lean over and kiss you like crazy, you won't run away?"

"I can't run from you anymore, London. It hurts too much."

He smiles shyly, and I see a sparkle of relief dance behind his eyes. There is something breathtaking about Loïc's genuine smiles. They're devastatingly beautiful.

He reaches out, cradling my jaw, and he draws my lips to his. He claims my mouth with his tongue, thoroughly kissing me with passion-filled movements. He salvages my flawed heart with his gentle caresses. With each lingering touch, I can breathe easier. It's different this time. The kiss is almost reverent. It isn't rushed with urgency because any moment might be the last before he runs. I can feel the change. This kiss is from a man who's going to stay.

That thought alone, the scenario where I get to keep Loïc, paired with the deliciousness of his tongue moving against mine make me so aroused with insane need. With my hands laced around his neck, I pull him onto me as I let my body fall to the mattress. I squirm beneath him as he deepens the kiss.

In a frenzy of movements, I try to take off his shirt, desperate to feel his skin. He sits back, and he grabs the base of his shirt before pulling it over his head. I follow suit, and then I make quick work of every article of clothing I'm wearing—which, admittedly, isn't much—until I'm left naked before him.

His eyes darken, and his gaze leaves a trail of heat with every inch it passes over. He starts to descend toward me.

"Nope. Stop," I say.

Confusion gleams in his eyes.

"Pants." I point to his fully clothed bottom half.

He laughs, all husky, and the sound resonates deep within my belly, filling me with warmth, until my entire body is burning for him.

Once we are both fully exposed, I don't stop him as his lips find passage across my skin, starting with my toes. Loïc's lips are skilled tools made for maximum pleasure. His kisses vary from soft to firm, dry and wet. They worship, caress, and tease. My heart races in anticipation as he works my body with his glorious mouth from my feet to my neck. My body hums with intense pleasure, the kind that is almost painful, making me so needy for more. He reaches my neck and applies soft nibbles, working up to my ear. He gently pulls my lobe between his teeth, and a jolt of pleasure hits me.

I want him. I want him more than I can remember ever wanting anything in my life. The need is urgent. I splay my hands across his tight ass and move my pelvis to position myself right where I want him.

God, I need him.

"You. Are. So. Fucking. Perfect," his gruff voice chants, each word a staccato.

His face begins to move back down my body, and I want to scream. I want to feel him inside me. He stops between my legs, opening me. His warm mouth finds me, and I expel a moan of relief, of pleasure. His tongue works me from the outside as his fingers enter me.

I scream his name into the lust-fueled air with a long-suffering sigh of ecstasy. My entire body vibrates in anticipation of what's to come, and I feel my release rising within me. A slow roll of pleasure courses through me, building, growing in intensity.

His hands grasp under my thighs, pushing me wide, allowing his tongue perfect access. My heart thrums wildly in my chest, and then I'm spiraling, shaking, assaulted with enormous jolts of pleasure. I unabashedly scream out, giving voice to the bliss that fills me.

As the cries of ecstasy racking my body slowly abate, I vaguely register the sound of a foil wrapper ripping.

Loïc kisses his way back up my body. He sucks on the delicate skin of my neck, and I sigh. His lips work across my cheek, and when his mouth meets mine, I feel a true connection as our tongues unite.

This man is meant for me. I will never want another. I wish I could push the pause button on the universe and just feel this moment for a long time, an eternity even. My body is sated, my heart is exploding with love, and my mind is at peace. Loïc is mine forever, and whether or not the notion is reciprocated, it won't change a thing. There is no negotiating with these sensations threatening to split me open. I pray that Loïc will always be with me because, after him, there could never be another.

I whimper as Loïc enters me. I've daydreamed about this event more times than I can remember, and not even my greatest fantasies can compare. This is everything.

Loïc grasps my hands, entwining my fingers through his, as he holds my arms above my head. His thrusts grow in urgency. His eyes lock on mine, dark with desire and need. His skin glistens with a faint sheen of sweat. The moisture seems to showcase his muscles as he moves in me. Staring at him above me, I can't help but take note again of how immensely drop-dead gorgeous he is. The sight of him alone is a never-ending aphrodisiac.

His pace quickens, and our breathing becomes labored, sporadic. He releases my hands to grab my thighs, holding each one out to the side, as he pounds into me. I can feel the build once more. It's blazing in intensity. My body loses all pretense of control as I cry out amid a current of pleasure.

"Fuck, London!" he calls out, his voice gravelly. His fingers firmly grasp my thighs as his face points toward the ceiling with his eyes closed.

He falls on top of me. Our chests push against each other as we work to take in air.

"Oh, London," he says on an exhale.

The awe in his voice causes goose bumps to prickle across my skin.

"I knew you were going to destroy me," he breathes against my neck.

I wrap my arms around his firm back and hold him tight. "I won't," I promise. *Please don't destroy me.*

I know I told him that I didn't care if we didn't make it because it was worth the risk regardless, but the truth is, I do care—like, a whole hell of a lot.

SEVENTEEN

London

> *"I'm so happy that I want to break into song,*
> *like a princess in a Disney movie, but I won't. That'd be weird."*
> —London Wright

The hot summer sun is beating down on my neck, causing me to sweat before I've even done anything. That, paired with the cheesy grin across Loïc's face, is really annoying me. "Stop looking at me like that."

"Like what?" he teases as he stands on one foot. His right leg is bent at the knee as he pulls his foot behind his ass in some sort of stretch.

"Like I'm stupid." I attempt to imitate his stretch, but I think better of it, as I'm sure I'd fall on my ass instead of balancing on one foot the way he is. Instead, I bend at the waist and touch my toes with both feet firmly planted on the ground.

"I'm not," he disagrees. "I don't think you're stupid at all. I think you're cute."

"No, you think I'm going to suck," I huff out as I stand up straight.

"Of course you will." He laughs. "But I think it's adorable that you want to try."

I cross my arms over my chest and glare at him.

He takes a step toward me. "London, I told you that we were running nine miles. Have you ever run one mile? You have to work up to bigger distances, but I think it's sweet that you're out here with me. It's fine. When you get tired, you can walk, and I'll run around the loop and catch back up with you."

Loïc and Cooper go running together a lot, and I insisted that I come with them today. We're at a park that has a three-mile loop around a lake, and they run around it three times. I'm actually second-guessing my decision to come along. Part of me just wanted to hang out with Loïc, regardless of what he was doing, and another part really wanted to meet Cooper.

"I'm not going to suck," I protest. *Yes, I totally am.*

"London, it's okay. Anyone, no matter how amazing they are, has to work up to running longer distances." He pulls me into a hug and kisses my forehead.

"Well, aren't you two cute?" An energetic loud voice startles me, making me jump back away from Loïc.

"London, this is Cooper. He's a bit obnoxious." Loïc gestures toward the guy who is now standing across from me.

He's sporting a huge grin, and I can already tell that I'm going to like him.

Cooper extends his hand toward mine. "You can call me David or Cooper. Either one's fine. Nice to finally meet the girl who has my boy here all gaga."

"Have I mentioned he's extremely annoying?" Loïc says with a laugh.

I shake Cooper's hand. "Nice to finally meet you, too. Loïc has nothing but great things to say about you."

"That's a lie, dude. I don't say anything nice about you," Loïc says to Cooper.

Cooper laughs and then turns his attention back toward me. "So, I hear you aren't much of a runner?"

The way he says it isn't accusatory in the slightest, and I'm surprised that his words don't bother me at all.

"No worries. I think it's great that you want to run with us. Just go slow. You can jog and then walk and then jog. But don't overdo it, or you'll end up pulling something. I sucked when I first started. Just ask Berkeley here. In basic, I was always one of the last ones to finish."

"Loïc, too?"

Cooper shakes his head. "Nah, that asshole was always one of the first. I think he had lots of practice running from trouble when he was out on the streets. That, and he always has to be better at everything than everyone else, you know?"

Loïc laughs. "You're such an ass."

Cooper grins. "All right, let's do this."

The three of us begin running along the paved path. I'm able to keep up with them for about two miles—just kidding. It's more like two football fields. That's decent though for my first time, I think. The ache in my side is so painful that I have to stop and walk.

Loïc turns around and runs backward. "I'll circle back around and see you in a few." He winks, and it's completely adorable.

"Stop being a show-off," I grumble.

He laughs and turns back around.

I continue walking, holding my side. *Motherfucker, it stings.* I enjoy the view of Loïc's backside for as long as I can before I can't see him anymore.

Over the next hour, Loïc runs past me three times. Each time, he smacks my ass as he passes, making me first jump and then giggle. During this entire time, I've gone around the loop once.

Eh, I could've done worse. I did manage to jog a few feet here and there.

When I've finished the loop, I'm a sweaty, disgusting mess. *Is this supposed to be fun?*

The three of us stretch afterward—well, at least the boys do. I attempt to copy them.

"Where should we go eat? London, what are you in the mood for?" Cooper asks.

"A shower," I respond dryly, eliciting a chuckle from him.

"Of course we'll shower first. But after?"

"I don't know. Maybe Mexican?"

"Dude! Let's go to Mexicantown. I haven't been there in forever," Cooper says excitedly.

Mexicantown is an area of Detroit that is mainly populated by Latino people, and they have the most authentic Mexican food around.

"That sounds good!" I agree.

"Sure," Loïc says.

"Will Maggie be able to join us?" I'm looking forward to meeting Loïc's other roommate.

"No, she's working a twelve-hour shift at the hospital," Cooper offers.

Maggie is a nurse at Mott Children's Hospital.

"Oh, that's a bummer. I want to meet her. Should we invite Paige?"

"Yeah, that's fine," Loïc answers.

"Great," I say happily.

I survived my first workout—okay, *workout* might be a stretch—with Loïc and Cooper, and now, I get to have fantastic Mexican food for dinner.

Loïc drops me off at my house, so I can shower while he goes back to his. Paige is game for a trip to the D—aka Detroit—and before I know it, the four of us are in Cooper's car, heading east.

We unanimously vote to go to Xochimilco. Their food is delicious, and their margaritas are even better.

Cooper parks in the lot next to the restaurant. Stepping out of the air-conditioned car, I'm hit with the thick and hot humid air. It's one of those days where there is so much sticky moisture in the air that I can feel it as I breathe in. I'm wearing a short little sundress, but it doesn't seem to help keep me any cooler.

I grab Loïc's hand and speed-walk toward the entrance of the restaurant before the minimum makeup I applied melts off my face.

The restaurant is styled in typical Mexican fashion—bright colors, flashing Dos Equis and Corona beer signs, and paintings of Latino women in flowy dresses, holding bouquets of white calla lilies. We're sat at a wooden table in the back of the room.

After ordering, Paige launches into her inquisition of Cooper and Loïc with endless questions about military life.

"So, like, what do you actually do when you're deployed?" Paige asks yet another question. She's extremely fascinated, apparently.

Cooper has been doing most of the answering, which I think is probably normal for him. He seems like the type of person who can talk to anyone. "It really just depends on what our mission is. The objectives vary, often daily. Many missions are reconnaissance in nature, which basically means that we explore enemy territories, hoping to gain some sort of desired information. Sometimes, we're involved in search and rescue. Other times, we take part in humanitarian assistance, especially if a location has recently been negatively impacted by war. Because Berkeley and I are in Special Forces, most of what we do is classified."

"Wow, that's so cool," Paige says with awe.

"Yeah, well, both Berkeley and I joined up right when we were eighteen and worked our way up to Special Forces. It definitely beats most jobs out there. Though, to be honest, a lot of what we do here is boring."

"What do you mean?" Paige asks.

"Just that the day-to-day stuff here is pretty standard, not much excitement going on. I suppose, like any job, it gets to be routine. Deployment is different though," Cooper says before taking a huge bite of his enchilada.

"All right, Paige, stop with the interrogation," I say with a chuckle.

"What? I'm just curious." She shrugs before taking a sip of her peach margarita.

"I know, but let the guys eat." I glance toward Cooper's mostly uneaten meal, which is huge actually, including several à la carte items in addition to his combo platter. "Though I don't know how you both eat so much and stay in such great shape."

"We work out a lot, so we get to eat a lot. It's a little perk." Cooper winks.

I can't help but giggle at his playfulness. I can see why Loïc loves him. He's one of those people who would be impossible not to love.

"You didn't think Berkeley here was born with that six-pack, did ya?" Cooper jokes.

"Yeah, we kinda did." Paige chuckles.

"Well, I'll agree that my boy here has to work a lot less than most for the same results. He's definitely gifted in the looks department—so the girls say."

"Oh, whatever, dude. I do just as much as you. Stop being a prick." Loïc shakes his head, sporting a grin.

Cooper shoots Loïc a sly smile before redirecting his attention to Paige. "So, Paige, what do you do?"

"Not much at the moment. London and I graduated from college a couple of months ago. Now, we're looking for jobs."

"Oh, yeah?" Cooper questions, sounding interested. "Where at?"

She shrugs unapologetically. "Well, nowhere yet. We're getting around to it. We've been busy."

I see the momentary confusion on Cooper's face as he assesses the situation even though he hides it well.

In the circle of people we normally hang around with, Paige's comment wouldn't have been questioned, but Cooper and Loïc have never been a part of that group of people. They belong to the crowd that has had to work for everything in their lives. I find that aspect of Loïc extremely sexy, and in this instant, I'm wondering how he finds me with my privileged life appealing in the least. I've never felt unworthy around anyone before Loïc. I don't like questioning my worth, but dating someone who's had to fight for every ounce of happiness he's experienced is sobering.

"Well, what was your degree in?" Cooper asks Paige a follow-up question.

"I majored in marketing, and London studied journalism."

"Very cool." Cooper nods his head.

Cooper and Paige continue to chat away, and I sip on the straw of my margarita while taking in their conversation. I turn my attention to Loïc, who is sitting across the table from me. His gaze is focused on my face, and it causes a torrent of goose bumps to populate the surface of the skin on my arms. He has this way of completely exposing me with a simple look. Though, with Loïc, nothing is ever simple.

The slurping sound of my straw searching for liquid no longer present among the ice in the large margarita glass fills the space, and I stop sucking. Yet Loïc's now seemingly darkened stare is still on me, and with nothing to occupy my lips, I start to chew on my bottom one.

His gaze is heavy, almost primal. It does something to my insides, and my body instantly responds to him. I feel the flush of desire creep up my neck and the familiar pull in my gut. His eyes dart from my lips to my eyes. Paige laughs at something Cooper said, but I barely hear it. My surroundings are now white noise to my sole focus—the gorgeous man before me.

I grab the bright yellow cotton napkin on the table, twisting and pulling it in my grasp. My palms feel sweaty as my heartbeat continues to accelerate. I've felt lust-filled want before, but it has never been this palpable, this urgent. With one look, Loïc has left me a fumbling mess of need with a craving so desperate that I would do almost anything to sate it.

I push back from the table. Clearing my throat, I say quickly, "I'm going to the restroom."

I walk toward the restroom like my ass is on fire, and while it technically isn't true, it sure feels like my entire body is ablaze. Inside the restroom, I wash my hands with cold water.

God, I'm a wreck.

My neck is splotchy, and my face is cranberry red. My pupils are dilated, and I look like I've just been thoroughly fucked or like I'm on drugs. Sighing, I shake my head to clear it. I don't do drugs, and unfortunately, I'm in a restaurant, so the initial one isn't true either.

I pull down on the paper towel from its dispenser and rip off a sheet of the brown paper to dry my hands. The restroom door swings open, and the air instantly changes. I turn, and my eyes go wide as I watch Loïc take two purposeful steps toward me. Before I can formulate a word, his hands grasp the sides of my face as his lips crash against mine. A whimper escapes my mouth as my hands frantically fist into his short hair, pulling him closer.

His hands drop from my face and hold my bare thighs beneath the sundress, lifting me off the ground. I circle my legs around his waist as he walks us past three empty stalls to the larger handicapped one at the end. His mouth continues to move against mine as he uses one arm to fumble with the lock on the door behind us.

I pull my lips from his as my back hits the hard wall behind me. "We're in a restroom." My voice is ragged as his body presses me into the hard plaster.

"Yep." Loïc produces a foil wrapper from his pocket and bites it between his teeth.

I'm contemplating protesting because it's a *restroom* when I hear him unzip his jeans.

I close my eyes, my chest rising and falling with labored movements. There's a rip of foil and some movement before Loïc's lips are on my neck—kissing, biting, sucking.

I'm about to be fucked against the wall in a dirty restroom, and oddly enough, I can't wait.

"You make me crazy, London," he whispers against my lips. "I can barely control myself with you. I want to be inside you all...of...the...fucking...time," he says between kisses.

Before I can respond, he pulls my thong to the side and enters me in one swift movement. I groan with the immense pleasure coursing through my entire body. Loïc kisses me hard, his tongue licking greedily, mimicking the movements of his body below.

I've never experienced a high like I do when I'm with Loïc. Everything about him—from his kisses to the way he touches me to the desperation in which he moves inside me, all of it—is so addictive. I need it. I need him. He's a drug I can't resist, and I would never want to.

This entire experience—the forceful way in which my back moves up and down against the wall, Loïc's urgent thrusts, our breaths, our kisses—creates a utopia of forbidden pleasure that sends me over the edge before I know it's coming. Loïc catches my cries in his mouth as he pumps faster and harder. He forcefully pushes in one last time as his body shudders against mine. I wrap my arms around him and hold him close as we both come down from our releases.

We stand this way for many heartbeats. The restroom is silent, save for our heavy breaths. After a beat, Loïc steps back, pulling me away from the wall. He pulls out of me, and I drop my feet to the floor. He disposes of the condom and buttons his jeans up. I take a moment to situate my clothing, and then we stand, facing each other.

His impossible blues gaze down at me with an expression of wonder. He lifts his hands to my face and runs his thumbs across my cheeks. "You are so amazing." He gives me a sweet kiss before resting his forehead against mine. "Well, I feel better. How about you?"

I giggle, my hands splayed across his T-shirt-clad chest. "Yeah, I'm feeling pretty good."

He moves his head back, assesses me again, and shakes it with a smile.

"I've never done that before," I admit.

"Been fucked up against the wall in a Mexican restaurant?" he questions with a smirk.

"Or any restaurant," I answer.

"Then, that's another first."

"Have you?" I question.

"Nope. Never in a Mexican restaurant."

"What about a restroom in any establishment?" I narrow my eyes at him.

"I plead the fifth."

"What?" I screech. "You're, like, a legit whore, Loïc."

Loïc laughs, and I hate that I can't help but smile when he does. He's so damn adorable when he's happy.

He leans down and kisses me on the forehead. "Babe, I've never experienced anything remotely close to the way I feel when I'm with you. You hold every first that matters because you're the only one I've ever wanted more with."

My heart is racing in my chest because he just called me *babe*, and he wants *more*, which I knew, but hearing him say it again is incredible. He's never used a pet name with me before, and I'm so happy that I want to break into song, like a princess in a Disney movie, but I won't. That'd be weird. Instead, I throw my arms around him and hug him tight. My face bears a huge smile as I snuggle into his chest.

"Should we go back?" he asks after a minute.

"Yeah, I suppose." I step back, releasing my hold. "Do you think they're going to know?"

"Probably. Does it matter?" He smirks.

"No, I guess not," I answer as Loïc opens the stall door. "I mean, to a whore like yourself who is no stranger to restroom fucking, I'm sure it really doesn't matter."

"If being a whore means I get to fuck you in other restrooms down the line, then I'll proudly wear that title," Loïc responds with a sly grin.

"You know, you can be cocky sometimes. It's kind of a flaw." I accusingly squint up toward him.

"Oh, I think you like that about me," he says matter-of-factly.

"Do I?" I huff in mock annoyance. "How do you know that?"

He shrugs. "I can tell."

"Whatever." I roll my eyes.

We exit the restroom, hand in hand, and come face-to-face with an elderly woman who is about to enter. She looks startled when she sees us.

"The men's room is out of order," Loïc says to the woman. He shrugs apologetically as we pass.

When the woman is inside the restroom, we both start laughing, and we are still smiling when we get back to the table.

"Did you get it all out?" Paige questions me as I sit in my chair beside her.

"Get what out?"

"Oh, I don't know…the fifteen-minute-long pee that you and Loïc both apparently had."

"No worries, Paige. We're good," Loïc answers for me as he shoots me a wink.

"Oh, I'm sure you are." Paige gives Loïc a knowing smile.

"Excuse me, Paige, but our restroom needs are not your concern," I say with a grin.

"Well, birds of a feather will flock together." She shrugs.

"Um...sure," I respond hesitantly.

"You guys want to order any dessert?" Paige asks us.

I shake my head. "No, I'm good. Thanks."

"I'm sure you are," Cooper chimes in.

I look to him, wide-eyed, before the four of us start to laugh.

This entire ordeal should be mortifying, but all I can manage to feel in this moment is pride because the handsome man across from me is mine—for all intents and purposes, at least. *In every way that matters.*

EIGHTEEN

Loïc

*"Slowly, I'm changing into the man I want to be—
one who can love London, truly love her, the way she deserves."*
— Loïc Berkeley

It's been a month since I finally decided to stop running from this connection I have with London. We haven't said the words out loud—perhaps because of my issues—but whether or not we verbally acknowledge it, I have a girlfriend.

Another first.

I guess for London and me, *No more running*, is equivalent to, *So, this means we're exclusive.* At least if I'm going to change into this person I barely recognize—this happy, open, loving sap—I can do it unconventionally and hold on to some of my autonomy.

The past month has been extremely difficult—at least for me. I've tried to keep the darkness away from London as I figure out my new normal. I text and call when I say I will, and I show up for our dates. And, at least as far as she can tell, I've stopped freaking out.

But nighttime—when my dreams come and the internal battles rage more than I would like—is hard. I'm a survivor. My body knows how to protect itself. It's instinctual.

This thing I have with London, although amazing, is going against everything that I am, that I've been forced to make myself be.

I know. I'm pathetic. I want to kick my own ass.

Poor Loïc has to date the girl of his dreams. It must be rough.

Logically, I know that London is the clear, sane choice. I wish I had control over my dreams—or more often than not, nightmares. It would be nice to shut out all my insecurities and self-defenses. If I were able, I would ignore them and solely focus on London and how *right* the world is when we're together.

Essentially, I'm reprogramming my entire being into the person I want to be. The mind is a powerful force. My thoughts, my brain, have saved me throughout my entire life. In doing so, I was made into this person who put up walls to protect himself from loss, someone who didn't trust, didn't take chances, and rarely loved. I know I can change. I am changing. It just takes time.

Thankfully, London is patient. I don't share my struggles with her, but I think she knows anyway. She's like Cooper in that way. She just gets me. It doesn't matter what I need—time, patience, reassurance, love. She gives it to me without me having to ask. Thank God because I would never ask.

Slowly, I'm changing into the man I want to be—one who can love London, truly love her, the way she deserves. I know I'll get there.

"Dude"—Cooper comes barreling into my room— "Maggie and I are thinking about going paddleboarding. Want to come?"

A smile comes to my face as I imagine London standing on a paddleboard. I wonder if she could balance for an entire minute.

"Oh, I would, man. I'd love to see London paddleboard. She's hilarious when she tries to do stuff like that, but we have plans already. I'm taking her to Lake Michigan for a 'relaxing' beach day." I do the air quotes with my fingers, and I can hear London's cute little whine in my mind.

"So, she hasn't found your love for outdoor activities yet?"

"Hardly," I say with a laugh. "She's more of an indoor type of girl."

"Right—so, like, completely opposite of you."

I shrug. "You know what they say...opposites attract or some shit."

"She does know that Loïc Berkeley doesn't just lie at the beach and sunbathe while eating bonbons, right?"

"She will," I answer smugly.

"You packing the boogie boards?"

"Already loaded," I say with a grin. I throw a few towels into my bag and zip it up.

"I kinda wish we were going with you two. I like London. Plus, Maggie still needs to meet her."

"You're welcome to come," I offer as I head toward the bedroom door.

"Nah, not today, but thanks. Maggie has plans with some friends this afternoon."

"Next time."

"For sure. Have fun, man. Have a nice *relaxing* time," Cooper calls after me.

"Don't I always?" I exclaim over my shoulder.

I hear his laughter as I exit the house.

"Oh, I love the beach," London says as I grab the cooler and supplies from the truck. "I mean, a beach in Florida or Hawaii would be better, but I'm sure this will be fine."

"Have you ever been to Lake Michigan?" I ask as I throw the boogie boards under my arm.

"No."

"Well, don't knock it until you try it. First, the sand in this area is the softest sand you'll ever find. The water isn't salty, so it won't sting your eyes, and it's really warm right now." It's almost August, which is the best time for Lake Michigan, in my opinion. "You've been living in Michigan for four years, and you've never come here?"

"Nope. I usually travel with my family during the summer months, so I've never been here."

"You're going to love it." I walk around the back of the truck to meet her.

"Um, what are those?" Her eyes dart to the boards beneath my arm.

"Boogie boards," I answer simply as I start walking toward the water.

"Why do you have two of them?" London calls out from behind me, the soft sand obviously slowing her down.

I stop walking to let her catch up. "Because there are two of us," I answer when she's next to me.

"I thought this was going to be a beach day. You do know what a beach day is, right? I'm talking about lying on a soft towel with a drink in hand, baking in the sun all day with an occasional short dip in the water. There are no surfboards allowed in this scenario."

I give her a quick kiss on her pouty lips. "Good thing I didn't bring my surfboards then."

"Loïc!" she says in a huff.

I continue my descent to the beach. I can't help the huge smile on my face. "Oh, chill, little spoiled one. You'll have fun," I call back to her.

The wind has picked up near the water, but I'm pretty sure I heard London let out a growl.

I find an empty spot located in a small dip of a large sand dune. It's perfect because the walls of the dune will keep out some of the wind and prevent our crap from blowing all over the beach. Plus, it's fairly close to the water.

I situate our large multicolored blanket, the beach umbrella, and cooler. "You ready to get in the water?" I ask London.

She has taken off her shorts and shirt, and she is facing me in her string bikini. I have no idea how she maintains such a smoking body when she enjoys physical activity less than anyone I know. She must come from good genes.

"You're exhausting," she says with a sulk, which elicits laughter from me.

I reach out my hand to take hers.

She wistfully looks down at the blanket. "Why did you bring the beach blanket? I have a feeling we're not going to be spending a lot of time lounging today." She sulks.

"I'm sure we'll need it at some point." I bend down and kiss her cheek.

I leave the boards by our blanket for now. She just grunts as we walk to the water.

"You know, for being so worldly, London, you're pretty sheltered."

"I am not. I've done lots of things. Just because my pastimes are different from yours doesn't mean they're wrong."

"You're right."

We walk through the waves where the water meets the sand. Michigan doesn't have brilliant waves like California does, but for a freshwater lake, they're pretty decent, especially on a windy day like today. It's a perfect day for boogie-boarding.

When we get out to where the water hits my chest, London wraps her arms around my neck so that our faces are level, and then her legs go around my waist.

"So, tell me what boogie-boarding is. Do I have to stand on the board?" she asks hesitantly.

"No, it's really easy and fun. You'll like it."

"Easy and fun to you maybe."

I expel a laugh. "I promise, you'll like it. We'll swim out to about there." I point to where the waves peak before they roll onto the shore. "See those waves? We'll be there. You can lie on your belly on the board. I like to go in on my knees."

She glares at me.

"But let's do stomachs for now." I smile. "So, you're there, lying on the board, and the wave will carry you onto shore. It feels like a mini roller coaster ride. Kids do it. It's easy. It doesn't require a lot of skill. Just wait, you'll have fun."

"Define *a lot.*"

I laugh. "Okay, it doesn't take any skill."

"That sounds more my speed." She giggles. "I like roller coasters."

"See? Perfect." I squeeze my arms around her, pulling her soft body into mine.

"Someday, are you going to get sick of me and my lack of outdoor knowledge? You might do better with dating a lumberjack or a professional outdoor person."

"An outdoor person?"

"You know what I mean." She grins wide.

"Do you know any female lumberjacks? Are they as hot as you?" I ask seriously.

"Not funny." She playfully hits my chest.

"Listen, London, I adore you just the way you are. I love that you haven't done a lot of the things that I like to do. It's fun to experience them with you for the first time."

"You have a thing about firsts, don't you?"

"With you, I do." My eyes capture hers, conveying all the things I want to say.

She places her lips against mine. I kiss her back, slow and worshipful at first, savoring the way she feels. I have an acute awareness of her, an inexplicable pull toward her, and I feel it all—the way her fingers caress the hair at the nape of my neck, her body wrapped around mine, and the sweet sighs that escape her mouth. All of it, all of London, makes me insane with need.

She is so different from me in every sense, but she couldn't be more perfect. Everything about her fills me with a sense of calm. With each kiss, each giggle, each pout, she is teaching my cold heart how to live again. Her presence alone is filling me up with the capacity to love.

I take the kiss deeper. I kiss her hard, my tongue licking greedily. Her taste is addictive. She whimpers into my mouth as her fingers pull through my hair, drawing me closer.

She pulls her mouth from mine, her lips swollen and red, sexy. "I'm clean, and I'm on the pill."

It takes me a second to realize what she's referring to, but when I do, I almost groan at the implication. "I'm clean, too." My words come out hoarse, my voice saturated in desire.

"Have you ever had sex in a lake before, Loïc?"

I shake my head.

"Me neither." Her voice is low and seductive.

With just a few words, London has the ability to make me crazy with desire. She is exceptionally skilled at it.

I look around to find us alone in the lake—at least, this far out. A few people are up on this section of the beach, but I know only our shoulders and heads are visible from above the water. We're far enough out that they would only be able to tell that we're out here, but they wouldn't be able to make out our actions.

My breaths come out ragged. London's eyes gleam in a silent dare.

"You know I have a thing for firsts." Using one of my hands, I slide my board shorts down until they are floating beneath the water around my ankles. I tightly hold London against me with one arm as my free hand pulls her bikini bottoms to the side, and two of my fingers enter her.

She bites her lip at the intrusion, and a small moan comes from her lips, but she doesn't look away. Our lusty gazes stay connected.

"Do you like that?" I ask as my fingers move deeper.

London closes her eyes and drops her face to my shoulder. "God, yes."

"Does that make you feel good, baby?" My thumb is moving in circles around her most sensitive area.

"Yes," she whimpers quietly against my neck. Her fingers grab at the skin of my back.

I pull out my fingers, and pulling the small fabric of her suit further to the side, I enter her. Every sensation of this experience is incredibly intense. The feeling of being out in the open and together in this way is hot as fuck. The warm water hitting my wet skin adds a different element and is highly enjoyable. And the way she feels without a barrier between us is incredible. More than that, the trust she has in me to allow me to feel her in this way puts me over the edge.

She continues to moan into my neck as my palms grasp her ass and push her onto me over and over again. I tilt my knees and bend my pelvis up, so I make sure that I'm hitting the exact spot that she needs. I can tell by the forceful way in which her hands grasp my back with her jagged breaths against my skin and the almost painful-sounding moans that leave her mouth that she is so close. My arms burn as I continue to move her onto me, increasing my speed with each thrust as I chase my own release.

Finally, we're both there, and as her body shatters around me, I let go. I capture her cries in my mouth as I kiss her hard. This is the single most satisfying moment in my life to date.

The two of us stay connected as we both come down from our moment of ecstasy. My mouth captures London's, the kisses slow and languid now. My lips and tongue cherish her with every soft movement.

Eventually, I pull my lips from hers. Our faces are still a mere breath away as we stare into each other's eyes.

I want to tell her that I love her because I don't know what else this feeling deep within my chest could be, if not for that. But I don't. Perhaps I'm a coward in that way. But I hope she sees it and feels it in me because it has to be exploding from my every pore. It's the most powerful emotion I've ever felt. It's not the type of love I felt for my parents or even Sarah. It's something more. It's raw, intense, and a little desperate. More than anything, it's terrifying because this feeling has the power to devastate me, to annihilate me.

London's eyes radiate with what I'm assuming mine do. Her expression is pensive, content, and a little fearful. But she doesn't say anything either.

Aren't we a perfect match? Yeah, I guess we are.

London's the first one to break the silence. "Well, I think I might be turning into an outdoor person," she says airily.

I can't help but laugh. "Is that so?"

"It's up for debate, but the outlook is good—especially if we can experience some more firsts together." She winks.

"I'm all over that," I say seriously, which makes her laugh.

Yeah, I'd risk complete annihilation to experience even one more first with London. And just maybe, if I'm really lucky, she'll get all the rest of mine.

NINETEEN

London

> *"Over the past few months—*
> *despite, or maybe because of, each varying aspect of him—*
> *I've fallen for the enigma that is Loïc Berkeley."*
> —London Wright

There. I've done it. I've officially applied to eight jobs, all within driving distance of my current residence. Granted, it took me longer than it should have to commence my job search. But getting Loïc to fall for me felt like a full-time job for a while. Then, once I got him, I was obsessed with spending time with him, and when he was at work, I was thinking about spending time with him.

But he's gone for two weeks for annual training, and there's no excuse not to get on with being an adult and finding a job. I have two Loïc-free weeks to fill. His training is up in northern Michigan where there is little but fields and forests, so his cell service is nonexistent.

He said he would try to call me a few times on the base phones.

I haven't applied to any jobs outside of Michigan—yet. I'm hoping one of the eight will work out, and I won't have to.

Truth is…I'm happy here. I don't want to move.

I close the lid of my laptop and make my way out to the living room where I find Paige eating a bowl of ramen noodles.

"You know, we're not in college anymore. There's no excuse to be eating those. Do you realize that each packet has sixteen hundred milligrams of sodium? That is well over half of the amount of salt you're supposed to have in a day."

"You sound like your mother," Paige responds before sucking a long noodle into her mouth.

"Shit, I do, don't I?" I plop down on the other end of the couch.

"Totally," Paige answers.

"I'm sorry."

"No biggie. What doesn't kill you makes you stronger, right?"

I squint my eyes toward Paige. "I don't know if that applies here."

"Sure it does. So, how's the job search going?"

"Oh, great!" I bounce up. "I'm done actually."

"Already?" Paige looks skeptical.

"Yeah, I know. I thought it would take longer, too. But, once I finished my résumé and cover letter, it went quickly."

"Where'd you apply?"

"Like, eight places—a few online news outlets, a couple of actual newspapers, and a few news stations."

"Sweet. I hope you get a job as the local traffic girl. That'd be fun, and you'd get to be on TV." Paige sets the now empty bowl down on the end table next to her.

"No way. I'm not going to be a traffic girl. That's lame. I want to write about real news."

"Well, you have to start somewhere."

"It won't be with me smiling widely, wearing an entirely too tight pantsuit and loads of makeup, while pointing to a screen where all the places with traffic backups or accidents on I-94 are lit up," I argue.

"Fine. Who knew you had so many scruples? I just thought you wanted a job."

"Not just any job. If I'm going to work, I'm going to be doing something that makes me happy even if I have to start off making next to nothing. Thankfully, I don't have to worry about money, and since I'm not desperate, I don't have to be a trashy traffic girl."

Paige dramatically leans back. "Yikes, what did traffic girls ever do to you?"

"You know what I mean." I laugh. "How's your job search going?"

Paige majored in marketing and wants to work for a promotions company of some sort. I just hope she doesn't use her backward knowledge of sayings as a foundation for marketing strategies.

"Eh."

"What does that mean?" I chuckle.

"We'll see. I've been applying. I haven't had any calls for interviews yet. Hopefully, something comes through."

"What should we do for the next ten days? I'm depressed just thinking about it." I sigh.

Creating my résumé, cover letter, and then applying to eight jobs only took up four days of my two Loïc-free weeks. Ten more days seems like an eternity.

"Is that how long you have until Loïc comes back?"

"Yeah."

"It doesn't matter. We can do whatever. Neither of us has interviews or anything lined up yet. Maybe we should go somewhere?" Paige suggests.

I nod thoughtfully. "You know my mom has been bugging me to come visit. Maybe I should suggest a girls' getaway. I don't want to hang out in Kentucky for a week though. Where do you want to go?"

"Let's do Vegas. We haven't been there since I turned twenty-one."

"So, you mean, in, like, a year?" I chuckle.

"Yeah, I guess. It seems longer." She smiles. "I've been craving that pasta we had at the bistro in The Venetian."

I groan. "Oh, that was so good."

"I know. I seriously dream about it."

"Okay, let me text her." I send a quick text to my mom.

Before Paige can find something we want to watch on the DVR, my mom texts back.

I look down at my phone. "She's in. She's calling her travel agent now to book it. She says to start packing. She's going to arrange for us to fly out tomorrow."

"Yay!" Paige claps. "Your mom doesn't mess around."

"She probably wants to lock us in before something comes up, and I change my mind."

"Well, whatever. She always plans the best vacations."

"It's our travel agent, Margaret. She's planned enough of our trips to know what we like."

"True. Let's go pack," Paige says excitedly, hopping off of the couch. "I hope I have enough cute outfits. We're not going to have time to go shopping tonight."

"It's fine. We can shop in Vegas." I follow Paige out of the living room.

"You're right. So true," Paige answers.

Well, I suppose if I have to spend the next week and a half without Loïc, there's no better way to spend it than with my mom and best friend in Vegas.

I returned from Las Vegas two days ago—well rested, tanned, overly fed, and shopped out. Actually, *rested* might be a stretch. Even though we spent many of our days lounging in the sun by the pool, Paige and I also spent an equal amount of nights out at the clubs. Anyone who has ever been to Vegas knows how exhausting that is.

So, in truth, I'm probably still slightly exhausted from the trip even though I slept the entire day after we got back. I might also be mildly jet-lagged as well. I'm using those two excuses as reasoning behind my current predicament.

Let's face it…I should just go to bed.

That would be the rational, logical behavior, but I've never been much of a rule-follower if said rules impede on my happiness. London first, logic second. At least I know myself enough to admit it.

It doesn't help that Paige went out with a group of our friends tonight, leaving me alone in our house to think. I don't do well with uninterrupted thinking time and no one around to talk me out of my actions.

So, here I am, driving to Loïc's, in just my PJs and flip-flops. My pajamas happen to be nothing more than a pair of yoga shorts and a flimsy tank top. My attire isn't even suitable to stop and get gas in. That's how much I wasn't thinking when I decided to bolt out of the house in my quest to get to Loïc. I blame Paige for not being accessible to talk me off of the ledge.

I let my gaze drop from the road to the car's front panel. *Phew, I still have half a tank of gas. Problem averted.*

I shouldn't blame Paige. She begged me to go out with her. Maybe I should have agreed. I just wasn't in the mood to go party. I hoped that I would be spending the evening with Loïc. I hadn't seen him in two weeks because he was at training. He'd called twice while I was in Vegas, but we weren't able to talk long either time.

I knew he was getting back today, and to say that I was excited would be a gross understatement. I'd practically been counting down the seconds until I would get to see him again, which was supposed to be today.

But then he called.

As soon as I heard his voice, I knew something was off. He said everything was fine, but I knew it wasn't. I could hear it in what he wasn't saying. His words were reassuring and placating, but in the empty spaces between each one were breaths of something that made my heart hurt. I suppose it was a sadness of sorts.

Red flags went up as soon as he told me that he couldn't see me today.

"I have a headache and just want to lie down. I'll see you tomorrow," were his words.

I have been missing him every second of every day for the past two weeks, and he'll see me tomorrow?

I reluctantly agreed and proceeded to sulk in my room for the next several hours. I refused to go out with Paige.

God forbid I do anything to take my mind off its current torture.

I let my brain wander aimlessly, going over everything that could be wrong with Loïc, until my thoughts were so loud that they demanded resolution. At which point, I jumped out of bed, grabbed my purse, and got in my car.

Undoubtedly, this wasn't the most suave plan I'd ever come up with. Perhaps Loïc just needed a night to himself. Maybe he did actually have a headache, and I was just being paranoid.

Too late to second-guess myself at this point. Operation Snuggle Time is in full motion. Headache or not, when he sees me, he's going to want to hold me. He'll be happy I came.

And if we want to get technical, it is just after midnight, which is really tomorrow, so all's good.

Over the summer, Loïc and I have grown so much as a couple. He still has his moments where he's closed off and times when he tries to shut me out, like tonight, but he has come such a long way. He's taken a while to get here, but I can't fault him in the slightest. He's gone through more in his life than most people have. He hasn't had an easy road, and understandably, his experiences have created defense mechanisms, some pretty foolproof ways of keeping others out. I get it. He was hurt by many people, so what better way to stop yourself from being hurt than by closing out the world, building walls?

I want him to know that he doesn't have to continue to keep me at arm's length. I'm not going to hurt him. I love him. I love him more than I ever knew was possible, and it's time I tell him. He deserves to know that I'm someone he can trust. I want him to understand that I'm in this for as long as he'll have me.

Loïc is a walking contradiction of emotions. He's hot and then cold, attentive and then elusive. He's gruff and domineering, and in the next breath, he's gentle and passionate. He's equal parts serious and funny. Within a span of seconds, he can be a complete jackass and then the most romantic man alive. I love all of him, every conflicting side.

Over the past few months—despite, or maybe because of, each varying aspect of him—I've fallen for the enigma that is Loïc Berkeley.

He needs to know that, whatever is troubling him, whatever insecurities he might have, we'll be okay. I'm not leaving him. I just know, beyond a shadow of a doubt, that he will own my heart forever.

God, I can't wait to see him, to hug him, to kiss him, to tell him that I love him.

I almost miss his street but manage to recognize it first. I've only been here once when Loïc just stopped by to grab something, and I didn't even get out of the truck. In the distance, I spot Loïc's gigantic truck parked in the road in front of his house. A smile immediately graces my face. I'm in deep when the mere sight of his vehicle makes me happy.

As I get closer, I notice someone walking up the front walkway to the house. It's not just someone. It's Loïc.

And he's not alone.

I slow my car to a crawl as I pass. My lungs burn as I hold my breath. I'm afraid to breathe with irrational fear that he'll hear me gasp for air and turn to see me—or perhaps the utter terror racing through me will demand to be felt with that breath. Somehow, denying my body oxygen, even for these few seconds, is allowing me to prevent my mind from acknowledging the sight before me. To take in air would be to accept my reality that I'm here, alive, in this space of time where Loïc is holding another girl in his arms. Right now, more than anything, I wish I weren't.

Hot tears burn down my cheeks. Loïc ambles up the sidewalk toward the front door with the girl. I can't see her face because it's nuzzled into his neck. Her long black curls fall over his shoulder, brushing his arm, as he walks. Her legs are wrapped around his waist, and one of his hands rests under her butt, securing her to him. Her arms cling around his neck with painful familiarity.

But all of this pales in comparison to the sight that hurts the most. It's not the fact that her lips are probably kissing his neck or the cozy way in which their bodies are responding to each other or even his hand on her ass that causes the most pain. The single vision that thrusts the dagger into my heart with unrelenting force is the vision of him throwing his head back in laughter. His beautiful face is lit up with happiness...because of her. Whatever she said or did to elicit that reaction from him is what kills me.

This isn't a one-night thing. He knows her. He loves her. If not love, then he holds a deep fondness for her.

His smile is genuine, and his laughter is real. In this moment, with another woman in his arms, he's truly happy.

He's giving her a side of himself that few people get to see. It's a piece of himself that I've had to work extremely hard to get glimpses of.

God, it hurts so much.

I drive to the end of the street and turn the corner. An elementary school is a block down, and I pull into its parking lot, stopping my car across three spaces. There's no one here to care anyway. I've barely moved my gearshift to park before I crumple against the steering wheel. My body vibrates as sobs rack through me. I cry into the dark space as howls of despair escape my lungs, and I ache everywhere. My entire body feels physical pain, as if it barely survived a cage fight with the current world champion.

How can emotional pain hurt this much? How can a stupid boy do this to me?

A vision of Loïc's face invades my mind before I force it out. It's too much. It's all just too much to take.

Why?

I don't understand why he would do this to me.

Was this some sort of a sick game to him? Was it all an act? Did he ever care at all?

So many questions plague my mind.

But I know that they don't matter. None of the answers matter. What's done is done. The reasons behind his actions will do little to pick up the pieces of my broken heart.

I hate him.

I hate him so much.

God, I wish that were true. I wish I could throw everything we had aside, like it meant nothing. I wish more than anything that I could take back the past three months. I wish I had skipped that stupid car wash. Who cares what the girls in the sorority would have thought of me?

It's just not fair.

My eyes burn, my chest aches, and my throat feels like it's on the second week of a bout with bronchitis. I ache—mind, body, and soul. It all stings, and in this moment, I feel as if it always will.

This is stupid!

I grab a handful of napkins from the glove box and clean up my face. Closing my eyes, I take a few fortifying deep breaths. No one has the power to destroy me, not even Loïc. I refuse to allow anyone to shatter me.

I put the car in drive and head toward my house. I take another route, not wanting to pass Loïc's house again. Errant tears course down my face as I tell myself over and over again that I'll be fine. *Loïc will not break me.*

I don't remember the drive back to my house, but I find myself in my driveway nonetheless.

Screw this! Screw Loïc! I'm going out.

I call a cab and run into the house. It's just after one in the morning. I'll have about forty-five minutes to accomplish my objective, which is plenty of time. I wash my face, throw my hair into a high ponytail, and put on one of my sluttier dresses.

I'm going to kiss Loïc out of my system. Even with puffy eyes and no makeup, I have a better chance of snatching a guy at the bar than half of the girls there. This will be cake.

I'm downing my fourth shot of vodka when I hear the cab out front. I throw the shot glass into the sink and race out the door. I could technically walk to the bar, but a cab will be quicker. I'm on a mission, and time is of the essence.

It doesn't take me long to secure a drink and find Paige when I get there.

She can't hide her surprise when she sees me. "What are you doing here?" She does a double take. "And why have you been crying?"

Out of everyone here, only Paige would know that I've been crying. She knows me better than anyone.

"I'm here to move on. Turns out that Loïc is a lying, cheating asshole. So, I'm going to find another hot guy and make out with him."

Paige looks legitimately confused and equally concerned. "Are you sure you want to do that? Don't rush into anything you'll regret."

I huff out an attempt at laughter. "Oh, I'm not going to regret it. Don't you worry about that."

Paige places her hand on my arm. "London, let's go home. I think this calls for a serious ice cream sundae session with at least three types of gummy bear toppings and extra hot fudge."

I shake my head. "Nope. You're the one who told me that the best way to get over a guy is to get under another one. I'm going to test your theory. Maybe not to the full extent—I'm not a complete hooker—but I think a heavy make-out session is in order."

Her eyes widen. "I said that? You know I give horrible advice. Since when have you ever listened to my words of wisdom? You know I don't make sense half of the time!"

"I'm fine. Relax." I spot a cute guy across the dance floor, and I start to walk in his direction.

"London!" my best friend shrieks from behind me.

I turn to face her.

"Don't do this. Let's go home," she pleads with genuine concern in her eyes.

"I have everything under control, Paigey Poo. Never fear, love!" I force a wide smile and continue my path to Rebound Suspect Number One.

The guy, albeit mildly wasted, is putty in my hands. It's too easy. But what did I expect? I've been off the market for a matter of months, not years. The Long Island he bought me goes right down. In fact, I barely taste it.

My head is heavy, and my thoughts are fuzzy, but that's a good thing. I need a break from my mind right now. Stupid thing keeps trying to remind me of what I lost, trying to make me think about *him*. I'm over it. I'm moving on. Can't my brain see that?

Rebound Dude holds me in his arms as we sway, I think, to music. Surely, we must be dancing.

228

What is his name? Mike, Matt, or maybe...Gallagher?

I can't remember. It doesn't matter. *Rebound Dude, it is.*

We've already established that he's going to take me back to his place and kiss me all night long. I was very upfront with my end game. Not surprisingly, he was all about it as well.

Stupid guys. They're so predictable and dumb...especially ones named Loïc. He's the stupidest one of all.

Loïc.

I open my eyes. Rebound Dude—or as I'm calling him now, R.D.—is talking to me. I blink a few times and focus on what he's saying.

"You ready to go?"

I have a feeling this isn't the first time he's asked.

I lift my heavy arm, and my palm holds his cheek. His face is full of stubble, like he hasn't shaved in a few days. I used to be extremely attracted to guys who had a five o'clock shadow like that.

Loïc never lets his stubble get that long. He has to keep it shaved for the military. Loïc's skin is soft beneath my touch. When I rub my hand in a certain direction though, I can always feel the tiny pokes of hair starting to grow. I miss that.

I haven't been able to run my hand across his smooth face in two weeks, and now, I never will again.

R.D.'s eyes are striking, big and brown. They fit his face perfectly. Pre-Loïc, I would have found his eyes sexy as hell. But, now, I can only be attracted to blue eyes—and not just any blue eyes. I'm in love with the type of eyes that contain countless shades of blue and look like an ocean is swirling inside them with a gaze that pins me with the weight of a majestic body of water.

229

Loïc might not want me, and he definitely isn't the guy I thought he was, but I can't deny the fact that I'm desperately in love with him. I have to figure out where to go from here before I do this. Being with another man when my entirety belongs to Loïc would break my heart, more than it's already been broken. I don't know how I'll recover from that. I know I'll have to get over Loïc, but this isn't the way.

I drop my hand from the handsome stranger's face. "Listen, R.D., you're a nice guy." I sigh.

"Arty? It's Ben." He sounds annoyed.

Ben! That's it!

"Right…Ben." I bob my head in acknowledgment. "*Yeah*," I draw out. "I gotta go." I point my thumb behind me. Then, I swivel and start to walk back to where Paige is.

The lights in the club are on now. It must be past two. I squint. The glare from the bright fluorescents is giving me a headache. I trip a little on my obnoxiously tall heels. Maybe they weren't the right shoes to wear when my night started by downing four shots, alone, in my kitchen. But nothing gives a girl confidence like her best fuck-me heels even if they are a bitch to walk in.

A set of arms wrap around my waist, holding me steady. "You ready to go home, killer?" Paige asks.

Aw, my Paige. How I love her.

"Yepper. Sure am." I nod.

She chuckles. "First, let's take these off."

She bends down and unhooks my shoe straps. I hold on to her shoulder as I step out of them. She hands them to me. Now that I don't feel like I'm walking on stilts, I'm much better.

"Let's get a cab, Paigey," I say weakly.

"No," she responds. "We'd have to wait forever for one, and I just want to get home. Plus, I think you could use a nice stroll with some fresh air."

"Yeah, fresh hair is nice, so soft," I say dreamily.

"*Air*, London…like the stuff you breathe."

"That's what I meant," I concur.

Paige and I walk home in silence. Our inner hands grasp on to each other as my outer hand holds my shoes. I bet she's dying to find out all the details about tonight, but she also knows that I need to focus on walking in my current state. She's a good friend, the best.

After eighty-five hours that fit into the space of probably fifteen minutes, we're home. The first thing I notice is Paige repeatedly squeezing my hand.

"Ow, Paige," I say for lack of a better response because it didn't hurt. It's just weird.

"Look," she hisses under her breath.

Look at what? What's her deal?

I lift my head that has been focused on my feet this entire time. On that journey, it took immense concentration to make sure I wouldn't stub one of my toes against the concrete sidewalk and ruin my perfectly painted nails. The entire walk, I was one step away from a massacre of ripped skin and gushing blood.

The interior of our house is dark, but the exterior is faintly lit up from the streetlights. I see a figure standing on our front porch. The world is starting to spin, but I would recognize that body anywhere.

Why is he here?

When we get to our front yard, Paige lets go of my hand.

What is she doing?

"I'll be right inside, London."

Why is she leaving me alone with him? Traitor!

I want to yell at her, but my head is too clouded to form thoughts quickly enough. When I'm finally ready to yell at her, she's already inside.

Instead, I'm left facing the man who broke my heart into a million pieces.

"You weren't answering your phone. I missed you," he says simply, as if he didn't destroy my entire world two hours ago.

"I hate you." I mean for it to come out as a loud, powerful declaration, but it leaves my lips on a broken whisper.

"I know. I'm sorry. I should have come over earlier when you asked. I feel horrible about it. But I had to see you."

"I hate you." This time, the words come out as a sob.

"London, I'm sorry. It was a dick move. I didn't have a headache. I'm sure you figured that out." He sounds sad, but I can't make myself care.

"I need you to leave—right now." These are the last words I say to him before a formidable explosion of vomit rips through me, causing me to bend at my waist and expel every last bit of vile liquid onto his feet.

TWENTY

Loïc

*"I've fallen hard for London.
Now that I've found her…I just hope I can keep her."*
—Loïc Berkeley

I spy with my little eye something fierce, stunning, beautiful, and mine.

At least, I hope she's still mine.

She kept repeating, "I hate you," over and over last night.

I didn't think she was such an angry drunk, but then I'd never seen her that out of it either.

After I gave her a shower last night to get all of the vomit off of both of us, I put her in a pair of simple cotton panties that I found in her drawer. I've never seen her in a pair like this. If it isn't silky, lacy, or a thong, she doesn't wear it. I thought this pair looked the most comfortable to sleep in. I'd be lying if I didn't acknowledge how incredibly sexy her ass looks in them right now.

I gave her some medicine and was able to get her to drink a full glass of water before she passed out, so I'm hoping she doesn't feel like complete shit when she gets up. And I know I'm a selfish prick, but I want her. My entire body craves her, and none of that will happen if she's still puking.

Part of me wanted to leave after she started throwing up. I know that's horrible to admit, but for me, watching someone that drunk brings back all sorts of unwanted memories. I could never leave her in that state, no matter how hard it is to be around it. She isn't them. I know that.

I'm propped up on my side on one elbow, watching London sleep beside me. Her chest moves quietly beneath the baggy T-shirt I put on her. She kicked off the blanket in her sleep multiple times last night, so I finally stopped covering her up, figuring she must be hot.

I shouldn't be creeping on my girlfriend when she probably feels like crap and more than likely will puke on me the second she wakes. But I haven't seen her in two weeks, and I've missed her like crazy—every single part of her, including her gorgeous ass.

Even if she feels fine, I'll have some explaining to do. She's never been so furious with me as she was last night. I knew she'd be mad, but I didn't expect that. Shows what I know. I'm always going to suck at this dating shit.

It was a jerk move. I realize that, but I'm the first to disclose that I'm not always going to handle things the right way—probably ever.

London starts to move beside me. I can tell the moment she realizes that I'm here. A serene smile crosses her face, and her body instinctually moves into mine. She wraps her arms around my back and snuggles her face into my chest.

God, I adore this woman.

I never thought I'd be here, in a place where I feel so much love and happiness. Truly, I didn't. I've fallen hard for London. Now that I've found her…I just hope I can keep her.

I return her embrace, dropping my face into her hair, smelling her sweetness. I pull her tighter against me, and my hands roam across her back.

Something shifts. London's body goes rigid. The languid caresses from moments ago have ceased. If I'm not mistaken, she's holding her breath, her back no longer rising and falling in contentment.

"London?" I ask cautiously.

Maybe she doesn't feel well.

Suddenly, she pushes away from me. Her eyes are dark with fury. "What are you doing here? Why are you in my bed?" She looks down to her bare legs before pulling the sheet over herself. "What am I wearing?"

I decide to first respond to the question with the most straightforward answer. "After our shower, I put you in the most comfortable attire I could find."

"Our shower?" she shrieks. "You got me naked?"

"We were covered in your vomit. I didn't think you'd mind," I answer dryly. "I've seen you naked before, London," I say, stating the obvious.

"But"—her voice is a high-pitched shrill—"you got me naked!"

I realize that I'm missing something. London and I are most definitely not on the same page.

"Are you still mad?" I ask.

"Am I still mad?" she yells. "You must be joking!"

"Listen, I said I was sorry. I knew it was wrong. You know I'm not good at this relationship stuff, London. You need to be a little more patient with me. Let me explain."

"I need to be more patient with you?" she screams.

I have an incredible desire to tell her to keep her voice down. She's giving me a headache. I might suck at relationships, but I have a feeling that wouldn't be a wise move. I've never seen her so mad.

She continues in her obnoxious tone, "So, I should just be patient with you while you stick your dick in some tramp? I should be understanding of that because you're"—she holds her fingers up in air quotations—"'not good at this relationship stuff.'" She ends the quote in a bitchy tone.

"Hold on, wait a minute," I stop her rant. "What are you talking about?" I ask, completely baffled.

"I'm talking about you cheating on me," she huffs. "What do you think I'm talking about?"

"Cheating on you?" I question. "I thought we were talking about me not coming over here when I got back last night, for telling you that I had a headache when I didn't."

"Well, that's how it started, but then it ended with you fucking some whore."

I shake my head. "I…what?"

London pulls the sheet up to her chest and crosses her arms. "Don't act confused. Please show me a little respect, and stop lying. I deserve that much."

"I didn't cheat on you, London."

"I saw you, Loïc! I saw you with her!"

"What are you talking about?"

"I knew you were lying about the headache. I thought there must be something wrong. I was worried about you.

Around midnight, I decided to go over to your house to comfort you. And that's when I saw you walking into the house...with her."

Walking into the house with a girl?

I think back to yesterday, and that's when it hits me. I can't stop the laugh that erupts from my throat. Now, it all makes sense. "I didn't cheat on you, London," I say with a chuckle. "That was my roommate Maggie. You know, my best friend's girlfriend? She's like a sister to me."

"Do you always carry around friends' girlfriends while groping their asses and letting them kiss your neck?"

"She wasn't kissing my neck, and I wasn't groping her!"

"Could've fooled me," she snaps. "Your hand was splayed across her ass, and her lips were on your neck."

"If my hand was on her, it was simply to help me hold her, and she was just resting her head on my shoulder because she was too drunk to keep it up."

"Or walk?" London huffs out.

"Yeah, or walk. Cooper and Maggie had a little too much fun a little too quickly at the bar and called me to go pick them up. I did, and I brought them back to our house. Then, I came over here and waited for over an hour for you to come back. That's all."

"Why couldn't Cooper carry her? I didn't see him anywhere."

"He was just as drunk and probably stumbled into the house right before you drove by. London, nothing happened with Maggie. I don't have any desire to do anything like that with her. She's family."

"You were laughing." Her voice is soft.

"Probably. Maggie says some hilarious stuff when she's wasted." I shrug.

"In your body language, I could tell that you were very comfortable with her."

"I am," I agree. "I love her, London…like a sister," I repeat slowly. "I would never cheat on you. Ever. That's not who I am."

"So, you didn't have sex with anyone last night?" she questions.

"No." I shake my head.

"You didn't kiss anyone last night?"

"Unfortunately, no. The girl I wanted to kiss had vomit spewing from her mouth, and that's a hard limit for me."

She starts to smile, and I can see the tension leaving her body.

"You didn't inappropriately grope anyone last night, especially on the ass region?"

"Maggie? No, not at all. But, in full disclosure, I might have washed your ass slightly longer than it needed, but I just wanted to make sure it was good and clean. It was purely unselfish on my end…for the most part." I smirk.

"Oh my God," London says before her shoulders sag. She wraps her arms around her bent knees, lets her face fall to her legs, and starts to cry with full-on shaking body sobs.

I sit up and wrap my arm around her shoulder and hold her as she cries. Her tears go on for a long time, and I continue to hold her and kiss the top of her head. I feel horrible that she thought I cheated.

"I thought I'd lost you," she eventually chokes out.

"You didn't."

"I was a mess. I just…it was horrible, feeling that way."

"I'm so sorry that you had to go through that."

"I almost kissed another guy to get back at you," she cries.

Wait, what?

My entire body stiffens. I have to focus on my breathing because I feel like I'm going to lose all control.

"I mean, I didn't," she continues. "But I wanted to. I wanted to hurt you. I went to the bar with every intention of making out with someone else. I thought I'd lost you."

"What happened with this other guy?" I say slowly, my words measured.

"Oh, nothing. I couldn't. Even shitfaced and brokenhearted, I just wanted you. I didn't kiss him. I think we danced. Or I might have just been standing there, and the room was moving. I can't be certain." She sniffs and wipes her eyes on the sheet.

I close my eyes and lean my head back against the wooden headboard. She was hurt and confused. I can't be mad, but, God, I'm so furious. She almost kissed some other guy, which would have most likely led to more. Okay, *almost* is a stretch, but she thought about it…and that's bad enough.

I'm trying to compose my thoughts when she jumps up and runs to the bathroom.

"I'll be right back," she says with extreme cheerfulness.

I hear the buzz of her toothbrush.

Despite my confused state, I can't help but smile. She has a thing about morning breath. So, the fact that she's in there, brushing, means that all is forgiven on her end, and she's ready to make up. Normally, I would be all about it, but I'm having a hard time getting over the reality that she just admitted that she had gone out with the intention of hooking up with someone else less than an hour after I supposedly cheated on her. It doesn't sit well with me or help my never-ending trust issues.

I understand why she did it and what she must have been going through. Logically, I can rationalize her confession. But, deep down, where my dark issues lie, I'm having a hard time, an extremely difficult time, letting it go. I don't want to fight with her. I definitely want intense, sweaty make-up sex, but I wish she had kept that confession to herself.

She comes bouncing out of the bathroom without a care in the world. She's so gorgeous. She jumps onto the bed and straddles me. "I can't believe you put me in these granny panties. I only wear these when Aunt Flo comes to town. I'm a little embarrassed."

I want to tell her that I find them extremely sexy on her, but before I get a chance, her hands take my face between them, and she slides her lips across mine. She holds my face and bites my bottom lip before pulling it into her mouth.

And with that, I'm completely ready for her. I'm ready to forget about the past twenty-four hours and fuck her so hard that neither of us will remember that we were fighting in the first place, let alone why.

But I can't.

I pull my mouth from hers. "London?"

"Yeah?" she says sweetly. Her lips burn a trail down my neck.

Blood pumps through my body at rapid speeds, fueling me with nothing but want and pure desire.

Focus.

"London," I breathe heavily. "I need to say something."

"Mmhmm…" she responds as her lips move down my chest.

"London, take your lips off of me."

She complies with a sexy grin. "But I like my lips on you."

"I do, too." I smile. "But, listen, I need to say something, and I can't concentrate with your lips doing that, okay?"

She nods.

"I understand what you must have been going through last night after you saw me with Maggie. But we are going to have other misunderstandings along the way, and it doesn't sit well with me that the first thing you wanted to do was hook up with someone else."

She opens her mouth to protest, but I put my finger on her lips.

"Let me finish. I know you didn't want to make out with someone else, but you thought about it. You know I have major trust issues. You know that this is all very new to me, but I promised you that I would try. I can't risk giving you my heart if I know that, at the first sign of trouble, you're going to destroy me with your actions. I can somewhat understand your reasons for wanting revenge, but I can't stomach it. The thought of you with someone else makes me sick. It sets fire to the part of me that can't trust others, the part that puts up walls. I don't give power to those who might hurt me. I can never be in a real relationship with you if I build walls. You and I both know that. I can't love you if I don't let you in, but I'm so afraid to let you in. You have the power to destroy me, London."

She does. With a few words, she could leave me in ruins, like an ancient city that can never be rebuilt.

"Oh, Loïc," she says on a whisper. Her eyes glisten with fresh tears. She holds my face between her hands and peppers soft kisses across the skin on my face, paying extra attention to my lips. She pulls back and captures me with her brown eyes. The gold specks that weave through her irises shine brighter through her tears.

She continues to cradle my face as she speaks, "So, we've established that I have another flaw, another one of many." She laughs lightly. "I will work on my communication. I promise you that, no matter how dire the circumstance or how awful it appears on my end, I will talk with you before I jump to conclusions. I promise you this, Loïc," she says the last sentence with so much conviction that I believe it.

"You have to know that I would never cheat on you," she continues. "Even when I was certain that you were screwing someone else and that I would never have you again…I couldn't. At my lowest point, with my heart completely shattered, I couldn't be with someone other than you. You have to believe me."

I nod because I do.

"And since we're talking about flaws, you, Loïc Berkeley, need to work on being honest with me. I know you're not telling me something. I know something is worrying you. I didn't believe your headache story for a minute. You promised me, no more running. You have to work on your communication, too. I realize that this is all new to you, so I'm being patient. But I can't be an open book for you when you're barely opening up a chapter of yourself for me. You have to trust me enough to tell me your fears and worries. Let me be there for you. I want to be there for you, too."

She kisses me again. Her lips caress mine, and right when I'm about to deepen the kiss, she pulls back one more time. Her face is a breath away.

"Do you know why I was going to your house last night? I was going to tell you that I loved you, Loïc.

I. Love. You. You can trust me with your heart because I'm not going anywhere."

Hearing those three words fall from London's lips helps me more than years of therapy ever could.

This time, I crash my mouth to hers. As my tongue swirls in her mouth, something that she said a minute ago confuses me, and I pull back.

"London, why do you only where these panties when your aunt visits?"

London starts to laugh hysterically and falls off of my legs onto the bed.

"What?"

"Loïc, Aunt Flo is another name for a girl's period." She giggles.

"It is?" I ask in astonishment.

"Yes! I thought you lived with a girl. You've never heard that before?"

"I don't talk to her about her period or whether or not she wears special underwear for it. How was I supposed to know that cotton panties are only for that?"

"You're so cute and naive." She laughs. "Don't worry. I don't let my real aunt see me in my underwear."

"I thought that was weird." I scrunch up my nose in disgust.

She just laughs. "Nothing like a conversation about good ole Aunt Flo to kill the mood."

"I know how to get the mood back. Tell me those three words again." I quirk up an eyebrow.

"Which ones?"

"You know which ones," I growl, pulling her hips toward mine.

She leans in. "I love you." Her breath from the words warms my face.

I groan as her lips find passage on the sensitive skin beneath my ear once more.

"I love you, Loïc Berkeley," she whispers against my skin, shooting chills through my body.

I roll her over until she's pinned beneath me. I'm aching with want but not with indistinct desire. No, this need is singularly focused, made for one woman only.

London is everything I could ever want but never knew to ask for. Even if I had known, I would have never wished for her. She's too beautiful and too perfect for me to be real. Yet here she is, and not only is she real, but she also loves me. I know I won't be able to hold on to her forever, but here and now, I'm making that wish anyway.

I hold her wrists against the mattress. Her hair is splayed across the pillow. She wears no makeup, and her eyes are slightly puffy from crying, but they appear to shine brighter in the morning light. She looks like an angel. I guess that is fitting since she's definitely saved me.

I pin her with my stare. "I love you, London Wright, more than I ever thought possible." My heart doesn't race with trepidation as the words leave my mouth. My palms don't sweat, and I have no desire to run. In fact, there is nowhere else I'd rather be than right here.

I do love London. It's my reality, and regardless of what happens in the future, I'm so thankful to have her now. She's told me many times, and now, I believe her. Love is worth the risk. These feelings of pure love and happiness coursing through me right now are worth it.

TWENTY-ONE

London

"I love you. Get it through your thick skull."
—London Wright

I'm presently in heaven, and I love it. Yep, I'm a huge fan of paradise on earth. And, to me, that consists of lying in my bed with Loïc with our naked limbs wrapped around one another, both of us in a sated afterglow of bliss.

I nuzzle my face against his firm chest. I could lie here all day.

It's been a week since we confessed our love for one another out loud. In truth, the L word must make Loïc extremely horny because we've spent the majority of the past week in this very bed in my room. Loïc leaves to go to work, of course, and we try to eat every now and then, but we're mainly here, wonderfully content.

Loïc wears happiness well, too. If anything, he's extremely irresistible when he's smiling—not that I'd want to resist him anyway.

He gently trails his fingertips across the skin of my back. "Hey, remember the last time I freaked out, after the sunset date a couple of months back?"

"Yeah." Of course I do.

"Do you remember when you gave your little speech at the end, telling me that not everything should be a battle and that I was a big, bad warrior?"

I huff out a laugh against his skin. "Yes, I remember."

"Why did you call me a warrior?" he questions thoughtfully.

"Early on, I looked up your name. It was probably because of that. Do you know your name means famed warrior?"

"I didn't know you'd looked it up."

"Mmhmm…I don't remember when. It was at the beginning though, maybe even after the car wash. I remember thinking your name was so unique, and I wanted to know what it meant. What made you think about that night?"

"I'm not sure. I meant to ask you about it before, but I forgot. I've always known what my name stood for. My dad used to call me his little warrior."

"Oh, I didn't know that." I sit up with my arm propped on Loïc, so I can see into his eyes.

I love when he tells me stories about his childhood, good or bad. It makes me feel closer to him, and I get a thrill every time he opens up to me. I know it isn't easy for him, and I love that he feels comfortable with me now. For some reason, every time he shares a detail from his past, I feel like we're a step closer to our future. I'm not sure why, but it's as if, when he shares with me, it is his way of mourning that part of his history, and after he lets it go, he's able to move forward with me.

Since we're sharing, I'm reminded of something I've wanted to ask him.

First, I bend down and kiss him, tickling my tongue with his. I'm so addicted to his taste, his kisses. I press my lips against his in one last chaste kiss before marginally leaning back.

"So, I wanted to ask you, what did you want to tell me last week when you got back from training?"

His body stiffens beneath me. "What?"

I attempt to keep the atmosphere lighthearted, ignoring his obvious discomfort from my question. I smile wide. "Don't think I've forgotten. You had something to tell me. You've kept me thoroughly entertained all week"—I give him a wink—"but I would like to know what it was."

"You're right. I did—I do have something to tell you."

The tone in his voice fills me with a sense of dread. The worry that has been absent from him all week has returned. I hate that I'm the cause of his shift in demeanor, but I have to know—now more than ever.

"You can tell me anything," I try to reassure him.

The hand that I have rested on his chest can feel his heart beating rapidly beneath his warm skin. The swift cadence now mirrors the beat of my own heart.

"Well, I knew it was a possibility, but I didn't know for sure if it would happen. I knew my unit was up, but I was hoping we wouldn't be called." He nervously searches my eyes.

"Loïc, you're speaking in riddles. Just tell me."

"We're being deployed."

I wait for him to continue, but he doesn't say any more.

"That's it?"

"London, I'm being shipped to Afghanistan where I will be for a *year*." He emphasizes the last word.

Then, I get it—his fear of losing me.

"Well, yeah, that totally sucks," I admit. "But you know it doesn't mean anything where we are concerned, right? I'll wait for you, Loïc. That isn't even a question. You know that, right? I'll miss you like crazy, but I'll be here when you get back, loving you just as much as I do now, if not more."

"A year is a long time, London. I can't ask you to do that for me. It isn't fair to you."

"Stop right there. I know you're new to this whole I-love-you thing, but when you love someone the way I love you, time and distance aren't issues. My love doesn't come with conditions. I don't love you because you're here right now. My feelings aren't going to expire because I'm not able to see you every day."

His eyes narrow. "Are you saying that you want to wait for me?"

He's so innocent in this moment that I can't help but laugh.

"Of course I will! I love you. Get it through your thick skull."

A slow smile crosses his face as he releases a huge breath.

I shake my head, huffing out a laugh. "Did you really think I'd want to break up because you're being deployed?"

"I don't know. I guess I didn't know what to expect. But I was prepared for anything."

"Loïc"—his name comes out as a whine—"you have a lot to learn about love." I squint down at him. "You don't want to date other people while you're over there, right?" I accusingly furrow my brow.

"No, of course not. You're the only person in this world I want, London."

"And you're the only one I want. You see how this love thing works both ways?"

"Yeah, I suppose I do." He chuckles.

"Plus, it will be kind of romantic. We can write love letters to each other while you're gone."

"I'll have access to the Internet when I'm on base." He grins.

"Fine, we can use your Internet connection for Skype and Internet sex, but other than that, I want letters, like snail-mail letters. That will be so romantic."

"Internet sex?" he questions with a huge grin.

"Of course. Just because you're a million miles away doesn't mean I'm not going to take care of my man," I say seriously.

"I think your mileage is a tad off."

I roll my eyes. "It will feel like a million miles, believe me. Anything more than a ten-minute drive away is too much." His smile falls a bit, and I quickly clarify, "But just because I'll miss you immensely won't change anything. You're stuck with me."

"Good." He grasps my face and pulls me in for a quick kiss.

"But, seriously…I can't wait to get your letters. You can tell me all the things you miss about me, what you'd be doing if you were with me, how much better your life is because I'm in it. You can write all your fantasies revolving around our future."

Loïc laughs loudly. "Wow, you've really planned this out in the thirty seconds since you found out I was leaving."

"What can I say? I like to plan."

"Really? 'Cause you haven't even applied for one job since I've met you. You seem content on coasting through life without planning a damn thing."

He smiles, and I know he's just teasing.

"That's not true! I've applied. I just haven't gotten an interview yet. I will though. Maybe my job search hasn't been as intense as it should be. But can you blame me? I've been preoccupied, trying to get the love of my life to like me back. Then, once he liked me, a whole other set of distractions came." I playfully wiggle my eyebrows.

He shakes his head in amusement, and his lips tilt up into a cute smirk. "Love of your life?"

"So far. So, don't mess it up." I poke him in the side.

He rolls us over so that I'm pinned beneath him.

"Wait," I say through a laugh. "I have a question," I get out as his lips start attacking my neck.

"What's that?" he breathes against my sensitive skin.

"How long do we have?"

"Until?" He lifts his gaze to meet mine.

"You leave."

"Two months. We head out the first of December."

"Perfect."

"Why's that?" His brows furrow, his eyes assessing.

"You'll be shipping out before Michigan's real winter hits, so I won't have to try to get out of all the outdoorsy crap I'm sure you would have planned."

"You're such a brat." He tickles my sides. "All of our time together this past week has been spent indoors. I don't know what you're complaining about. Plus, remember that means I will be getting back right before winter starts the next year, so I'll make sure to plan all of our reunion dates to be outside."

"I vote that I'm in charge of all reunion-date planning."

He grins, and it's carefree and sexy. Grasping my face in his hands, he says, "I vote that we worry about that in a year and two months. For now, you can tell me all about this Internet sex that you have planned. Or, better yet, you can show me." His expression is lusty and primal.

His words shoot chills through my body as I draw in a deep breath. My body is instantly needy for him.

"I can do that." I stare up into his amazing blue depths, immediately lost in my Loïc obsession.

His lips find mine, and I'm so thankful that, out of all the obsessions I could have chosen, I got him. There is no one else I'd rather get lost in.

"You know what I was thinking?" I ask, my limbs once again jelly as they entwine with Loïc's.

He props himself up on his elbows. "What's that?" He smiles down to me.

"That we leave this bed today."

He cocks his head to the side in a distractingly charming way. "Why would we want to do that?"

"I know, right?" I giggle. "I was just thinking that, because it's Saturday, it might be a good day to meet Maggie. I've never even met her. I mean, you're so close with Paige that you've witnessed her in all her bed head and morning-breath glory, and I haven't even been introduced to one of your best friends. If I had, we wouldn't have had the drama of last week because I would have known it was Maggie."

He studies my face, like it's a puzzle he can't solve. "You're right. God, I'm sorry, London. I hope you don't think I've kept you from her like I didn't want her to see you or anything like that. She knows all about you—obviously. The few times you've seen Cooper, she's been at work. It wasn't intentional."

"I know that."

He reaches for his phone on the bedside table. "Let me text Coop and tell him we want to hang out tonight." He swipes his phone. "Oh, Cooper sent me a text a few minutes ago, telling me to come home, that he has something to show me. Cool," he says to himself. He types something out and puts his phone down.

"What'd you tell him?"

"That I'd be home in an hour."

"Why an hour?"

"So, we can shower first." He raises a brow.

I throw a pillow at him as I get up. "Hell no. I need a reprieve. I'm going to shower without you."

"That's no fun," he protests. "Fine, we shower together, and I'll promise to keep my hands to myself."

"You'd better." I accusingly point at him. "I'm serious. Shower only."

He gets out of bed. "You can trust me."

I huff out a laugh. "That's what you said the last time."

"Well, last time, I was lying." He walks past me into the bathroom in all his naked glory.

I check out his ass some as he passes because, damn, it's delicious.

"So, you're not lying this time?" I yell into the bathroom over the sound of the running water.

"Get your ass in here, London. We only have an hour. We wouldn't want to be late."

"I hate you." I giggle as I step into the shower.

"I thought we were working on that flaw?" he asks before his wet hands take my face between them and pull my lips to his.

It's a glorious fall day, simply beautiful. The sun is shining, casting its warm glow on the trees. The leaves are still on the branches, but they've started to change into a kaleidoscope of autumn colors. The breeze blowing through the open windows of Loïc's truck is warm and soothing as it glides across my skin.

It's a magnificent day, and I'm incredibly in love. I wonder if I will see the upcoming cold winter differently under my new state of mind. For some reason, I doubt it. Love can only tint my vision so much.

We turn onto Loïc's street almost exactly an hour after he told Cooper he would be there. My entire body hums with giddy excitement to meet Maggie. I know Loïc doesn't let many people in, so the fact that he's so close to Maggie means that she must be a pretty amazing person. I know Cooper is. I hope she likes me.

Who am I kidding? Of course she'll love me. We'll become great friends, and then the four of us can double date all the time. It'll be perfect.

As Loïc's truck slows, he says, "What the fuck?" under his breath.

I turn to ask him what's wrong, but I stop myself. His entire body is shaking, vibrating with a deep emotion that I can't yet decipher.

"Holy shit. Oh my God. Oh my God," he chants. His knuckles are ghost white as they clutch the steering wheel.

My chest pounds with fear—of what, I'm not sure. But seeing Loïc this shaken is worrying me.

"It can't be. Holy shit," he whispers to himself, tears now falling from his face.

"What is it, Loïc? What's wrong?"

He doesn't hear me. Instead, he parks the truck with a jerk. His breaths are short and rapid as his chest rises and falls while his tears fall onto his T-shirt.

I finally pull my attention from Loïc and follow his gaze to the front of his house where a girl is sitting on his porch steps. I can't see the details of her face, but from here, she looks like a Victoria's Secret model. She seems tall and looks very thin with long, wavy blonde hair.

Loïc is out of the truck before I can even process what's happening. He runs to her as she lunges toward him with equal fervor. He says something, but I can't make it out. I quickly exit the truck and watch as she jumps into his arms, wrapping her legs around his waist. The two of them bury their faces in each other's neck and cry.

I watch, mesmerized, as their bodies convulse with sobs, each holding on to the other with such passion and commitment. Their arms strain to pull the other in tighter. The sounds of their cries truly break my heart, and I realize that I, too, am crying.

I pull my eyes off of Loïc and the blonde to find Cooper and Maggie on the porch. Cooper has his arm around Maggie as she leans into him, tears rolling down her cheeks. Cooper raises his free hand to wipe the corner of his eye.

My attention falls back to Loïc and the display of utter heartbreak and joy before me. The reunion between them seems so sacred that I feel like I should go somewhere else to give them privacy. Not only do I not have anywhere to go, but I also can't turn away.

The five of us stay like this for what feels like an hour before Loïc finally releases his death grip on the blonde and starts peppering kisses all over her face. She untangles her legs and lets them fall back to the ground. The two of them stand with their foreheads together. They're whispering to each other while his hands hold her upper arms, and hers are wrapped around his waist.

Finally, Loïc takes a step back, and I can see the moment when he remembers that I'm here. His body tightens, and his head turns in my direction. His glistening eyes meet mine, and he smiles weakly. He reaches his hand out toward me, inviting me forward. I close the distance between us and put my hand in his outstretched one.

He squeezes my hand in his before addressing me, "This is my Sarah."

Sarah? I'm sure my eyes go wide when I say, "Sarah?" in complete amazement.

"Yeah, Sarah," he repeats, his voice equally astonished.

He turns his attention toward her. "Sarah, this is my girlfriend, London."

She smiles at me, and I return it with one of my own.

"London?" Her brows go up in question as she and Loïc exchange a look.

He chuckles. "I know. What are the odds, right? We have a lot to talk about."

Well, if that isn't the understatement of the year.

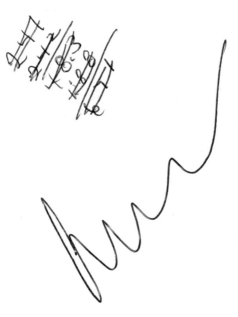

TWENTY-TWO

Loïc

> *"Hope is the building block for miracles,*
> *but it is also the catalyst for disappointment,*
> *depending on which way the coin falls."*
> —*Loïc Berkeley*

It's impossible for me to wrap my mind around my reality at the current moment.

This is reality, right? Not some sick dream designed to completely destroy me?

This is real.

I grasp Sarah's soft skin in my left hand, and her fingers entwine with mine. She squeezes back.

She's here. She's alive.

She's here. She's alive.

I repeat these thoughts over and over in my head. It's still unbelievable. I don't know how one should respond when someone he loves comes back from the dead, but

I'm sure I could be handling it better. I'm one gigantic mess right now.

Driving toward my house minutes ago, I knew it was Sarah before I could even make out her features. The curve of her body and her posture as she sat on my porch steps was so familiar, even from a distance. For the past eight years, I've had all the infinitesimal details that made Sarah who she was running through my mind on repeat. Much like I do with my parents and my dad's stories, I would play the two years that I spent with Sarah over in my mind until each memory was so ingrained in my brain that I could never forget it.

When one loses someone he loves and all that's left are memories, one makes damn sure he will never forget any of the details, not one. So, I remembered her every single day. I might not have broadcasted my thoughts to the world or even to my one confidant, Cooper, but they were always there for me, in my mind, where I would have mourned her forever.

But, now, she's here—alive, breathing, real.

It's the most amazing moment in my life, and at the same time, it's the worst. Thoughts of the past eight years plague me.

Where's she been? What's she been doing? Has she been sad? Alone?

I haven't been there for her. I left her alone when she was so broken. I shudder as I try to imagine what our time apart has been like for her. I need to get her by herself, so we can talk. There is so much to say, so many questions to ask. More than anything, I just want to hold her and allow her presence to fill me up because, despite getting her back, I feel so lost. My world has been completely thrown off its axis, and I need to find my new normal. I'm off-kilter, and that isn't a good place for me to be.

I'm reminded of London when I feel her small hand in my right one.

The three of us walk toward the house.

I'm literally holding my past in one hand and my present in the other, and the three of us are on a path to...*where? My new future?* I haven't a clue. Of course, I'm not certain of much right about now. My mind's a jumbled mess of confusion.

Cooper holds the door open for us, and we step inside. I release the two hands I was holding and wipe my sweaty palms against my jeans before bringing them to the base of my neck.

I'm mildly aware of the introductions happening as Cooper introduces Maggie to London. I make my way to the kitchen and fill a glass with water before chugging it down. I set the empty glass on the counter and turn to find Sarah behind me.

"I'm sorry. It's a lot. I should have probably warned you before showing up."

"No...it's fine. I mean, yeah, it's a lot"—I grin—"but never apologize. This is like a dream come true for me. I just need a moment to process it, is all. Don't apologize, Sarah." I let out a large breath. "Come here." I pull her against my chest. Wrapping my arms around her, I hug her tight. I'm still so amazed that I'm standing here, embracing her, my Sarah.

I close my eyes and relish in the sensation of having Sarah in my arms. We stand like this as my mind continues to try to wrap itself around this new reality. It's like I need to keep touching her to reassure myself that she's really here. It's so surreal.

I open my eyes when I sense the presence of others. Cooper, Maggie, and London stand at the entrance of the kitchen. They all wear odd expressions. A mixture of happiness, confusion, and unease grace their faces. I want to laugh because this entire ordeal really is strange. It's not like someone who was presumed dead shows up on my doorstep every day.

Cooper—gotta love him—breaks the awkward silence first. He has this innate gift to know what others need, and right now, we need some lightheartedness to break up this intense atmosphere. "So, I'm sure you two have tons to talk about, given the fact that you thought she was dead when you woke up this morning—and every other morning for the past eight years, for that matter. Do you two need time to talk? Do you want us to take London back for you?"

"Oh, that would be great, Coops. Thanks." I turn my attention to Sarah. "Can you give me a minute?"

"Of course." She grins up at me. Her big blue eyes shine bright with joy and something that I've never seen in them before—peace.

She looks the same as she did when she was sixteen but completely different at the same time. She's healthier and happier now, which makes her even more beautiful.

I walk over to London and take her hand in mine as we exit the house. Maggie and Cooper get in his car. They close the doors behind them, leaving London and me alone outside Cooper's vehicle.

We stand, facing each other.

"Are you okay?" she asks, concern etched across her face.

"Yeah, I'm fine," I admit. "It's just a lot to take in."

"Are we okay?" Her voice cracks with emotion.

I'm momentarily taken aback. "Yes, of course we are. Why do you ask?"

"I just wanted to make sure," she answers softly.

"London, we're fine. We're great. Okay?"

She nods, but her brown eyes still hold concern.

"Look, I know this day is ending on a weird note. I guess I never really told Cooper that I was bringing you with me when I texted him earlier. I'm sure, had he known, he would have told me not to. Not because I don't want you here, but obviously, I have a lot of catching up to do with Sarah. So, I'm sorry our evening is being cut short. But we're good, okay?"

"All right." She nods before turning to open the car door.

"Hey"—I grab her wrist and turn her until she's facing me—"I love you." I give her a quick kiss. "I'll call you."

"Love you, too." She gives me a weak smile before getting into the backseat of the car.

I watch as Cooper's car backs out of the drive, and then I head back into the house.

I find Sarah where I left her in the kitchen, and now that we're alone, I'm overcome with another round of unbelievable happiness.

I take her face between my hands and kiss her forehead. "God, I can't believe this. Is this real?" I shout with what I'm sure is a crazy grin on my face.

Sarah giggles before wrapping her arms around my waist. "I've missed you so much."

"Oh, me, too." I kiss the top of her head. Stepping back, I grab her hand in mine. "Come on."

I lead her to my bedroom. We both kick off our shoes and climb into my bed without discussion.

The rituals of our teenage selves come back full force, not missing a beat. I held Sarah in my arms every night for two and a half years. We weren't always in a bed. In fact, a high percentage of those nights, we weren't. But, no matter where we were—city benches, alleyways, shelters, under an overpass, or atop the grass of a park— we were together, and she slept in my arms. I never wanted her to feel alone.

We lie, facing each other.

"They told me you were dead." I pause. "Well, I guess the hospital receptionist actually told me you were gone, and I assumed." The last two words come out with so much regret. "I couldn't feel a pulse before the ambulance came. I guess I thought you were already gone before you even got to the hospital. But, regardless, I waited in that lobby for two days, begging anyone to tell me something. They wouldn't. They wouldn't let me see you, wouldn't tell me anything. I felt so helpless. Finally, the receptionist came out on the second day and told me to go home because you were gone."

"I'm so sorry," she says, her eyes filling with tears. "I'm sorry I did that to you. I'm sorry I couldn't find you sooner."

"Tell me what happened."

"Well, I think I was in the hospital for two days before I was transferred to a treatment facility. I had asked for you, but I was in and out…" She hesitates. "I don't remember a lot about it. I just know, when I got to the rehab place, I wasn't allowed to call anyone for what seemed like forever. When I finally was able to make a call, I called the motel, but they said that you had left, and I had no idea how to find you."

"So, what happened to you?"

She laughs dryly. "Well, I wish I could tell you that I got better after that, but I didn't. I was in and out of a couple of group homes that housed mainly teenagers."

My body goes stiff.

She notices and rubs my arm. "No one hurt me…again. No one touched me—well, at least no one who I hadn't asked to." She frowns. "You know how I was. I was really messed up for a long time, Loïc. I'm sorry. I wish I could have been stronger. But I'm finally okay. I've been to more therapy sessions than I can count, and I go to meetings every week. I've been clean for two years."

"How'd you find me? Why didn't you look sooner?" I question.

"I did. I've looked for you on and off the entire time. You do realize that you have zero social media accounts. You're, like, impossible to find. I didn't look all the time because it would drive me mad, but every month or so, I would do an Internet search with your name. I just did one, and I found a military article that mentioned you and David Cooper. So, I looked up David and stalked his Facebook. He'd posted a picture with you. In his post, it showed the city, so I came here. When I got here this morning, I messaged him and told him who I was and that I needed to see you. When he told me that you thought I was dead, I figured it would be best to meet you here versus having him tell you over the phone. I didn't want you freaking out and driving."

I take in her words. "This is just so insane."

"I know," she agrees.

"I thought I'd lost you," I say sadly.

"I know. I'm so sorry. You look so good though, Loïc. You look happy, and your girlfriend seems nice."

"She is. She's amazing." I huff out a humorless chuckle. "London's actually my first girlfriend…ever. She's kind of a recent development. I wasn't good for a long time. After I lost you, I shut down completely. I couldn't imagine losing anyone else. So, I never got close to anyone again—besides Cooper because he's persistent like that." I smile.

"He seems great." She smiles.

"He is."

"So, what happened to you after you left the hospital?" she asks.

"I went back to the motel room and packed up my stuff. Then, I left. I couldn't stand to be there without you. I aimlessly traveled around for a couple of months before turning myself into the system, so I could get an ID. At that point, I was just shy of eighteen, so I didn't have to go to a home or anything. I got my GED, joined the Army, and met Cooper. That's about all. I lived a pretty emotionally closed-off life until this summer when I met London."

"What's up with the name? You think it's a sign?"

I know what she means. Some days, I think it might be—well, at least I would if I believed in that sort of thing.

During the time I spent with Sarah, I turned my dad's stories of London into a fantasy for the both of us. I told her story after story until, eventually, we both dreamed of making it to London where we could be happy and free.

"I don't know. Her name definitely caught my attention, that's for sure."

"Have you been to England? Did you check on your grandparents, let them know how you were?" she asks eagerly.

I shake my head. "I couldn't."

Her face drops, sadness lining her features. "Why?"

"They left me. They didn't deserve to know that I was okay." I use the last word in the loosest term of the word.

"But they're family, your only family."

"Family doesn't abandon a child who's lost everything, Sarah. They're not my family anymore. I have Cooper and Maggie, and now, I have you again. And maybe, if I don't scare London away, I'll get to keep her in that category, too."

She laughs. "Why do you say that?"

"Because, since I lost you, I've kind of turned into somewhat of a jackass. I'm not what you would call a relationship kind of guy."

"Well, judging by the way she looks at you, I'd say you have her fooled. I'm sure you're doing just fine."

"I'm trying. It's been a bit of a train wreck, but she continues to like me. So, I guess we'll see." I shrug.

She runs her hand along my cheek. "You still don't get it, do you?"

"What?"

"You're impossible not to love, Loïc." Her expression is so sincere, and her words make me uncomfortable.

I shake my head. "That's not true." My voice cracks.

"It's very true. I told you when we were kids, and I'll tell you again...you are special. You have the kindest heart. You are brave. In this world of ugliness, you are a beacon of gleaming light. You are impossible not to love."

"You don't know me at all, Sarah."

"Wrong. I know you better than anyone. Your experiences might have left you jaded, but they haven't dulled your shine. Something about you makes you this enigma, Loïc Berkeley. Something about you makes you great."

She scoots her body closer to mine until our faces are mere inches away. I can see the dark blue ring that circles her brilliant eyes.

"Once upon a time, you saved my life. The hope that I would find you and see you once more saved me again and again every day that we've been apart. You are my angel," she says.

"And you are mine." I wrap my arms around her, relishing in her living, breathing warm existence.

"I'm never leaving you again."

"Promise?" I say against her soft hair.

"I promise you." She nuzzles her face against my chest.

I sigh as my current life comes to the surface.

"What is it?" she asks.

"I'm leaving in two months on deployment. I'll be gone for a year."

I used to love being in the military. I lived to go on deployments. While overseas, I volunteered for numerous missions that didn't need me. I'd be lying if I said that I had done it because of the love of my country. I know that's the right answer, but it's not my answer. I put myself into dangerous situations because I felt disposable. And to be honest, if I were going to go out, why not go out with some excitement, fighting for some cause? It felt good to fight for something when there was nothing good left in my life to fight for. I wanted to die as a man with convictions even if they weren't mine. I'm not sure if that makes any sense, but it's the truth. The other glaring truth is that I had no one on this earth who needed me or would miss me. Yes, I'm sure Cooper would have missed me some. But he's in the military, so he would have understood.

266

But, now that I've fallen in love with London and gotten Sarah back, I'm leaving. And though a year isn't forever, it sure seems like an eternity in this moment. The timing of all this just blows.

Sarah's voice is calm and measured, as if she senses my inner turmoil, which she probably does. "It's okay. We'll be in contact while you're gone, and I'll be here when you get back."

Her statement makes me realize that I have no idea where she lives.

"Where have you been living?"

"All over. That part hasn't changed much. I'm currently in Orlando, Florida."

"Oh, yeah? What do you do there?"

She giggles. The sound does something to my insides, bringing me back to when it was Sarah and me against the world.

"I work for Disney. I'm Princess Aurora. You know, Sleeping Beauty?"

"You're a Disney princess?" I ask in amusement.

"Yeah, I dated Aladdin for a while. He got me the job," she says casually.

I can't help but laugh. The vision of her out with a guy in poufy silk pants and a barely there vest is a priceless sight.

"That's bloody brilliant, Sarah."

"Oh, I love when you use your British words!"

I chuckle. "It happens a lot less than it used to. Being around you makes me think of the past and my parents. I guess that's why some of my dad's phrases slip out. So, who would have guessed you would grow up to be a princess?"

"Yeah, not what I thought I'd be doing with my life, but it pays the bills."

"I think it's great. You deserve to be a princess."

She lets out a disapproving sound. "It's not really all it's cracked up to be. Ninety percent of the days in Florida are scorching and humid as hell. The princess dress is heavy, hot, and stinky. The makeup that I have to cake on my face makes me sweat more than I already do, and to top it off, I get to have thousands of grimy kids' hands pawing me all day. I'd gladly leave that job to move up here."

"Well, maybe you should wait until I get back. The winters up here are no joke, and if you thought that the winter months in Texas were cold, just wait until you live through one up here. There's no point in being here and suffering, like I know you would be, if I'm not here anyway."

She groans. "Why did you choose to be stationed here?"

I chuckle. "Cooper wanted to live with Maggie, and he's really all I had, so I agreed to follow him up here. Actually, you get used to the winters. I kinda dig 'em. I love snowboarding and skiing."

"If you say so," she says with definite speculation lining her voice. "Maybe I will wait until you get back."

"How long can you stay?"

"I have a week's vacation."

"All right. Then, we have a week to figure out what you want to do."

"Sounds good," she agrees.

The two of us talk for hours, both eager to know every detail of the other's life that we missed in the past eight years. When I think about it, it seems like we've been apart for a lifetime. The person I was back then and the person I am now are so vastly different. But, at the same time, lying here with Sarah in my arms feels like no time has passed at all.

I'm not sure how late we stay up, talking, but at some point, we start to drift off. Right before sleep takes me, I am overcome with complete and utter contentment, and for the first time since I was a little boy, a powerful emotion is present in my chest. It feels a little like hope.

Hope is the building block for miracles, but it is also the catalyst for disappointment, depending on which way the coin falls. But, maybe for once, the coin will land in my favor.

TWENTY-THREE

London

"Love makes me weak—it's true—
but it's in that fragility where I will find my true strength."
—London Wright

"How do I look?" I ask Paige.

"You're a hot babe, as always," she responds.

"I don't need you to blow smoke up my ass, Paige. I need the truth," I say, irritated.

"Rawr," Paige growls like an angry cat. "Don't bite the hand that feeds you."

"You rarely cook." I roll my eyes. "Sorry. I know my earlier comment was a tad bitchy, but I need honesty."

Paige lets out an exhausted sigh. "I was being honest."

I exhale loudly, pouting out my lips. "Okay. Just checking."

"You're so annoying sometimes."

"Thanks," I say as I spray myself with more body spray. "I'm sorry. This is serious. I need to be hotter than everyone else today."

"Loïc doesn't love you only because you're pretty. I'm quite sure he likes you as a person as well. You should focus on that aspect a little more." She gives me a pointed stare. "You have no reason to worry. Seriously, stop getting your chickens in a twist."

"Isn't it panties?"

"What's panties?"

"Ugh, never mind." I let out an exhausted groan. "I'm sorry. I don't like feeling like this. This is new territory for me, and I don't like it. I'm telling you, when you meet her tonight, you'll see. She's a freaking model."

"So what? There will always be tons of gorgeous women in this world. You can't freak out every time Loïc talks to one."

"I know, I know. But they have history."

"Not that kind."

"Right. I know…I'm being stupid."

"Yeah, you totally are. You're not acting like the London I know and love. No offense, but this whole week, you've been rather whiny and annoying. Just being honest."

"You're right." I sigh. "Please feel free to kick my ass."

"That won't be necessary." Paige laughs.

"Remember back when you were in love with Troy? Did you feel neurotically jealous all the time?"

"Yeah, but that's because I could sense something wasn't right. Turned out, he had been cheating on me with every Delta Zeta who would put out. I had reasons. You don't. Loïc is a man, not an immature douche bag, like Troy was. Totally different."

"Fine. So, I don't have any good reasons? I'm just a dumbass?"

Paige chuckles. "Everyone handles love differently. You've never truly been in love before. You'll figure out how to navigate through this without all the jealousy. It's a learning process. Plus, Loïc isn't always the most open, so you have some additional obstacles."

"True. All right, let's go hang out with the woman Loïc loves." I grab my purse and head toward the door.

"Like a sister," Paige says behind me with obvious mirth in her voice.

"Whatever."

Paige and I are meeting Loïc, Sarah, Maggie, and Cooper at the bowling alley. Loïc's been hanging out with Sarah the past few days, but he really wanted everyone to do something together before she leaves on Saturday morning.

I see Cooper's car in the parking lot when Paige and I arrive, so I know they're already here. We find them sitting at a table in front of a lane, ready to go. They've already input the six of our names into the computer, evident by our names being up on the monitor above our lane.

They're all laughing at something Cooper said.

"Hey," I cut in, waving to the group.

Loïc stands and pulls me into a hug, a huge smile on his face. "Hey, I've missed you," he says before planting a quick kiss on my lips.

I introduce Paige to Maggie and Sarah. Sarah gives me an awkward hug. All right, maybe it's just weird on my end.

Why do I make everything so uncomfortable? Ugh, I hate emotions.

"So, Loïc tells me that you want to be a journalist?" Sarah asks with what appears to be sincere interest.

Fine, maybe she is truly a nice person.

"Yeah. I actually got a call yesterday to interview with a local paper. It's a small writing gig, but if I get it, I'm hoping it will grow into more," I say to everyone, as they are all listening in on the conversation.

"That's awesome, babe. Why didn't you tell me?" Loïc asks, grabbing my hand and squeezing gently.

"I don't know. I forgot. I guess I just figured I'd tell you the next time I saw you." I shrug, smiling weakly, before taking a drink of pop that Maggie just poured for me.

"That's awesome. When's your interview?" Cooper asks.

"Next Thursday."

"Make sure to let us know how it goes," Maggie chimes in.

"I will. Thanks. So, what have you all been up to?" I direct my question to everyone.

I know that Loïc and Cooper had to work the past three days. They usually get home from work around three in the afternoon.

"Well, it's been great because Maggie has had the last few days off, so I've been able to spend time with her during the day while Loïc has been at work," Sarah says.

"Yeah, it's been great. Unfortunately, I have four straight twelves, starting tomorrow. So, tonight's going to be the last time I really get to see anyone again until Monday." Maggie makes an exhausted face.

"What does that mean?" Paige asks. "Twelves?"

"Well, London's probably told you that I'm a nurse?" Paige nods her head.

"Well, at the hospital where I work, we do twelve-hour shifts, but if you include driving time and the amount of time I have to stay extra to finish charting, I can be gone for up to sixteen hours on the days I work. So, I basically just come home and go to bed. I don't have much time to do anything but work and sleep."

"Ugh, that sounds horrible." Paige scowls.

Maggie chuckles. "It's really not bad because I only work three days a week. Depending on how my workdays fall in the week, I can have a bunch of days off in between. So, that makes up for it."

"So, what did you do after the guys got home?" I direct my question to Sarah.

"Just hung out basically. It's been such a gorgeous week, so Loïc and I spent a lot of time outside. We went kayaking and hiking, and he took me to the shooting range. That was fun!"

Of course it was. I have to stop myself from rolling my eyes. I hate feeling like this.

I plaster on a smile. *Fake it till you make it...right?*

"What are you going to do tomorrow while everyone's at work?" I ask.

"Loïc's going to let me borrow his truck, and I'm going to drive around to look at some possible apartments and check out a few jobs."

"Oh, wow. So, like, you're moving here?" I try to mask the worry in my voice.

"At some point, yes. I'll probably wait until Loïc comes back from deployment, you know? But we'll see. If I find an amazing job before then, I might move up sooner."

A long lock of her beautiful Rapunzel hair falls over her shoulder and comes close to the plate of pizza in front of her. My eyes bulge as Loïc reaches over and places her hair behind her ear, so it doesn't fall onto the greasy pepperoni.

What the hell?

"Oh, great!" I exclaim a little too cheerfully.

Paige squeezes my knee under the table. I turn to her, and she smiles reassuringly. She knows I'm about to lose my cool.

At least when Loïc leaves me for the blonde beauty, I'll still have Paige.

Can the confident London, circa June, please return? This current model is driving me insane.

"So, should we get this game started or what?" Cooper asks.

"Yes, let's do it!" I cheer. *God, who am I?*

Bowling is actually really fun. I haven't bowled since I was little. I suck—like, totally suck—but that works in my favor because Loïc spends a lot of his time helping me get my form right.

The annoying Sarah-focused conversations are gone as well. In between turns, everyone chats about random stuff or jeers the current bowler. Loïc and Cooper have this crazy competitive thing going, and it's quite hilarious. I think Paige and I are also in a rivalry, but we are duking it out to see who's the worst bowler.

Many times throughout our game, I find myself laughing until my sides hurt, and to be honest, I need it.

We're all in a fit of giggles as Cooper completes his pre-bowl ritual. He's standing in front of the lane. First, he places the ball down on the ground between his feet while he stretches his hands up and then out in both directions, swinging his arms back and forth in front of himself. He ends his stretch by shaking out his hands. Then, he touches his toes before completing some sort of lunge. That move is followed by the rolling of his neck.

Finally, he picks up his ball, blows on it, rubs it, and appears to whisper to it.

"Fucking-A, Cooper! Bowl!" Loïc laughs.

"Don't be a hater just 'cause I'm going to kick your ass," Cooper calls out.

"You can sprinkle pixie dust on that shit, and you still won't beat me, so stop making a fool of yourself." Loïc shakes his head in amusement.

"Who knew bowling was so competitive?" I laugh, leaning my head onto Loïc's shoulder as he sits next to me.

"Everything between Cooper and me is a competition. When we were stationed at Fort Sill in Oklahoma, we went bowling all the time. There seemed to be nothing to do in that city, but for some reason, there were four bowling alleys really close to the base. So, Cooper and I spent a lot of our free time trying to beat each other at this game." Loïc smiles.

"I'm glad we all got to do it. It's fun. I haven't bowled since I was a kid," I say.

"Yeah, it's cool having everyone out together."

"It is," I agree.

"You sure you don't want to get together tomorrow or Friday? Sarah will love it. I promise," he says.

"No, really, that's okay. You two haven't seen each other in years. You should spend her last two evenings catching up. It's fine. I'll see you Saturday after she flies out."

"Are you sure?" Loïc doesn't sound convinced.

"Totally." I pat his leg. "Enjoy your time with Sarah, but when she leaves, you're all mine. Got it?"

He laughs. "All right. I can handle that."

I have Loïc all to myself today. *Finally.* I've been patient for a week now.

That's a lie.

I let Loïc believe I was being patient when, in reality, I'd been complaining my ass off to Paige for seven days straight. She'd had to endure my bitching and moaning from sun up to sun down.

That's also a lie.

I wouldn't get out of bed until at least noon—most days, two in the afternoon—so the complaining was endured from lunchtime on, at best. But, regardless, I'm a nightmare when I'm in a foul mood, and Paige is the best for putting up with my shit.

The crazy thing is, I can't complain to Loïc. *What kind of insensitive bitch would I be?*

Hey, you, boyfriend. I know that one of the only people you've ever loved, who you thought was dead, just showed up, undead, and you're over the moon with joy as your heart unshatters from the million pieces in which it had previously shattered. But do you think you could pay me more attention?

See? It wouldn't work.

In truth, I truly am so happy for Loïc. He has had such a hard life, and he received such a gift last week. He deserves it. He's such a great man. He is worthy of happiness. I can't even imagine how he must be feeling, having Sarah back. The entire ordeal is hard for me to wrap my mind around, and she's not even my long-lost best friend/sister.

So, while my head tells me to stop being selfish and to think about someone else's happiness for once, my heart is beating with more urgency this week…in warning. Of what though?

Loïc's told me many times that he's always loved Sarah like family, like a sister. There has never been anything romantic between them. But I have a hard time sitting back while my love spends quality one-on-one time with a gorgeous woman he loves and cherishes, regardless of the way in which he claims to love her.

Rationally, I know I have to give him this. I have to trust him. But I've never loved anyone the way I love him. My fragile heart is so fearful of the things that could happen. Because, let's face it, stuff can happen. I have friends who have had betrayals happen with boyfriends who had a lot less invested in their mistresses than Loïc has invested in Sarah.

Bowling on Wednesday went well. Loïc was completely sweet and attentive toward me. He treated Sarah with the same type of admiration he showed to Maggie and Cooper. Nothing seemed amiss, but the underlying feeling of dread remained.

Loïc did invite me over to hang out with him and Sarah several times this week. I knew he was just doing it to be nice, so I always declined. The mature girlfriend in me gave him time to get reacquainted with his dear friend. I know he needed it, and I hope that his heart was able to mend itself some this week.

Yet I miss him so much it hurts. I just need him to get here, so I can reassure myself that everything is right between us.

The rumbling hum of Loïc's truck's engine sounds through my bedroom walls.

He's here!

I don't even wait for him to make it to the front door before I throw it open and leap into his arms. He catches me, and I wrap my legs around his waist. His strong chest vibrates from laughter as I cling to him like a spider monkey.

"Miss me?" He chuckles.

His full lips plant soft kisses on my neck as I hold him tight, burying my face against his shoulder.

It feels so good to have him in my arms again. *How am I going to make it a year when I couldn't even make it three days?* Good thing I saw him midweek, or I would have been more pathetic than I am at the present time.

That's a lie.

I couldn't possibly be more pathetic due to the fact that I'm currently crying. *Damn it.*

I'm not exactly sure when I started, but I'm sobbing on Loïc's soft T-shirt that smells like fabric softener and the sexy-as-hell cologne he uses.

God, he smells good.

Pull yourself together, London, before he notices.

"London, are you crying?" he asks, concerned.

Well, shit.

"No," I lie through a sniffle.

Loïc laughs. "London, why are you crying?" He sounds completely amused.

"I don't know," I mumble, my throat tight, as my arms continue to cling to his neck.

"Look at me."

I shake my head.

"London, please look at me," he says gently, placing a finger beneath my chin.

I let him guide me, slowly lifting my head, without attempting to wipe my tears. *What's the point?*

"What is it?"

"Do you still love me?" The words tumble out of my mouth before I can stop them. This isn't me. In fact, I hate this weak version of myself. Yet, apparently, where Loïc is concerned, I'm not very strong.

His big blue eyes widen. "Of course I do. Come here." He moves us to the bench on my front porch and sets me down. He takes a seat next to me and grabs my hands in his. "Tell me what the issue is, London. I can't fix it if I don't know what's wrong."

I wipe the wetness on my cheeks. Now that my face isn't buried in Loïc's shirt, the tears have stopped coming, which I'm thankful for. I take a large breath and steady myself. "I'm just afraid."

Loïc urges me on with his kind expression.

Why is he the one comforting me?

In a matter of a week, our roles seem to have reversed.

I sigh, letting a gush of air out through my lips. "I'm just afraid that I'm going to lose you. I...I've had a lot of time to think about us this week, and I really don't want to lose you. I think I need you more than I realized."

He cocks his head to the side. "Is this about Sarah?"

"Maybe." I shrug.

"Do you think something happened between us?"

"No." I shake my head. "Maybe. I don't know."

He wipes his thumb across my cheek, catching an errant tear. "London, nothing happened with Sarah." He regards me with a thoughtful expression. "She knows that I love you, and I know that I love you. Plus, throw in the fact that she and I don't have that type of relationship, and we never have. I know we're close, and that can be a little off-putting if you don't understand it, but I promise you that I don't love her in a romantic way. I've always cared for her like family, someone that I needed to protect. I will love her in that way forever, and she will always have a huge part in my life. But I will never love her the way I love you. You own my heart in that way. You're the only one who ever has."

I allow his words to fall around me, soothing my frazzled nerves like a warm heating blanket. "Okay." I nod, feeling relieved and mildly idiotic. "I'm sorry. I don't know why I'm being so emotional. I guess the mind can do some damage when it's left to think of all the worst-case scenarios for a week straight."

He pulls me into him. My head is beneath his chin as his strong arms hug me.

"Is it bad that you freaking out like that made me a little happy?" he asks.

I lean back, so I can see his face. "Why?" My lips turn up into a grin.

"It makes me feel better about leaving you for a year. It gives me some hope that you will wait," he says simply.

"And me telling you that I will doesn't?"

He gives me a crooked smile. "You aren't the only one whose mind likes to think in worst-case scenarios."

"Who knew we had so many flaws? How can we even stand each other?"

Loïc throws his head back in laughter. "I think you'll find that more people are screwed up than you think. The trick is finding the person whose flaws are compatible with your own."

I remember something he said to me months ago. "So, we can be fucked up together?"

"Perfectly fucked up together," he says before kissing my forehead.

"Until we're just together?"

"Exactly. Look at that; you listened to me," he says with mocked shock.

"I remember everything you've ever told me. The question is, whether I choose to believe you or not."

"And what's the verdict?"

"I believe you," I admit. "Next time my heart tries to be all dramatic, I will have my brain remind it of your words."

"Sounds like a plan. So, are we good?"

I nod. "We're good. What do you want to do today?"

"It's such a nice day. I thought we could go on a hike and maybe go apple-picking."

I sigh.

"What?" Loïc laughs.

"I know I'm being a downer and all, but I was promised two months with you, and though I'm truly happy for you and Sarah, I feel like I was robbed of a week. The one month and three weeks we have left need to be more epic than, 'Let's go walk around the wilderness.'" I use my fingers to make quotations in the air while my voice goes low in a horrible impression of a dumb Loïc.

My joke has the desired effect as Loïc laughs. It's full-on and carefree—my favorite.

"Oh, it's going to be epic, little spoiled one. We have the entire day. Don't worry. We'll end it in bed where the magic happens." He playfully waggles his eyebrows, eliciting laughter from me.

"Or we could skip the nature part and just go there now." I pout my lips.

"Though I still find that pout extremely adorable for some reason, I'm thinking that, eventually, it's going to be time for you to let it go. And we can't spend our entire lives in bed, London."

"That's not what you said two weeks ago."

"Yeah, I'm fickle about my convictions in that way," he teases. "It's a flaw."

"I hate you." I giggle.

He wraps an arm around my middle, pulling me against his body. His hand cradles my jaw. "And I love you," he says before he drops his full lips onto mine. His lips are soft and full against mine, and his touch is warm.

Instantly, I'm lost in him, and the truth is, I go in gladly with my eyes closed and my heart open, leaving me exposed.

Love makes me weak—it's true—but it's in that fragility where I will find my true strength.

"Admit it!" Loïc tickles my sides until they ache, but I refuse to give in.

Tears of laughter fall down my face, and I gasp, "Stop! Stop!" I kick my bare legs, trying to buck a naked and extremely sexy Loïc off of me.

"Nope, not until you admit that you are a stubborn woman." His fingers work their way up to my underarms.

I can't stand underarm tickles. To me, it is the cruelest type of torment.

"Okay! You're right!" I laugh.

He stops tickling me, and I catch my breath. My chest expands as it recovers.

"Right about what?" He quirks up a brow.

I exhale. "You are right. It was an amazing day out in *nature*," I say the word like it's poison.

"And?"

"And I had fun! You happy? You win. Okay?" I stick my tongue out at him.

He chuckles and rolls off of me until we are lying side by side in my bed.

In reality, I had an incredible day. The warm autumn weather made it a perfect day to walk through the woods. And Loïc was right. The apples in the store do not even compare to the deliciousness of a crisp apple straight from the tree. Though I'm trying to fight him, he's turning me into an outdoorsy girl.

Okay, maybe that's a bit much. I'm not going to subscribe to *Field & Stream* magazine anytime soon, but I will admit that some outdoor activities are fun...enough.

But I love to rile him up. It's one of my favorite pastimes.

"I hate when you tickle me. That's a weak form of torture," I huff out, my sides still tingling from where his fingers just were.

"No, you don't," he answers lazily.

"Um, yes, I do," I respond with a slight attitude.

He turns to his side and props his head up with his arm. His blue eyes squint, assessing me. "What did I say to you right before I tickled you?"

"I don't remember." I shrug.

"Stop being a hard-ass for two seconds, London. What did I say?" He shakes his head in disbelief with a huge grin on his handsome face.

"You said that if I didn't tell you the truth, you were going to tickle me." I sulk.

"Exactly."

"Exactly what?"

"I gave you an out. You didn't take it, so you wanted me to tickle you. I got your number, oh spoiled one." A cocky expression graces his face and, damn it, if that look isn't gorgeous on him, too.

I laugh. "You're ridiculous."

"Ridiculous for you."

"That doesn't even make any sense," I tease right before he bends and takes my exposed nipple into his mouth. The sudden pull startles me, and I yell out.

He releases it just as suddenly and plants light kisses up my chest, across my collarbone, and up my neck. I hum with contentment as his lips caress my skin.

He sucks on the sensitive skin of my neck for a minute before he leans over my face. His fingers run through my hair as his eyes take me in.

"So, today was good enough for you?" His lips press into a line as he tries not to smile.

"Yes, I will allow today to be counted toward the month and three weeks I have left with you."

"Well, I'm glad because I don't know what I would do if it wasn't good enough." He chuckles.

"Try extra hard tomorrow," I quip.

He shakes his head. "You're kind of insane."

"Insane for you."

His head falls back in laughter, and the sound is so beautiful. "What did I do before you?"

"I have no idea."

He runs his thumb across my temple, his face serious. "I spy with my little eye someone who's so beautiful that it hurts, someone so caring that she was able to break down my solid walls, and someone with ridiculous flaws that perfectly complement my craziness." A slow smile forms on his lips, lighting up his eyes.

"You know, growing up, I held on to this dream of London being this magical place where I would eventually go. It was going to be the place that would save me and shelter me from all the evil in the world. I knew that, when I got there, I would be happy. I would be safe. My dream of London helped me get through some of the darkest times in my life. I knew that I could endure anything because, soon, I would get to London, and all the bad would be replaced with nothing but goodness." He pauses, taking me in with such reverence that my heart twists.

"Along the way, I lost some hope. I started to believe that maybe this miraculous place wasn't meant for me, that I would never get there. I would never be rescued. I would never be happy.

"Then, I met you, London. You refused to give up on me. You fought for me time and time again when I was nothing but cruel. Somehow, you saw something in me that even I couldn't see. You saw worth. You made me believe in myself, so I could believe in us.

"*You* are my *London*, my safe place. You rescued me, made me happy. You are so much more than the woman I love. You are my entire destination. Wherever you are is where I'm meant to be. I was never meant to make it to some fantastical place overseas, made up from a little boy's imagination. My entire journey has been steering me toward you. It has always been you."

His blue-eyed gaze captures mine. My heart, full of gratitude, pounds beneath my chest.

"I don't even know how to respond to that," I choke out. "Those are the most beautiful words I've ever heard in my life." Tears fall from my eyes. "I love you, Loïc, so much. This"—I bring my finger between his chest and mine—"is meant to be. We are meant to be. I know it. I know we'll make it, no matter what happens."

"No matter what," he echoes my thoughts.

He brings his lips to mine and thoroughly kisses me. Yes, this day definitely counts…in a big way.

Dueling emotions swell beneath my chest. I have never been so amazingly happy in love before, and at the same time, I've never been more scared. Maybe that's what love truly is—complete and utter loss of control, your heart beating outside of your chest, fragile and open.

With real love comes unyielding fear because, when you really love someone, you never want to know what it feels like to be without that person.

But maybe that's what makes love so great. The risk is so worth it because you know what it's like to have that all-encompassing love. True love brings the knowledge that you're one of the lucky ones because not everyone gets this.

I know I'm so fortunate to have Loïc in my life, and I'm not going to take a second of it for granted.

I'm going to face the fear head-on. It's the presence of fear that means the love is worth fighting for.

We're going to make it, Loïc and me.

Of this, I am certain.

KEEPING LONDON

BOOK TWO IN THE FLAWED HEART SERIES

COMING JUNE 2016

ACKNOWLEDGMENTS

I just love this story! I hope you all enjoyed it, too. I love the characters. They are all so interesting to me and were fun to write. I wanted to write a story that had two differently flawed characters falling in love. Though dissimilar from each other in many ways, London and Loïc are just two people trying to figure out who they want to be in this world. Both are a big change to what my usual hero and heroine are like, and I adore them.

The next two novels in this series are going to give you all sorts of feels! I'm excited to see what you all think as you read them.

It is so crazy to me that I am publishing my sixth book, and what makes it more surreal is the fact that I'm doing it as a full-time writer! This is no longer my hobby but my legit job—the best job. I never thought I would be sitting here, saying this, yet here I am, people! Amazing. Dreams do come true! ☺ What a gift. ♥

I want to thank my readers so very much. Thank you for reading my stories and loving my words! I wouldn't be living this dream without you. Thank you from the bottom of my heart!

In every one of my acknowledgment sections, I get quite wordy when expressing my love to all the amazing people in my life. I am so fortunate to have this life I've been given. I have a wonderful husband, healthy and happy children, an astonishing extended family, the best mother in the world, and friends who would do anything for me. I am so blessed and grateful to be surrounded by so much love that I want to shout it from the rooftops.

A special shout-out will always go to my siblings, who were my first soul mates. You will find them in every story I write because so much of what I know of love has come from them. One of my biggest wishes for my children is that they will always love each other unconditionally and fiercely, the way my siblings and I love each other.

There is a core group of people who go above and beyond in helping me with my books—most of whom, I didn't know prior to becoming a part of this crazy book world—and I am so thankful.

To my beta readers and proofreaders—Gayla, Nicole, Amy, Tammi, Elle, Heather, Terri, and Angela—You all are so awesome. Seriously, each of you is a gift, and you have helped me in invaluable different ways. I love you all so much. XOXO

Angela, my cupcake—I've said it before, and I will say it again. I love you big time, like hard-core, intense love! I am counting down the days until we meet in person! I can't thank you enough for all you do for me on a daily basis! I am so truly blessed to know you. ♥

Gayla—Thank you for taking time out of your busy life to help me, no matter what I need. You are so smart and talented. You are a blessing, and I love you more than I could ever express.

Nicole, my BBWFL—You are my biggest supporter and ally in this crazy book world. You will always get the credit for starting it all. Our mutual love of books and our late-night chats reignited my dream to write. None of my books would be the same without your input. Your friendship means the world to me. Love you forever.

Tammi—I've said it before, and I will say it again. I will forever continue to write as long as you continue to read because your feedback alone is enough. *You get me.* Thank you for being you because you are perfect. I live for your comments and feedback. Not only do you fill my heart with so much gratitude, but you also make me a better writer. *Tight Hugs* I freaking love you!

Amy, my BBFFL—What can I say that I haven't already said? You know how much I love you! I have cherished your support from the beginning. Six novels later, you continue to bless me with your feedback and support. You get me and my writing. You make my books better. You are one of the kindest and most supportive people I know. I love you to pieces! ❤

Terri—I'm still so grateful that I met you and thankful that you continue to beta! You know exactly how to make my work better. Thank you for your honest feedback. You are such a kind, smart, and giving person. I hope you know that, now that I've found you, I'm not going to let you go! ☺ XO

Elle—I love you for so many reasons! I especially love how you make me laugh when I need it! Thank you for loving and supporting me. You are such a good person. Thank you for all you do to help me! I am so grateful. ❤

To my cover artist, Regina Wamba from Mae I Design and Photography—Thank you! Your work inspires me. You are a true artist, and I am so grateful to now have six of your covers. People do judge a book by its cover, so thank you for making mine *gorgeous*! XO

To my editor and interior designer, Jovana Shirley from Unforeseen Editing—You are, simply put, the best. Your talent, professionalism, and the care you take with my novels are worth way more than I could ever afford to pay you. Finding you was a true gift, one that I hope to always have on this journey. Thank you from the bottom of my heart for not only making my words pretty, but for also making the interior of the book beautiful. Thank you for always fitting me in! I am so grateful for you and everything you have done to make this book the best it can be. XOXO

Lastly, to the bloggers—Oh my God! I love you! Since releasing *Forever Baby*, I have gotten to know many of you through Facebook. Out of the kindness of your hearts, so many of you have reached out and helped me promote my books. There are seriously great people in this blogger community, and I am humbled by your support. Truly, thank you! Because of you, indie authors get their stories out. Thank you for supporting all authors and the great stories they write.

Readers—You can connect with me on several places, and I would love to hear from you.

Find me on Facebook:
www.facebook.com/EllieWadeAuthor

Find me on Twitter: @authorelliewade

Visit my website: www.elliewade.com

Remember, the greatest gift you can give an author is a review. If you feel so inclined, please leave a review on the various retailer sites. It doesn't have to be fancy. A couple of sentences would be awesome!

I could honestly write a whole book about everyone in this world whom I am thankful for. I am blessed in so many ways, and I am beyond grateful for this beautiful life. XOXO

Forever,

Ellie ♥

ABOUT THE AUTHOR

Ellie Wade resides in southeast Michigan with her husband, three young children, and two dogs. She has a master's in education from Eastern Michigan University, and she is a huge University of Michigan sports fan. She loves the beauty of her home state, especially the lakes and the gorgeous autumn weather. When she is not writing, she is reading, snuggling up with her kids, or spending time with family and friends. She loves traveling and exploring new places with her family.

Made in the USA
Middletown, DE
29 September 2016